Being a thief [...]
way Alex exp [...]

Keeping her back to the security cameras, she opened her purse and slid out a bracelet. It was a poor imitation of the one in the display case, but it should fool someone who only looked at it in passing.

Five seconds until the cameras completed their sweep. One thousand one. She lifted the real bracelet. One thousand two. Laid the fake one in its place. One thousand three. She slid the door shut. One thousand four. She had barely straightened before the cameras came back to her.

She closed her hand securely around the genuine bracelet and casually slipped it into her purse. She'd done it. A sense of satisfaction settled in.

She began slowly moving away from the counter, but she stopped dead when a deep male voice said, "All right, put it back."

She jerked around and found herself staring into eyes so green that they looked like emeralds. This wasn't the security guard—so who *was* he?

Dear Reader:

We at Silhouette are very excited to bring you this reading Sensation. Look out for the four books which appear in our Silhouette Sensation series every month. These stories will have the high quality you have come to expect from Silhouette, and their varied and provocative plots will encourage you to explore the wonder of falling in love – again and again!

Emotions run high in these drama-filled novels. Greater sensual detail and an extra edge of realism intensify the hero and heroine's relationship so that you cannot help but be caught up in their every change of mood.

We hope you enjoy this Sensation – and will go on to enjoy many more.

We would love to hear your comments and encourage you to write to us:

Jane Nicholls
Silhouette Books
PO Box 236
Thornton Road
Croydon
Surrey
CR9 3RU

MARY ANNE WILSON
Liar's Moon

Silhouette Sensation

*First published in Great Britain in 1994
by Silhouette Books, Eton House, 18-24 Paradise Road,
Richmond, Surrey TW9 1SR*

© Mary Anne Wilson 1989

Silhouette, Silhouette Sensation and Colophon are
Trade Marks of Harlequin Enterprises B.V.

ISBN 0 373 59067 9

18-9401

Made and printed in Great Britain

Other novels by Mary Anne Wilson

Silhouette Sensation

Brady's Law

For Jeremy—
who stubbornly made liars
out of the experts
for almost fifteen years.

Much love

Prologue

Paris

The lies that had seemed so necessary and logical to Jon Stanhope twenty-seven years ago, made him feel vaguely sick now. *What a tangled web we weave,* he thought, his hands clenched tightly behind him. After fifty-eight years of living, more than thirty of those years with the Agency, he finally understood the burden lies could lay on a person.

"They tell me these operations are pretty successful, Ian," he said aloud as he stared out the multipaned window, determinedly keeping his back to the green hospital room, which smelled of medication and sickness. He couldn't look at Ian Hall now, not yet, so he glanced up at the night sky, the stars obliterated by the glow from the city, but he could clearly see the moon. The silver crescent of light, haloed by mists and shadowed by passing clouds, hung in the blackness overhead.

A liar's moon, shrouded and elusive.

The irony of its appearance tonight wasn't lost on Stanhope. As his regret deepened, he looked away from it down at the city ten stories below. But he barely saw the sea of lights in the late-June night. Regret all but choked him. He'd altered Ian's life twenty-seven years ago. Now his only comfort was the fact that he thought he might have the power to make a difference, but he wasn't quite sure how to use it.

"Good odds, Ian, damn good odds with this operation," he murmured, as much to reassure himself as his friend. "Damn good. Damn good."

"Odds don't matter," Ian said, breaking his prolonged silence, but his usually strong voice was weak and unsteady. The sound tightened Stanhope's gut. "I've done what I've wanted to do, Jon, what I had to do. Just the way you have."

Stanhope finally turned to face his friend and partner. Lean and strong just a month ago, now Ian lay in the narrow bed, ashen and starkly gaunt. A full head of gray hair swept back from a pale, tight face, the eyes under straight brows as dark as the night sky. Stanhope himself might have succumbed to middle-aged spread along with thinning hair and the need for bifocals, but Ian hadn't. He'd seemed indestructible—until now.

"Have you done everything you'd wanted to and done it your way, Ian?" Stanhope asked, almost dreading the answer. "Any regrets?"

Medication-dulled eyes took on a shocking intensity for a full second; then the emotion dissolved on a ragged sigh. "Regrets? Yes, there are some, but the bottom line is that I've done what I've had to do," Ian muttered.

"Working for the Agency tends to make any other life a bit impossible, doesn't it?"

Ian frowned, a deep furrow forming between his dark eyes. "For the most part." He chuckled, but it ended in a soft cough, and he closed his eyes for a moment. "When I signed on all those years ago, I never thought I'd go like this—in a damned sickbed, waiting to have my heart rearranged."

Stanhope had faced death so often in his life that he would have sworn he'd come to terms with it. Another lie. He felt shaky just looking at Ian. "Neither did I," he conceded. "We always expect it to be fast, to be over quickly—mercifully." He shrugged and pushed his hands in the pockets of his tweed sports jacket. "But this isn't the end, you know."

"Isn't it?" Ian asked softly.

"No, this sort of surgery goes on all the time." He tapped his own heart under the brown fabric. "You get to our age, now and then they have to fix the old ticker. You'll be up and around in a week or two."

Words meant to comfort seemed to do just the opposite. Ian paled until his skin almost matched the white of the crisp linen, and his mouth drew together in a tight line. "What's left for me?" he whispered harshly. "A desk job? A few years of writing memoirs that will never be published? Living alone with memories to keep me company? I don't think so."

Defeat, pure and simple, laced Ian's voice, and Stanhope's guilt and regret took on the heaviness of a millstone. He'd been so certain about his actions back then. So damned sure he'd done the right thing for everyone. He, above anyone else, had known Ian's life-style—an echo of his own. And he'd known the situation was impossible. Dangerous in the truest sense. Now, with the wisdom of hindsight, he knew how wrong he'd been. "If things had been different with Meg. If you had . . . ?"

"No." The single word cut off any reminiscences and brought a flush to Ian's cheeks. But it wasn't a healthy color. "The past is dead and buried. I was one month too late, one damned month." He took a heavy breath. "And I won't live on 'what might have been,' not now, now ever." He clutched the hem of the sheet, tangling the material in his large hands. "This is the way it should be. No one to grieve for me, to worry or to hurt. It's over and done."

It's not over and done, Stanhope thought. Far from it. He moved closer to the bed and laid a hand on Ian's shoulder, the body heat reassuring under his fingers. "The past is never completely gone, my friend. Never."

Ian met his gaze, then, without saying a word, closed his eyes, shutting out Stanhope and the whole world.

For hours Stanhope sat by his friend's bed, checking his watch over and over again. The nurses who came to check on Ian didn't bother him, knowing that he wasn't about to leave even though visiting hours were long over.

Those hours of waiting gave him time to think, to lay out mentally what he was going to do. When his watch showed one hour past midnight, Stanhope stood, took one last look at his friend and went out into the hallway.

Quickly, he walked off down the brown-tiled corridor toward a bank of pay phones near the windows at the end of the silent hallway. He was the only person who could give Ian Hall a reason to fight, to survive the operation. And he couldn't use the Agency, not for this job.

He got the long-distance operator on the line. It would be nine o'clock in Santa Barbara, California, the beginning of business hours. He gave the operator a Santa Barbara number he'd used enough over the past five years that he knew it by heart. Somehow it seem appropriate to use his contact there for this job, since that was where his web of lies had begun to form.

When a secretary answered, he stood straight and said, "This is Jack Stanley. I need to speak to Michael Conti right away."

Chapter 1

Santa Monica, California

Alexandria Elizabeth Thomas wasn't lost anymore.

Michael Conti glanced at his watch and grimaced. He'd found her three hours ago, and he'd been sitting in his blue rental car waiting for the woman to reappear ever since then. Being the youngest in a large Italian family had taught him patience, a patience perfected during his time in prison, but he was getting restless. He wanted to get on with his job.

He narrowed his green eyes against the stark gleam of the clear afternoon sun bouncing off the white stucco and the red tiled roofs of the ocean-view condos on the quiet, tree-lined street. He had parked under a spreading jacaranda tree, thankful for its thick shade and the fact it was directly across from the Thomas woman's condo, which was clustered with three other residences serviced by a single courtyard. It was only the last day of June in California, yet the thermometer had topped ninety by noon.

The sky over the deep turquoise of the distant Pacific held no clouds at all, and in some way the early morning fog and cool temperatures of the Santa Barbara he'd left three days ago seemed like another world. Mike shifted on the velour

seat, carelessly raked his fingers through his thick brown
hair and prayed for one of those famous ocean breezes.

With a sigh, he readjusted the heavy thirty-five millime-
ter camera with the extended telephoto lens that rested on his
lap. He scanned the BMWs and Mercedeses of the up-
wardly mobile residents, which lined the narrow roadway on
both sides, and knew he fit the image of this conspicuously
affluent neighborhood as surely as the cars did.

The expensive tan polo shirt that he wore with trim brown
slacks and hand-stitched leather moccasins could have been
the casual clothes of an attorney or any upper-level business executive. He wore them because they were comfortable. He even had the haircut—no sideburns, brushed
straight back from his face and left long enough to brush his
collar at the back—but he'd preferred the style before it
came into fashion. There was nothing to label him as an ex-
con or, as the slogan on his business card said, Finder of
Lost Persons.

He brushed a hand across his damp face and looked toward the entrance of the wrought-iron-enclosed courtyard.
Not a person stirred, so Mike settled back and closed his
eyes for a minute.

It had taken him three days since Jack Stanley had called
and he'd started the search in Santa Barbara to find the
Thomas woman. He'd started at the St. Thomas Home for
Girls, a series of old brick buildings attached to a Gothic-
looking church by arched walkways. One of the nuns who
had been there for years remembered that Alexandria
Thomas had spoken about heading for Los Angeles after
Sister Elizabeth had died. So Mike had made a few calls,
then flown down and begun looking around here. He'd finally found her through the Department of Motor Vehi-
cles. A driver's license made someone so traceable.

He'd found out she'd worked at eleven different jobs, and
that she'd left her last position eight months ago. She had
never married—at least he'd found no record of a marriage—and her last landlord at a tiny, nondescript apart-
ment in Westwood had given him her forwarding address.

"Nice little thing," the man had said. "Real quiet. Hardly knew she was there."

Mike had easily located this address and had barely had time to check the mailbox, finding only a number on the panel, then park under the huge tree before a black BMW had pulled up to the curb across the street. A woman with ebony hair caught in a high ponytail, and a wispy figure under jeans and a loose sweatshirt, had stepped out and hurried up the short walkway to the courtyard gates. She had quickly opened them, gone inside and disappeared into the first house to the left of the gate.

The woman had to be Alexandria Elizabeth Thomas. The house number had been right, and she fit the description he had from the DMV and her old landlord. "A big name for a tiny woman," the man had chuckled. "She's no more than five foot two and maybe a hundred pounds soaking wet."

Mike agreed with his assessment. A very big name and a very expensive address for someone who, as far as he could tell, hadn't had a job for over eight months. A beautiful woman with lots of money and no visible means of support.

If Mike had one flaw, he knew it was probably caring about his clients too much. There had been cases where he hadn't taken a fee because he knew the client couldn't afford it. Or cases where he'd put in extra time without charging for it. Or last year, when he'd stuck with a case for over a month because he hadn't wanted to go back to a mother and tell her that the evidence pointed to her daughter being dead. The extra work had paid off. The child had been found alive and well, and Mike had felt great.

He didn't feel too great now. He opened his eyes to the sunlit day and wondered why he had an urge to dig deeper than the surface on this case. He'd found her; he would get his pictures and contact Stanley. But it bothered him that the woman hadn't made any effort to hide or stay anonymous, not like the other people he'd located for Stanley. She was much prettier than the others, too. And the way she'd walked up to the house hadn't added up. She'd looked up at the sky, taken her time, with nothing furtive in her actions.

He'd wondered about the elusive Stanley from time to time over the years, who Stanley was, why he wanted the information he asked for. But he'd pushed his concerns aside until now. The man with the faintly British accent had been a client. Pure and simple. Until now. Questions about the man began to nudge at Mike, and he didn't understand why this time should be different. Something didn't add up, leaving Mike with a tingle of uncertainty, much like an itch that couldn't be scratched. He hated that feeling.

"Come on, Ms. Thomas," he muttered to himself. "Let's get this thing over and done with."

Right then the door of the condo opened. Mike sat up straight, lifted the camera and pressed its viewfinder to his eye. He adjusted the zoom lens until it focused on the tiny figure who came through the gates.

Her jeans and sweatshirt had been replaced by an elegant dress. Her ponytail had been restyled into a neat twist at the back of her head, but Alexandria Thomas still moved quickly and surely, with a hint of sensuality that Mike had noticed from the first. Maybe it was the rhythm of her hips, or her small high breasts, but she had a look that he'd always called "neat." Tidy, compact and very interesting.

She lifted her face to the sun as she stepped through the gates, her creamy skin glowing in the clear light. Mike trailed the lens along the line of her graceful neck to her chin, up across the hollow of her cheek to brown eyes luxuriously framed by dark lashes.

Her generous lips parted slightly. *Click.* He caught the action in freeze-frame. She walked toward the street. *Click.* She approached the black BMW sedan. *Click.*

Although Mike had been married for almost eight years and had four older sisters, he didn't know much about women's clothes. But the simple dress that molded perfectly to her narrow-waisted figure looked as expensive as the diamond teardrop earrings that flashed with reflected brilliance at her ears. She lifted her face again. The lens opened and closed, Mike's finger snapping the trigger almost on its own. *Click.*

She reached the BMW. *Click.* She circled it, a sweep of surprisingly long legs exposed as the skirt of her dress drifted above her knees. She pulled the door open. *Click.* Settling into the two-door sedan, she closed the door and turned to look over her left shoulder. *Click.* The car started and pulled away from the curb.

Mike watched her drive slowly down the street; then, instead of doing what he knew he should—going back to contact Stanley—he acted on impulse and followed the BMW. With the camera safely on the seat by him, he gripped the steering wheel with his square-fingered hands and concentrated on keeping a bit of distance between his car and hers.

Stanley had been specific on the phone. *"I want you to find Alexandria Elizabeth Thomas. She was put in the St. Thomas Home for Girls in Santa Barbara twenty-seven years ago. She left there when she was eighteen. Find out where she is, then get back to me. You've got a week."*

The expense account was open; Mike knew that from the other jobs he'd done for Stanley over the years. And it wouldn't add anything to the bill to spend another half hour or so following her, and he might be able to make a bit more sense out of what he'd found.

He watched the black car as she threaded it easily through the heavy afternoon traffic, and he sorted out what he had to tell Stanley. *I found her this morning and maybe she's a prostitute, or maybe she has an independent income, or maybe she won the Lottery.*

He saw her adjust her rearview mirror, and instinctively he slowed enough to let another car cut between him and the sedan. When the BMW took the off-ramp, Mike followed it into Beverly Hills. This job was almost done, and something in him wanted the report about a girl brought up by nuns in a dull brownstone home for girls to end on a positive note.

Hell, this is all business for Stanley, and he probably won't care what Alexandria Thomas's methods for making money are, Mike thought. And he knew he shouldn't care, either.

Being a thief never felt quite like Alex expected it to. Her heart beat steadily against her ribs. Her breathing stayed deep and even. Strange. She always expected a rush, but it never came, just a clear vision of what she would do.

She parked the BMW right in front of Aria's Diamonds on Rodeo Drive, got out and walked to the entrance of the tiny shop. With one black-gloved hand, she pushed back the glass and brass door and walked out of the June heat into cool quietness. "Elegant and expensive," her contacts had informed her when she asked around about Aria's. "Their security system is fairly new." But Alex was banking on her sense that the system had some serious flaws.

The high heels of her black leather pumps sank into deep beige carpeting, and her gaze swept right and left to rows of glass display cases set on marble bases. At the far end of the twenty-foot central aisle there was an area that had been designed to look like a living room. Two wheat-colored linen couches faced each other, separated by a round marble table with a square of black velvet laid smoothly on top.

Just as the door swung silently shut behind her, Alex noticed a surveillance camera tucked behind a six-foot palm to the right. Then she saw another camera fastened to the gold leaf base of the middle of three crystal chandeliers overhead. Her gaze slid along the textured walls, then dropped to the glass cases. It took her only a moment of intense scrutiny to spot skillfully camouflaged wires entering the display cases from the marble stands, wires used to monitor the weight of each piece of jewelry on pressure-sensitive spots. If a piece was moved without shutting off the alarm, a central control area would be notified. A neatly tied up security system, Alex decided. But not too neat.

Her hand tightened on her black silk purse when she spotted her target in the nearest case to her right. The bracelet. Just as she'd been told. Perfect. Three large diamonds set in a filigree of platinum and ringed by ruby chips. *Now* her heart began to beat faster. The bracelet was displayed next to ruby earrings.

"Welcome to Aria's."

Alex barely kept from jumping when a man's voice intruded on her concentration. With great deliberation, she took time to smooth the Dior original she'd bought for fifty dollars in a used-clothing store in Hollywood yesterday; then she looked toward the back of the store. A thin man in a subdued gray suit was coming toward her along the aisle. Pale eyes partially hidden by wire-rimmed glasses studied her. Albert Simon, she thought as she recognized the manager of Aria's from the pictures she'd been given.

Alex knew she was playing her part well when the man smiled at her. "I'm Mr. Simon. May I help, madam?"

As he stopped about two feet from her in the aisle, she nodded. "Yes. A friend recommended your store to me." She saw him glance at her diamond earrings, the only piece of good jewelry that she'd ever owned.

She smiled, knowing well the effect the expression had on men—on people in general. She'd practiced it often enough in the orphanage in front of the old mirror. Lift the faintly generous lips, crinkle sable brown eyes and sweep long, dark lashes low. People loved delicate children. Men loved women they perceived as delicate. "What about rubies and diamonds?" She shrugged with what she hoped was casual uncertainty. "Maybe earrings."

I haven't lost it, she thought with a degree of pleasure as the man nodded and said, "But of course. I have the very thing for madam."

Alex felt her heartbeat speed up even more as he moved to the case she'd targeted. Taking a silent breath, she followed and looked down into the display case. As she rested her purse on the glass top, the feel of the faint bulge in the purse under her gloved hand gave her a degree of comfort. Her excitement steadied as the anticipation of doing the job took over.

With a flourish, Mr. Simon laid a square of velvet on the top of the case, then silently unlocked it. He inserted a second key to cut off the alarm system in that section, took out the ruby earrings and arranged them on the velvet.

"Very special pieces," Mr. Simon murmured as he looked at Alex expectantly over the top of his glasses. "And the deep red would be perfect with madam's coloring." The earrings, two perfect diamonds encircled by tiny rubies, glittered in the overhead lights. "Two one-carat stones surrounded by rubies set in fourteen-karat gold."

Alex leaned forward and studied the earrings. Beautiful, she thought with inward appreciation for the exquisite work, but she waved them aside with the flick of one hand. "No, I don't think so."

The clerk peered at her. "Does madam have an idea of something else she might like?"

"Aria's has been going for more flash lately," her contact had told her. "Mixed gems, rubies, emeralds, some topaz and opals, all accenting perfect diamonds. If you ask for something plain, he'll have to go into the back of the shop."

She lifted one finely drawn brow and asked for what she knew he wouldn't have on display. "Perhaps a pendant, a simple teardrop—a diamond. Maybe two carats."

"I have exactly what you want," he said as he slipped the earrings back into place in the case.

When his hand went for the lock, Alex spoke up quickly. "I'm in a rush. Maybe I should come back later."

He waved that aside, his pleasant expression not completely masking the thought that he might be losing a nice commission if she walked out the door.

"No, no, no. It won't take me a moment," he said quickly and did what Alex had hoped he would. He left the case vulnerable by not rearming the system because of his rush to please the customer. "I know exactly what you'll like," he said over his shoulder as he hurried down the aisle.

"Fine," she murmured and watched until the man disappeared through a door near the left couch. Quickly, she opened her purse and, keeping her back to the cameras, slid out a bracelet, a poor imitation of the one under glass, but one with just the right weight. It could fool someone who only looked at it in passing.

She watched the cameras' actions out of the corner of her eye, counting while they swept away from her, then moved along the right side of the cabinet to the back corner. Five seconds for the cameras to complete their sweep. She hid the fake bracelet in her hand, pretended to be studying rings in a wall-mounted display case while she waited for the cameras to move away from her a second time. Then she reached into the case to her left.

One thousand-one. She lifted the bracelet. One thousand-two. Laid the fake in its spot. One thousand-three. She slid the door shut. One thousand-four. She had barely straightened before the cameras came back to her.

She closed her hand securely around the genuine bracelet and casually slipped her hand into her purse. She'd done it. She let a sense of satisfaction settle in as the weight of the bracelet slipped off her fingers.

Slowly she inched backward toward the front of the counter, but stopped dead when a deep male voice said, "All right, put it back."

She jerked around so sharply that she knocked her hip against the counter, and a real rush *did* fill her, then. A rush of fear. Her heart lurched, her breath caught in her chest, and her stomach knotted with shock when she found herself staring into eyes so green that they looked like emeralds. She damned herself for being careless enough to get caught, so careless that a security man had caught her red-handed.

Then she realized he couldn't be a security man. She knew all the staff at Aria's by sight. He wasn't one of the owners, or part of the management.

The knowledge that the man wasn't security should have helped, but as long as those eyes held her gaze, her heart refused to settle. With an effort, she looked away, but that only meant she finally saw the rest of the man. Thick brown hair swept back from a strong, angular face where deep lines bracketed a wide mouth and a cleft vaguely showed in a clean-shaven chin.

This man disturbed Alex, and not entirely because he'd caught her stealing. It was something more basic. Something in his strongly built body clearly defined by an expensive tan polo shirt and snug brown slacks. And she wasn't quite sure how to handle it. No more than how to act at being caught. Neither had happened to her before.

He'd neatly trapped her, his frame squarely blocking any chance Alex had of escaping into the aisle and through the door.

"Give it to me, and I'll put it back. Or do it yourself." She was thankful that he kept his voice low enough that it wouldn't be heard in the back room and draw Mr. Simon out. His eyes narrowed under a slash of dark brows as he darted a look to the back of the store; then he faced Alex and thrust out a strong, ringless hand, palm up. "Now!"

She moved back half a pace, trying to gather control. She had never felt quite so off balance, so unable to think clearly. But something in her let her know that this man in front of her wouldn't be fooled easily by lies. That didn't mean she wouldn't try anything to get away, but she didn't have high hopes of it working. She matched his whispered tone and hoped that she sounded authoritative enough. "I don't know who you think you are, but you're crazy. I didn't steal anything." She held the purse protectively against her middle. If the man would move just a bit to the left, she might be able to make it past him and run for the door.

But he held his ground, his hand still extended toward her. "Give me the damned bracelet," he said. "*I'll* put it back for you."

She cocked her head to one side. Would he react to a "helpless female" act? Probably not. He looked about forty, with gray brushing the temples of straight hair worn long enough to touch the collar of his shirt. And his tanned, not quite handsome face looked as if its owner had seen life in its many guises. The vaguely crooked nose might be from nature or from a fist.

Alex took a deep breath. She could pretend to faint. No, she could see intelligence in his eyes. That wouldn't work. So all she had left were indignation and attack. "I'd be careful, if I were you. You can't go around acting like this, accusing people of stealing!"

He came even closer, so close that she could feel the heat of his breath brush her face. "Damn it, listen to me! I'm trying to give you a chance to get out of here without being taken out by the police in handcuffs."

"*You* listen to *me*. This is none of your business." Alex had no idea what he was up to. Why would a customer get so involved? "Just leave me alone," she whispered. "I know what I'm doing."

"So do I. You're stealing a piece of jewelry."

"Listen, I . . ."

"Madam? Sir?"

Alex turned and saw Mr. Simon coming down the aisle. As he came closer, his eyes narrowed; he obviously sensed a confrontation, but didn't understand it. "May I be of some assistance?"

"I gave you a chance," the stranger whispered, low enough for only Alex to hear. When she turned back to him, he'd put two feet of distance between them, but his green eyes never left her face as he spoke to the manager. "It seems this lady . . ." He lifted one dark eyebrow inquiringly at Alex. "What was your name?"

This had turned into a fiasco, a real farce. First he'd seemed intent on helping her escape; now he was probably going to turn her over to Mr. Simon. This had never happened before. She'd never broken concentration in such a damaging way.

"You do have a name, don't you?" he persisted.

She moistened her lips. Damn, she hated failure. This job was a bust. She looked right into those intense eyes and spoke with sarcastic sweetness. "Mrs. John Robie."

A full heartbeat passed before Alex saw the stranger's re-action. The green eyes flashed with what might have been a burst of humor, but the reaction was gone so fast that she wondered if she'd imagined that he'd seen the movie *To Catch a Thief* with Grace Kelly and Cary Grant and gotten her joke. When she saw the total lack of a smile on his lips, her heart sank.

"Mrs. Robie?" he asked.

"Yes. Mrs. *John* Robie," she muttered.

Mr. Simon cleared his throat. "Er...Mrs. Robie, I don't understand...."

Alex drilled the stranger with her best glare of disgust, then looked at the clerk. She slipped her hand into her purse and took out the bracelet. "I removed this from your dis-play case," she said before the green-eyed man could inter-fere any more, and she dropped the piece of jewelry on the countertop.

"I can see you have everything under control," the stranger murmured, and Alex looked back at him at the same time that he abruptly turned away from her. The air stirred from his action, and Alex inhaled the essence of the man—after-shave, and something she could only label as "male."

Silently, she watched him head for the door, off balance from her reaction to him, and more than a little annoyed that he had so easily made her job secondary in her mind, something she couldn't afford to allow if she wanted to sur-vive.

As the door closed silently, Alex touched her tongue to her lips and turned to look down at the brilliant flash of diamonds and rubies lying on the black velvet square. Now that the man was gone, Alex realized that being caught had been embarrassing, but it could be only a minor setback if she played her cards right. With luck, she could still make it work.

"Well, well, well," Mr. Simon murmured as he scooped up the bracelet. "We regret it, but we must call the author-ities."

Alexandria Elizabeth Thomas pressed one hand flat on the glass top of the case and smiled her best smile. "If you'll call the owner, I think I can clear this up."

Within an hour Mike was back at the hotel near Los Angeles International Airport, in his silent room and on the phone to Paris.

"I didn't have much trouble finding her, Stanley."

"I didn't think you would. What's she like, Mike?"

"She's tiny, dark, beautiful and, I suspect, very bright."

"But? I can hear a qualifier in there. What's wrong with her?"

Mike debated for only a heartbeat, then spoke the truth. "She's a thief. Not to mention a consummate liar."

The silence came back and began to set Mike's nerves on edge. Then Stanley spoke in a low, tight voice. "Explain everything to me."

Mike went over the past three days, then the finale at Aria's. When he came to a stop, he waited for Stanley to make some comment.

"Are you absolutely certain there isn't a mistake, that you have the right girl?"

"She's Alexandria Thomas, all right." He, above anyone, should know how mistakes could be made by trusting in appearances, how it could destroy people, but he couldn't hedge with Stanley. "I saw her steal the bracelet."

"Why did she do it? What was her explanation?"

"She didn't offer one, and I wasn't in any position to demand one from her." *And how do you explain grand theft?*

"Mike, I need that girl. But I can't use her if she's what you think she is. I have to be certain her presence will do good . . . not harm. She's vital to me."

You're out of luck, then, Mike thought, but kept his own counsel.

"What happened to her?" Stanley asked.

"I didn't hang around to find out, but my best guess is that she's on her way to jail by now." The words brought bitterness to the back of his throat. "That bracelet wasn't some cheap fake.'' Mike hesitated, then said, ''I just wanted you to know the job's done. I found her. I'll send the information to the box number, and you can—''

''No.''

The single word stopped Mike. ''What?''

Stanley took an audible breath before speaking quickly, ''I want you to stay with this for a bit longer, Mike. Is there any way you can get information from the jail?''

''There might be. I've got an old friend working for the LAPD. He might be able to get something for me.''

''Good. Good. Check with him and find out anything you can. I'll make it worth your while.''

Mike didn't care about extra money right now. All he really wanted to do was go back home and forget about Alexandria Thomas, but he found himself agreeing. ''All right.'' He glanced at his watch. ''It's too soon to get anything. She wouldn't be processed yet.''

''Maybe things aren't what they seem to be.''

Despite his statement, Stanley didn't sound any more hopeful that there had been a mistake than Mike felt. ''Sure,'' he agreed softly. ''I'll get back to you as soon as I can.'' And he hung up.

He looked at the stock hotel room, neutral and boring, done in dull beige and green. He'd give the police another hour to get the woman booked; then he'd contact Gil Barrows and see what he could find out.

Abruptly he stood, tension knotting the muscles at the back of his neck, and he walked into the bathroom. He stripped off his clothes, tossing them carelessly onto the floor; then he stepped over the pile and into the tiny shower stall. Flipping on the water, he stood very still while the hot stream washed over him.

Suddenly he realized he'd omitted telling Stanley that he'd tried to stop the woman from stealing the bracelet. Maybe he'd kept that quiet because he didn't understand it himself. What had possessed him to do that? Momentary insanity? Stupidity? Hormones?

From a distance he'd admired her, even felt vague stirrings in his body as he studied her. Up close he'd been bombarded by her. Lust he understood, but he didn't understand the overriding instinct he'd succumbed to when he'd realized what she was up to. He'd thought only of getting her out of there, of protecting her. It stunned him even now thinking about it. "For Pete's sake," he muttered and reached for the soap. "A knight in shining armor? Rescuing a thief and a liar." He thought of how ridiculous that sounded.

He picked up a washcloth and began to scrub his skin. But he couldn't quite put the questions out of his mind. What was this woman to Stanley, a man he'd never once met, who never said whom he worked for, who paid the bills, or why he needed people located from time to time. He'd never even questioned why Stanley had run a security check on him before giving him that first assignment. Now Stanley wanted Alexandria Thomas for some reason—but not if she was a thief.

He rubbed his skin with a vengeance. She hadn't looked like a thief to Mike. And he'd known enough thieves in the prison to spot one when he saw one. Then the answer came. Her appearance was her gimmick. Every crook had one. She certainly did. Beautiful. Tiny. Neat. Delicate. Wide-eyed.

Careful, he told himself with real feeling. *Careful.*

Mike stood very still, unable to understand why some woman who was a thief could make him wish he wasn't alone tonight. The cloth slipped out of his fingers and tumbled to the shower floor. Despite the force of the water, he felt a familiar tightness in his loins, a tightness he knew would turn to much more if he let it.

Abruptly, he reached for the faucet, turned off the hot water and let the cold take over. He gasped as the coolness washed over him and stopped the real ache before it began. Damn it. He didn't want to feel this way about someone like her. A thief and a liar! He'd had his fill of lies years ago. He knew the price they exacted from people.

Then things shifted as he remembered the name the woman had given—Mrs. John Robie—and he began to laugh, the sound echoing all around him in the shower stall.

Chapter 2

It had taken almost two hours for Alex to get things worked out at Aria's, and she felt very tired by the time she got into the BMW and headed back to the house in Santa Monica.

She drove slowly through the congested, late-afternoon traffic on her way to the freeway, thankful to be done with the Aria's job. As she swung onto the freeway, she snapped on the radio. "And the weather forecast for Southern California is perfect for the beginning of the Fourth of July weekend. Hot and clear, with the ocean temperature heading into the high seventies. Inland, the days will soar into the eighties. Enjoy the Fourth and head to the beach to see the firework displays at . . ." the announcer was saying.

The Fourth of July. Alex could almost feel the delicate gold of the heart-shaped locket lying between her breasts under the black dress. *Alexandria, July 4th,* the inscription read. She was so used to wearing it that she often forgot about it completely. But that date brought a lot back to her.

She'd claimed the day as her birthday simply because she didn't know the real date. Now it *was* hers. The way her name had become hers. She was Alexandria Elizabeth

Thomas, though she used other names from time to time when she had to. She took an unsteady breath and stared straight ahead at the rush-hour traffic. Like Mrs. John Robie.

The name brought a flashing memory of the stranger who had called her a thief. Odd that he had seemed bent on protecting her from being caught at first. Maybe he was one of those do-gooders out to make everyone in the world fit their mold of morality.

As she took the off-ramp near the beach, she caught a glimpse of the blue of the Pacific splashed with the rich colors of twilight. In just a few minutes she was on her street. She slowed, pulled the BMW to the curb and turned off the motor, but she didn't get out immediately.

She stared at her gloved hands on the wood-tone steering wheel. Today had been strange, with nothing turning out the way she'd planned, yet in the long run she'd done just fine. She tugged off her gloves and dropped them along with the car keys into her purse. She caught a glimpse of the check for her work at Aria's.

The owner had been generous, even more so than when he had first approached her with his request. "I heard from a client that you really know security systems," he'd said less than a week ago. "I'm willing to pay whatever it takes to make sure my establishment is secure."

Whatever it takes. She stared at the amount on the check, then tucked it more securely into her purse and snapped the fastener. He'd added a good bonus to their agreed-on payment. Some day, if things kept going this well, she'd be able to afford a few luxuries herself.

She sank back in the leather seat, and for a moment she simply let go and allowed the dreaming to take over. That ability to pretend had been her salvation for as long as she could remember, a comfortable escape from a crazy world that she had never quite fit into. If she closed her eyes, it was so easy to pretend this was all hers. She could lose herself in the dream of having this car, these clothes and this condo at the beach. She inhaled the rich scent of the leather interior. In dreams, anything was possible.

No more rentals, no house-sitting for a year while the owner was on sabbatical in Europe, no using the owner's car. The BMW and the two-story, Spanish-style condominium with a view of the ocean were hers. And when she went in the front door, she wouldn't be facing rooms draped in silence and dust sheets, but a home warm with loving, where he'd be waiting for her. She didn't know who "he" would be, but she knew they'd talk about their day, curl up in front of the fireplace with glasses of wine, hold each other and make love.

She looked up into his face over her and into the greenest eyes...Alex opened her own eyes abruptly and sat up straight. "Enough of that, Alex," she muttered and, with a shake of her head, got out of the car. Enough of dreams. After a lifetime of nothing but made-up stories and yearnings, she had finally begun to make a life for herself. She still made up the stories, but now she got paid for them. They helped her survive. And that's what she was above all else— a survivor.

She strode up the walkway and through the gate toward the house. Eight months ago she'd left her last job, a boring sales position, but she'd left with enough savings to last six months. Up to now she hadn't had to touch her nest egg. The jobs had come slowly at first, by word-of-mouth, taking time to gain momentum. But satisfied customers recommended her to others, just as someone had mentioned her to the owner of Aria's, and now she was making enough to actually put some money away.

She fumbled for her key in her purse, unlocked the door and pushed it back. She swung the door shut, threw the bolt and walked quickly through the silent, shadowed rooms without looking right or left. The owner had given her unconditional use of the entire house, yet she'd chosen to stay in one room, a bedroom at the back on the first floor, that had a view of the ocean. She suspected it was meant to be a maid's room, but it felt right to her. And that meant a lot.

There hadn't been too many places in this world where she felt comfortable.

As she stepped into the darkened bedroom, the flashing red light on the answering machine by the bed caught her attention. Stepping out of her shoes on the way to the bed, she crossed to snap on a light. The soft yellow glow barely touched the pastel-toned room done in natural wicker and brass.

Alex dropped down on the double bed and reached to push the *play* button. But nothing was there except buzzing from three callers who had hung up instead of leaving their messages.

As she pushed *rewind* the phone rang, and she picked it up immediately. "Hello?"

"Alex Thomas, please," a deep, rough male voice said.

"This is Alex Thomas."

Total silence met her words, and for a moment she thought the connection had been cut. Then the man spoke abruptly. "I didn't know Alex Thomas was a woman."

Alex wanted to tell him that this Alex Thomas had never been anything else, but she held her peace. "Who is this, please?" she asked evenly.

"My name's Lincoln."

"And you wanted to speak to me?"

He hesitated, then said, "I was going to talk to you about a job, but..."

She wasn't going to lose a prospective assignment just because some man couldn't handle the fact that Alex Thomas was female. "Mr. Lincoln, if you have a job, I assume you need something done—something you can't do on your own?"

"Yes, but—"

Before he could say any more, she cut him off. "If you'll tell me what the job is, maybe I can offer *you* a deal?"

"Oh, a deal, is it?" Condescending humor touched each word.

She kept her annoyance under control. "If your job sounds interesting and I think I can do it successfully, I'll take it on. If I fail, you owe me nothing at all. But, if I succeed, I'll accept a bonus." It was a gamble, just as it had been when she'd used it before. It had worked then. Now she held her breath.

A long silence hung on the line, followed by a gruff laugh. "That's quite a deal, little lady."

She cringed at the "little lady" expression, but made herself ask, "Do you want to take a chance and tell me what the job is, Mr. Lincoln?"

"Sure. I'm game. I want the security system at the Elysian Hotel and Casino in Las Vegas checked."

"The whole hotel?"

"No. We have three different systems. One for the casinos, one for the hotel rooms and one for the tower. I only want the system for the tower area checked."

Hotel/casino combinations usually had multiple systems, and Alex knew most of them thoroughly. She asked him the make of the system, and when he gave it, she didn't hesitate. "I can do it . . . if you want me to."

"I'm not sure. I heard that you check them in a rather . . . er . . . unique way."

"What exactly did you hear?" Alex asked and scooted back on the bed until she could lean against the high wicker headboard. She pushed a mauve throw pillow behind her head.

"That you figure out the flaws in a system by getting past it without anyone knowing about it until you're done."

Alex closed her eyes and pushed the silky blue and mauve bedspread with her heels. She could relax a bit now that she knew she had him interested. "That's about it."

"And what are the odds of a system being faulty?"

"Seventy-five percent of the systems I test are inadequate in one way or another. It's hard to make a foolproof system, Mr. Lincoln. They just get more complicated."

"*If* our system is faulty, what do you do?"

"I get into the secured area, retrieve something, get back out, then give it to you as proof that I broke the barriers." She wouldn't think about today, when the owner of Aria's had rushed into the store, worried that there had been a scene. She ignored that because everything had worked out in the end. She'd gotten her fee and earned the man's respect by pointing out how his system had failed. And there wouldn't be a green-eyed stranger at the Elysian to mess things up. She took a breath. "Included in my fee is a written report on the strengths and weaknesses of the system. How to improve it, and, if I think it's necessary, a recommendation for replacing it with a better system."

"And this can all be kept quiet? I don't want our guests to lose confidence in our hotel."

"You're head of security at the hotel?" She couldn't remember if he'd said that or not.

"Exactly, and I need to keep things going smoothly with the guests. A hint that the Elysian isn't absolutely safe could do a lot of damage. Gamblers are well-known to be paranoid, and even a suggestion that they can't count on our security procedures could be devastating."

"I understand completely. This won't go any further than you and me and whomever you report to."

"You don't have a partner, do you?"

"No, I work completely alone. The fewer the people involved, the better the chances of success."

"Good enough. If you can guarantee absolute discretion, you have a deal."

"I *do* guarantee it. Now, I need details."

"I'd rather go over them in person with you. How soon can you fly into Las Vegas?"

"How about after the holiday? I can . . ."

He interrupted her. "How about tomorrow morning?"

Alex sat up straight and opened her eyes. She could do the report on Aria's tonight. She didn't have any job waiting to be done, so the timing wasn't too bad for going to Las Vegas. "The flights out might be full, and I don't want to drive."

"Most tourists are coming in today, and I know that United has a flight out at eleven from LAX, flight 1250. I'm sure you can get on it. When you get here, wait inside the terminal doors, and I'll find you. Then we'll talk." He hesitated. "You're sure this won't go any further than us? If anyone knows you here, or recognizes your name . . ."

"I'm not famous, Mr. Lincoln. It's to my benefit to keep a low profile when I work, but I can use another name if it would make you feel better."

"It can't hurt. An ounce of prevention. You know."

"Of course."

"Better safe than sorry, little lady." She was waiting for him to say "loose lips sink ships," but instead he asked quickly, "What name do you want to use?"

Alex had known from the first that her work was like a game to her. A job, yet one she approached like a game of wits. And she got into the swing of it with Lincoln. "What color will you be wearing tomorrow when we meet?"

"Oh, um . . . gray, I suppose."

"All right, I'll be Mrs. Gray. One thing I've learned is to keep any deception simple. There's less to go wrong, fewer ways to get tripped up."

"You sound like a real pro."

"Then it's settled?"

"Get a reservation on flight 1250 in the name of Gray and call the hotel for a room reservation. I'll make sure you get one."

"Fine."

"How will I know you when I see you?"

Alex exhaled and thought. "I'll be carrying a blue tote bag with a big 'A' on it."

"All right."

"See you tomorrow," she said and hung up.

She sat in the silent room for a while without moving, just thinking it all over; then she reached for the telephone again. She asked for Las Vegas information. "The number for the Elysian Hotel and Casino, please."

When she had the number, she dialed it and asked for security.

There was a pause, then, "Security. Taggert speaking."

"I'm Sara Blair with the Trans-West Credit Bureau."

"Yes, ma'am. What can I do for you?"

"We've been contacted by a client to check on Mr. Lincoln who works at the Elysian."

"Yes, ma'am, Milt Lincoln. He's worked here for a long time, longer than me. Probably ten years or so."

"What I need to know, Mr. Taggert, is exactly what Mr. Lincoln does at the Elysian."

"Security, ma'am. He's head of it, making sure that everything works right. He's really good at spotting trouble areas. He's tough to work for, real demanding. I mean, I wouldn't want you telling him I said that, but he does the work real well. Personality isn't everything, is it?"

"No, it certainly isn't," she said.

"That's the way I figure. Just because some guy's got a short fuse and wants everyone to be perfect, it doesn't make him bad. Milt's damn good at what he does. I think he's..."

Alex thanked her lucky stars that Taggert wasn't involved in national security. She had all she could do to cut him off before he gave her any and all the informational tidbits she could ever want. "You've been a big help, Mr. Taggert. Thank you. Oh, one other thing, is Mr. Lincoln in the position to hire people?"

"He hired me, and he's hired all the staff since I've been here."

"Is Mr. Lincoln there now?"

"No, ma'am. He left a few minutes ago. He's got something he's working on. I don't know what. That's another thing, he's real closemouthed about things. I don't ask him too much. He doesn't like talking about the work a lot."

Not like you, she thought. "Thank you, Mr. Taggert. Thank you." And she hung up, making a mental note to tell Lincoln about maintaining security even over something as trivial as getting information from an employee over the telephone.

She hit the redial button on the phone and asked for reservations for the hotel.

* * *

In the darkened hotel room, Mike lay on the bed wearing just his jockey shorts. Finally, he sat up, swung his legs over the side and snapped on a table light.

He lifted the telephone receiver and pushed the button for information. "I need the number for the Los Angeles Police Department. This isn't an emergency."

The operator told him the number, and he hung up, then dialed it."

"Police."

"I need to talk to Detective Barrows in vice, please."

"Who's calling?"

"Michael Conti."

The line buzzed with emptiness for more than a minute; then Gil Barrows answered, his deep, smooth voice instantly recognizable. "Hey, Mikey, is that you?"

The use of his old nickname made Mike smile. "It's me all right, Gil. How're things with you?"

"Since I haven't talked to you for almost a year, I hate to tell you they're about the same as always. Married, happy, two kids, lots of bills, a steady job that pays me enough to make ends meet."

"So goes the life of a cop, full of excitement and danger." Mike laughed.

"You got that right. Last I heard from your mother, you were licking your wounds from the divorce. What're you up to now and where are you calling from?"

The reference to the divorce sobered Mike. "I'm long past the 'licking my wounds' stage, and I'm keeping busy working. Right now I'm working on a case down here in L.A."

"Hey, if you're in town, maybe we can...?"

"No, sorry, I'm on a tight schedule." Somehow, it didn't sound appealing to get together for drinks right now and talk over the old days in the old neighborhood. Gil and he had been close years ago, but things had changed so much, starting right after Mike's arrest. Gil had gone off to the police academy, while Mike had gone to prison. "Next time I'm down, we'll get together. All right?"

"Sure. If you didn't get in touch to visit, what's this call for?"

"Information."

"Shoot."

"I need to find out about a prisoner who was arrested in Beverly Hills a few hours ago. Can you get information on the arrest for me?"

"Sure, if you give me a few minutes to call over there."

"No problem."

"All right. Male or female?"

"Female. Alexandria Thomas."

"Alexandra Thomas?"

"No. Alexandria, like the city in Egypt. Thomas. T-h-o-m-a-s. She was picked up on Rodeo Drive today—late afternoon—grand theft."

"Hold on."

Mike stared into the shadows until Gil came back on the line after two minutes. "No one by that name's over there."

"Was there anyone booked, then let out on bail or O.R.?"

"I checked that, too. Nothing."

He frowned, then remembered Mrs. John Robie. "Maybe she used an alias. Could you look . . . ?"

"I could, but it wouldn't do any good. There hasn't been a grand theft arrest on Rodeo for a week. That isn't a real hotbed of crime, Mike."

"I appreciate the help."

"What's it all about?"

"The case I'm working on."

"A missing person?"

"She used to be. I'm not sure exactly what she is now."

"Mikey, is there anything I can help you with?"

Mike heard the same tone in Gil's voice that had been there when they had both been eighteen and Gil had been the one to see the police arrest Mike and take him in. Gil had sounded the same when he'd said, "Can I help, Mikey? Tell me what to do for you."

Gil hadn't been able to help then, and it seemed that he couldn't really help now. "No, Gil, nothing. But thanks for the offer."

After talking generalities for a few minutes, Mike hung up and fell back on the bed. What had happened? He stared into the shadows of the acoustic ceiling over him. Had the woman talked the clerk out of calling the police? Had she made a deal with the owner? Had someone important pulled strings? Had she escaped from Mr. Simon? Had there been a partner waiting to help?

He sat up, reached for the phone again and dialed the overseas number. Stanley answered with a single word. "Yes?"

"It's me. I just called the police."

"What happened to her?"

"Nothing. She wasn't arrested. I don't know why."

"Where is she?"

"I don't know."

"Find out."

"Then what?"

"Don't let her out of your sight, Mike. I've got a few days before I need to make a decision about her. And who knows, maybe things aren't as bad as they look. After all, she wasn't arrested. Circumstantial evidence can be misleading."

"Yeah, it can be," he agreed.

"Find her and don't lose her, Mike."

"I'll do my best," he murmured.

"I'm counting on you," Stanley said, then hung up.

Mike dropped the receiver back on the cradle, then stood and slipped on a pair of Levi's. After pushing his feet into sneakers, then putting on a white shirt, he left his hotel room and went down to get into his rental car. Quickly, he drove through the night back to Santa Monica.

Circumstantial evidence—evidence that implies the existence of a fact. He knew the definition by heart. And if seeing Alexandria Thomas stealing wasn't enough to infer grand theft, he didn't know what was.

Almost simultaneously, the idea of her in jail brought sickness to the back of his throat and the idea that she'd escaped going to jail made him angry. Mike gripped the steering wheel more tightly. Damn it, he knew she'd stolen the bracelet. He'd seen it with his own eyes.

He stared out at the night, at the lights of cars passing him by, until his eyes burned. But why had he tried to stop her, to make her get out before she could be caught? "Protector of the world," his mother had often teased. Maybe she had been right. He had simply hated the idea of Alexandria Thomas being in jail.

He drove slowly onto the residential street in Santa Monica and pulled over to the curb a few doors down from her condominium. For over an hour he stared at Alex's home, but the windows never showed any light. Short of going up to look in the windows, he didn't know how he could prove whether she was there or not.

With a low oath, he started his car and drove away. When he got to the hotel, he looked through his notes and found the phone number for Alex's address. He dialed the number and waited for two rings; then an answering machine picked up. "Sorry, no one can take your call right now, but if you leave your name and number after the beep, someone will get back to you as soon as possible."

Just when he was going to hang up, he heard a double click, then a sleep-filled voice murmuring, "Hello? Hello?"

Alex. And the image her soft voice conjured up, her dark hair tousled from sleep, her brown eyes heavy... He hung up quickly. At least he knew she was back at her house.

He waited a minute to collect himself; then he put in a call to Stanley.

By seven the next morning, Mike was back at the condominium, parked down the street a short distance from the BMW, his suitcase in the trunk. Stanley hadn't been at the number last night, but the man who'd answered had asked for a message. Mike had made it simple. He knew where the girl was. "Stay with her, don't let her disappear and call back by noon your time tomorrow," he'd been told.

Mike settled back in his car and waited, but by nine o'clock he was beginning to wonder whether Alex was really at home or if he'd been wasting precious time watching an empty house. Then a taxi cab drove past Mike's car and double-parked beside the BMW. The driver honked once, and a moment later Alex came out into the clear sunlight of morning. Mike actually had to look twice to make sure it was really her. She looked so different from yesterday.

Her dark hair had been pulled back from her face with clips; it was parted in the middle and curled softly against her neck and around her ears. The elegant dress had been forsaken for an oversized pink cotton blouse and white walking shorts that showed off surprisingly long, tanned legs. Leather-thonged sandals and oversize sunglasses gave a feeling of "tourist," an impression accentuated by the huge blue tote bag she carried.

Whatever had happened with her yesterday, she didn't show any signs of worry or fear. She wasn't in jail, but she *was* going somewhere. Mike started his car as she tossed her bag into the back of the taxi, then got in after it. Pulling his rental car out into the street, he followed the yellow cab.

After a long trip in and out of traffic on the congested freeway, Mike followed the taxi off at the exit for Los Angeles International Airport. He stayed one car back while it funneled into the multiple lanes that led past the terminals. Alex's cab pulled up at the unloading area for United, and Mike drove slowly past to stop at an unloading zone farther down the way. He got out and motioned to a skycap. As the man hurried over to him, he held out twenty dollars. "Can you take care of this for me? Just park it and take the key to the rental station on the tag. Tell them where it's parked."

The man hesitated. "I'm not sure I can do that, sir." Then he saw how much money Mike had given him and smiled. "Sure thing, mister. No problem."

With a hurried "thank you," Mike got his bag out of the trunk and took off at a jog toward the United terminal. Alex was nowhere to be seen, at first; then Mike spotted her in the crowd just inside the glass doors by the luggage carts. He went after her, barely managing to keep sight of her dark head.

When he got within a few feet of her as she neared the counter, he veered off to a television screen that showed the flight schedule. If he concentrated and blocked out most of the general noise all around, he could hear her talking to the counter agent and only miss a few words here and there.

"...and flight 1250 leaves in fifteen minutes from gate 70," the clerk said. "Thank you for...United."

"Thank *you*," Alex said.

"Have a good time...enjoy your flight, Mrs. Gray."

Mrs. Gray? Mike turned and saw Alex walking off in the direction of gate 70. When she was out of sight, he looked back at the screen in front of him. Flight 1250 was on time and going to Las Vegas.

If he wasn't going to let her out of his sight, that meant he was going to Las Vegas, too. He didn't have time to contact Stanley right now. He got in line; then when he approached the clerk, he asked, "Is flight 1250 full?"

The uniformed man checked the computer screen in front of him, then shook his head. "You're lucky. It was, but we've had a few cancellations."

Mike hesitated. "I have a friend on the flight, Mrs. Gray. Is there any chance of getting a seat near hers?"

He checked again, then looked up at Mike. "Sorry. She's way in the back. The empty one's in row four at the front, by the window."

Good. Now he knew where she'd be—and that she wasn't likely to spot him. The farther away he was from Alex, the better he'd be. It would be hard enough getting on without her seeing him, and he didn't want any more contact with her unless he could control the circumstances. "Thanks. I'll take it."

Chapter 3

Alex was one of the last passengers to step off the plane into the hot desert air. She squinted at the glare of the terminal shimmering in the brilliant sun. Las Vegas. She'd wanted to come here for a long time, to look into the job market. After all, what Lincoln had said was the truth. Gamblers were paranoid. But not quite as paranoid as the hotel owners. She would have a bit of free time this trip, so she could check out some hotels. Because of this job, she had an excuse to be here and all her expenses were being paid.

With the sun hurting her eyes and her hair vaguely damp from the heat, she went down the steps and onto the blacktop. Slipping her sunglasses on, she took one step away from the stairs, then someone touched her on the shoulder.

"Really nice meeting you, Mrs. Gray."

Alex glanced at the middle-aged woman who had sat by her on the flight, a Mrs. Erskin from San Diego, a brilliant vision in a flowing purple shift. Alex nodded and smiled. "Nice meeting you, too." She motioned to the terminal. "Let's get out of this sun."

The two women walked quickly toward the building along with the other passengers. "Never did like the heat," the heavyset woman said, a bit breathless from the fast walk toward shade and coolness. She pulled a huge, floppy-brimmed hat out of her tote and plunked it on her head. "Hate the sun, but love to gamble. Just love it. I can't believe you've never been to Vegas. Didn't know such a person existed in the world."

"I never had the chance before. But I'm excited about being here—finally." Alex was being pleasant, but she hoped that the woman would disappear as soon as they got into the terminal; at least before Lincoln showed up. "Are you meeting someone here?" she asked to make conversation.

"Sure thing. Friends of mine. They'll be waiting in the bar with a cool drink. How about you? Is your husband coming?"

Alex could have said there was no Mr. Gray, and she knew she should to keep it simple, but she couldn't resist. "No, he's too busy. He's an artist, a portrait painter. And he's getting ready for a showing of his pictures."

"Oh, how exciting." The woman looked very impressed. "I'm not one who knows much about art, but you must be so proud. It's too bad he couldn't come here with you, though."

Alex nodded. "I know. But Dorian just seems to thrive on the work. It keeps him youthful, but I needed a vacation."

"I love a good vacation," the woman said at Alex's side as they stepped into the terminal.

Alex relished the refreshing coolness that washed around her like a cool drink of water. She stopped just inside the doors and smiled at the other woman. "Good luck to you, Mrs. Erskin."

Mrs. Erskin looked around, then pointed down the terminal to the left. "There's the bar." She looked back at Alex. "Have a good time," she said. "And next time you come here, you bring your husband, Dorian, with you."

Then she strode off into the crowds milling around the doors.

Alex set her tote down by her feet. Dorian Gray? A portrait painter? Where had she come up with that one? She hadn't felt like playing games with people for a long time. She stopped. That wasn't right. Just yesterday she'd given her name to the green-eyed stranger at Aria's as Mrs. John Robie.

She chuckled softly to herself. Even Sister Elizabeth would have loved that one, Alex conceded. The sister would have enjoyed it, then punished Alex for lying, but not too severely—never too severely. There was a lot of remembered gentleness and affection, and maybe that was why Alex had asked Sister Elizabeth once if she was her mother.

The gentle woman had hugged her so tightly that Alex had barely been able to breathe. "No, child, I didn't give birth to you." She'd moved back and laid a hand on her ample breast. "But in here . . . deep down inside my heart, I think you just might be my child, that you were meant to be with me."

Alex exhaled, unnerved at the prick of tears behind her eyes. Quickly, she rubbed a hand over her face. Why was she thinking about the orphanage now? That was another life, a life Alex had deliberately put behind her after Sister Elizabeth died. A life she never admitted had even existed anymore. The story of being from a big family, of being the child who set out on her own, made things better, easier.

And maybe she believed the story herself just a bit. Maybe that was why she could survive. Believing was half the game. The lying didn't count.

"Alexandria," Sister Elizabeth would say in her tiny voice when she caught Alex in one of her lies. "Truth is a weapon. Truth is its own defense. Truth is its own reward. You must learn the value of truth in all things."

Alex remembered standing with her head down, nodding very solemnly, agreeing with every word. But that hadn't stopped her from trying to figure out who she *really* was. The problem was, she'd never found out. The records had been sealed; then, when she could have seen them, they had been destroyed by fire, and Sister Elizabeth had been gone. Now she would never know. She accepted that intellectually, but in her heart she never would. That was why she made up stories.

They weren't really lies. I've got a vivid imagination, an exceptional way of expanding the truth and pretending to have what everyone else in the world has had, but me, she thought. Good rationalization, Alex, she told herself.

She leaned back against the cool wall by the door as the old ache settled in her stomach. She'd always expected that to decrease with time, but it didn't. It just hid a little better as she grew older.

Enough, she told herself and concentrated on what she was doing in Las Vegas. This was work time, not play time. She scanned the milling crowds for a man who could be Lincoln. She'd formed a mental image of him while she spoke to him on the phone. From his voice, Alex had guessed that Lincoln was tall, well built, maybe forty. He probably dressed in a sports shirt and cords, along with dark glasses. "Wait by the door when your flight gets in," he'd told her. "I'll find you there."

A short, balding man came toward her looking nothing like she expected; then she realized that the Bermuda shorts and matching shirt in bright blue eliminated him from the running. No gray there, and he passed her by, going out the door. Just when she was beginning to think Lincoln had stood her up, she spotted another man coming through the crowd in her direction. Tall, slender, in gray slacks and a white linen shirt, possibly fifty years old. He looked exactly as Alex had pictured Lincoln, only a bit older. She stood straighter, pushed her sunglasses up on her head and smiled.

Wiping her damp hand on her shorts, Alex was just ready to step forward when the gray-haired man veered off without even looking at her.

She slumped back against the wall.

"Mrs. Gray?" a man asked.

Alex turned to her right and found a skycap looking at her questioningly.

"Mrs. Gray?" he asked again.

"Oh, yes," Alex managed.

"A gentleman asked me to give you this." He handed her a folded piece of paper and a single rose in white tissue paper. She took them both, and the skycap turned and walked away. Alex shrugged, flipped the paper open and read the scrawled writing done in black ink.

Accept this rose and my apology for not being able to meet you. An emergency came up at the hotel, and I had to get back. I would appreciate you catching a taxi and meeting me in the security offices of the Elysian, downstairs, at 12:30. Come right in. I'm in the last office.

Lincoln

Alex glanced at the rose, then at her watch. Half an hour before she had to meet Lincoln. Just enough time to find a rest room and catch a taxi to the hotel. Automatically, she tore the note in half and tossed it into a waste basket nearby; then she looked for a rest-room sign.

Mike cursed himself for being so stupid. He'd watched Alex from a safe distance for almost ten minutes; then he'd taken his eyes off of her just long enough to ask where the nearest telephones were, and when he'd looked back at the doors, she'd disappeared. He looked in both directions, but he couldn't see her anywhere.

He moved quickly, weaving his way through the jostling crowds, but he arrived at the entrance to the terminal without catching sight of her. He stepped outside into the furnacelike heat, then looked up and down the area where buses and taxis pulled away from the curb in a steady stream, but there was no tiny, dark-haired woman anywhere to be seen.

Finally he went back inside and decided to watch the entrance from a safe distance. If he was very lucky, Alex was still in the terminal. If not, he'd call Stanley and tell him that Alexandria Thomas was missing again. He hated to do that.

He looked at his watch. He'd wait a half hour, then go to the telephone by the bar and contact Stanley.

Alex stepped out of the rest room and smoothed her vaguely clammy clothes. She wished she had the time to change, but splashing cool water on her face and combing her hair had helped a bit. Gripping her purse and tote bag, she headed for the entry.

She went through the crowds of people that all looked as if they had come ready for a party, wearing bright clothes and laughing at the least little thing. They must have come to celebrate the Fourth of July, she thought. Birthdays and celebrations. She closed off that subject, keeping the past, which seemed intent on intruding, at bay.

She neared the door of the terminal, then reached out and touched the cool glass to push it back. The heat she stepped into almost took her breath away.

"Can I help you, ma'am?" a skycap asked immediately.

Alex slipped her sunglasses down and nodded. "I need a cab to the Elysian."

"Yes, ma'am. That's downtown on the Strip," he said as he took her case from her. "Come with me."

She followed him to the curb and watched him wave to the next cab in line. It pulled forward, the man opened the door, and when Alex got in, he put her tote on the front seat. "The Elysian," the skycap said to the driver.

Alex handed the man a tip and sat back. But before the door closed, the skycap looked back inside. "Would you be willing to share your cab with another person going to the Strip, ma'am?"

"Sure," Alex agreed as she settled back in the coolness of the air conditioner and closed her eyes for a moment.

"Thanks, I appreciate this," a deep, masculine voice said.

It took a moment for the sound of the voice to register with Alex, but when it did, it drew her up sharply. She turned and found herself looking into eyes as green as emeralds.

"Hello again," the man said as he leaned back and the cab pulled away from the curb.

Alex stared at him, her mind spinning. He didn't seem the least bit shocked to see her, but all she could manage was a single word. "You."

"Yes. Me." He turned in the seat and studied her from under thick, dark lashes. "And who are *you* today?"

Alex touched her tongue to her lips and couldn't think what he was talking about. All she understood was the fact that he had been in her thoughts a lot last night under the guise of "what went wrong" with the Aria's job. Even though she'd always had a good eye for details, she couldn't think why this man had been so thoroughly imprinted on her mind.

His eyes were memorable—she freely admitted that—but what was it about the rich, brown hair or the lean strength of his build that had stuck so firmly with her? Now, sitting just inches away in the tight confines of the cab, he looked annoyingly relaxed and cool. A white shirt, with the sleeves rolled up to expose arms roughened by dark hair, was worn with faded Levi's and blue running shoes. The well-worn denim molded his muscular legs, and Alex watched him spread his hands on his thighs. Square nails. Long fingers. No rings.

He'd asked her a question, and she didn't have any idea what it had been. "What did you say?" she managed in a voice that came out almost as a croak.

"The last time we talked, you were Mrs. John Robie." His lashes hid none of the humor in the green depths of his gaze. "Who are you today? Grace Kelly?"

So he *had* understood her reference yesterday. Alex released a breath, but found that her lips wouldn't respond with a smile. "No, I'm not. I'm Alexandria . . ." She hesitated, but had enough control to stay with her cover. "Alex Gray."

"Is there a Mr. Gray?"

She fingered her purse in her lap, nervously smoothing the soft leather. That direct question put her in a corner. "There ... there used to be, but he's gone."

"Gone?"

"We're divorced."

"What a relief. I thought the poor man had died."

Alex paid no notice to the fact that the cab was going at a snail's pace, along with the other taxis and buses on the way to the exit. This man held her full attention. "Who *are* you?" she blurted out, unable to hold in the question any longer.

"Michael Conti, and yes, there is a Mrs. Conti. My mother."

Thoughts tumbled over each other in Alex's mind. *He's not married, he's here, and something about him is making me crazy.* She moistened her lips. "Mr. Conti, I . . ."

"Mike," he corrected smoothly.

She ignored his interruption. "Why are you here?"

"I came to Las Vegas to get away from it all for a few days."

"I mean, why are you *here* in this taxi, with me?"

He studied her openly for a full moment before he asked, "Do you want the truth?"

Boy, did she ever. "Yes."

"I spotted you in the terminal and bribed the skycap to put me in this cab."

That brought her up short. "You what?"

"I wondered why you weren't in jail, and I needed to get downtown to the Strip. So I figured sharing a taxi with you would do two things. It would get me where I'm going, and it would give you a chance to tell me why you're in Las Vegas instead of in the Beverly Hills Jail."

He didn't beat around the bush, and Alex felt heat flood her face. "I . . . I think you have the wrong idea about me."

"Do I?" he murmured.

"I wasn't stealing the bracelet." She turned in the seat to face him more squarely, but she kept on her sunglasses. "I know it looked like I was, but it wasn't like that, not really." She was babbling, words spilling over words; then the perfect story came to her in a flash. She grabbed at it and jumped in with both feet. "I'm friends with the wife of the owner of Aria's, and she and I—we were playing a joke on her husband. She dared me to get that bracelet."

He studied her with those incredible eyes, then shook his head in disbelief. "That was all for a joke?"

"It wasn't terribly smart of me to agree to it, but—" She shrugged. "—it could have been funny."

"Why would a wife...?"

Don't ask that, Alex wanted to scream, a part of her already wishing she could end the lies with this man. "How would I know? I've never..." She stopped herself before saying she'd never been married. And she finished with, "I've never done that sort of thing before."

"Was he amused?"

"Who?"

"Your friend's husband."

"No." She'd only placated Aria's owner by demonstrating how simply she'd circumvented his system. Mr. Simon wouldn't get off lightly though, she bet. Poor man. "He was pretty angry at first. No sense of humor. He wasn't pleased that I made a scene in his shop." She crossed her arms over her middle in an attempt to stop her nervous fingering of her purse. "Which, by the way, was your doing."

His eyes widened. "Mine?"

"If you hadn't interfered, I could have done it and gotten away without embarrassing anyone. My friend could have given him the bracelet in bed last night, and then he would have been...in a better mood."

He held up one hand, palm out, toward her. "Hey, don't blame me. I thought you were stealing the damn thing."

She studied the man, the pulse that beat rapidly at the open neck of his shirt and the way his dark brows slashed a line above his narrowed eyes. "Why did you try to help me like that? Why did you get involved at all?"

His hand dropped to his thigh. "The truth?"

Why did he keep using the word—truth? She swallowed hard. "Of course I want the truth."

"I didn't want you to go to jail."

"I wasn't going to jail. I . . ."

"I know that now. I didn't then. Yesterday I was certain you were going to be arrested any minute."

"So you took it on yourself to be a white knight and rescue me?"

He nodded, and Alex could have sworn he almost looked embarrassed at her choice of words. "My mistake," he murmured.

Actually, Alex kind of liked the idea. A knight in shining armor. "Do you always go around trying to save the world from itself?"

That brought an easy smile, a flash of white teeth, and his whole face changed in a wonderful way. "I've been told that's a bad habit of mine," he murmured.

The cab turned onto the street, and its speed increased considerably. "You certainly didn't do what most people would have done. They would have screamed for the police right at the start," Alex said.

"The police can do their work without my help. Besides, I've never been very good friends with most of them."

That intrigued her. "Why?"

"The truth?"

Damn it, that phrase was driving her crazy. "Of course," she said with a bit more tightness than intended.

He hesitated, then spoke abruptly. "I've been in prison. That doesn't make you buddy-buddy with the boys in blue, or particularly partial to getting them into the act."

"Are you serious? You were in prison?"

"Dead serious." He said it so calmly. "It happened a long time ago, but not so long that I don't remember the feeling of being caught, trapped and put in a cage." The smile was gone completely. His tone was almost neutral, yet his eyes were anything but. "I wouldn't wish for my worst enemy to do time."

It fascinated Alex that despite the fact he admitted to being in prison, she didn't sense any sort of threat from this man. "What did you do to be put in prison?"

"Nothing." He cast her a sidelong look. "They picked me up for robbery and grand theft, auto. I was innocent." That brought a tight smile to his lips. "Yes, it's true. Everyone in prison is innocent, if you listen to them."

"You really were innocent?"

"Absolutely. I had a bad reputation, and it came back to haunt me," he said cryptically. "I used up almost two years of my life before I could prove I didn't do anything. A lot of wasted time before the truth came out." He exhaled sharply. "But that was over and done with years ago. Trust me, I'm terribly respectable now."

Trust me. The words came easily from him, yet—strangely—Alex thought she probably could trust him. She seldom felt that way about anyone, and it fascinated her that Mike, a near stranger, could draw that from her. "Did you come to Las Vegas to gamble?"

"I love to gamble. How about you?"

She nodded. "I never have very much, but gambling sounds like fun."

"Is that why *you're* here?"

Keep it simple and ambiguous, she told herself. "No, I'm here on business."

"What business?" he asked with jarring directness.

She hadn't expected that question, and for a second she regretted her assurance of confidentiality to Lincoln. With great care, she hedged. "Nothing interesting, I promise you."

"I thought you might be here for the Fourth, or maybe a college reunion. You went to college, didn't you?"

She had no idea why he'd said that, but she didn't hesitate before nodding. "Of course."

"What college did you go to?"

She'd always wanted to go to the University of California at Berkeley. "UC Berkeley," she said quickly.

"I'm impressed."

I would be, too, she thought, if I had been anywhere near the place. "It was hard, but I graduated with a business major."

"I bet you graduated summa cum laude."

She felt suddenly uneasy. Was he teasing her? "No, I came up a few points short of that," she muttered.

He glanced out the window at broad stretches of land being bulldozed for construction. Alex followed the direction of his gaze, seeing the raw land and huge real-estate signs in the dusty earth. POTENTIAL COMMERCIAL SITE, the largest sign read.

Then Alex realized they had reached "the Strip," a broad street lined on both sides by hotels, casinos and signs that flashed with lights even in the daytime.

Abruptly, Mike turned back to Alex and asked, "What hotel are you staying at?"

"The Elysian."

He flashed a sudden grin that all but took her breath away. "Another coincidence. So am I."

Right then the taxi pulled in to the curb, and Alex tore her eyes away from Mike, away from his smile that had hit her like a bolt of lightning. She looked out the window again, but this time she saw a glass-and-steel structure that soared at least thirty stories into the cloudless sky. A huge sign shaped like a unicorn and outlined with flashing lights proclaimed "The Elysian! The Palace of Supreme Delights!"

A doorman dressed as an Arabian sultan opened the taxi door and nodded to Mike and Alex. "Welcome to the Elysian."

Mike got out, and as Alex stepped onto the walkway after him, he turned and looked down at her. His eyes narrowed against the brilliance of the sunlight, and he offered his hand to her. "Nice meeting you, Alexandria," he said softly.

For an instant she hesitated, uncertain whether she wanted a solid contact with this man. But she couldn't ignore his offered hand, so she took it and found she wasn't any more prepared for the contact than she had been for his smile. Heat and strength surrounded her hand, and an actual physical jolt ran through her. Every part of her being responded to Mike, and she knew she'd been right that first moment in the taxi when she'd looked at him. It had all begun with his eyes.

But she couldn't figure it out, not now, not here, while he held her hand. Reluctantly, she pulled free and held tightly to her purse. In some way she hoped the feeling of the leather would kill the tingling on her skin, where the imprint of his touch still lingered.

"N-nice meeting you, too," she finally managed when she realized she was expected to say something.

Sharp shadows from the overhead sun hid any expression in his eyes, but he smiled again. "Thanks for sharing your taxi with me. Maybe we can get together for a drink when you're not working?"

Alex found the idea very appealing, but only after she'd finished with Lincoln. She needed to give her whole attention to this job. "I might have time—later."

"You can't work all the time."

"Of course not."

"How about later today?"

"I'm not sure what I need to do," she said quickly.

"I'll call you around five. You can let me know then, all right?"

That would give her some much-needed time to think this through. "Five," she echoed and turned to follow the bellhop who had her tote bag.

Mike watched Alex go, letting his gaze slide over her tiny frame as she climbed the red-carpeted steps and disappeared through the entrance doors. He'd never felt more confused in his life. Business? What business?

With a sinking feeling, he knew it wouldn't have done any good to try and pin her down any further on that, either. The woman was a consummate liar. He knew she'd never been married or gone to college, and he'd hated setting traps for her like that. But he knew any regret on his part for his actions was very misplaced. He'd realized that when she'd told the stories without hesitation, without faltering.

Lies, all kinds of lies, and they frightened him. Their cost could be monumental. Lies had already cost him so much.

And it threw him off balance that he really *did* want to see her again. He didn't know a single thing about her beyond what he'd found out on his own, yet he felt a need to help her. He wanted to stop the lies. To feel she trusted him, no matter what was going on. He wanted to have drinks with her and talk to her and find out why she was lying.

Protector of the world? Right now it wasn't the world he wanted to protect, but a tiny, dark-haired woman who claimed all his attention.

Circles within circles. And nothing settled on as fact. Logic told him that he would do well to walk away from her, to tell Stanley he was done with the job. He could tell Stanley there wasn't any more to learn about her, then let him know where she was located. He himself would never look back. But the thought had barely materialized before he knew he couldn't do it. He would stick with this job.

With a deep sigh, he walked up the red-carpeted stairs to the entrance of the hotel. He knew her phony name, so he could find her again. Right now, he had to try to get a room at this hotel.

Mike stepped into the coolness of the vast, domed reception area, a space with all the trappings of a sultan's harem, from its red velvet walls, simulated Persian rugs lying on marble floors and gold-shaded chandeliers hanging from an intricately painted ceiling, to gold-leafed columns and music that seemed to be more chimes than notes.

Then, through the haze of cigarette smoke and across the milling crowd of visitors, he saw Alex. She was already at the check-in desk on the far side of the lobby, nodding at something the desk clerk was saying to her.

Mike hesitated. He couldn't walk up to the desk and ask for a room when he'd told his own lie, that he already had one. So, not taking his eyes off her, he walked across the lobby, staying to the right, passing people, heavy drapes twined around the gold columns, and potted plants set in strategic places.

When he neared the counter, he saw pay phones to the far left of the desk—about three feet from where Alex stood talking to the clerk. He could stand there and wait until she left. He didn't move until she leaned forward to sign in; then he quickly walked past her to the phones. He lifted the receiver of the first one he reached, turned his back to the desk and held the cool plastic to his ear.

For some reason he didn't understand, he seemed capable of picking up Alex's voice, even over the perpetual din in the lobby, just the way he had at the airport terminal in L.A.

"I'm looking forward to this visit," Alex was saying.

"How long will you be with us, Mrs. Gray? You didn't say when you called in your reservation."

"A few days, maybe three or four."

"All right. Here's your key to 1058."

"How about your penthouse suites?"

"You're interested in one of the suites in the tower?"

"Not for me, but I have some friends coming who might be. Do you have any available?"

There was a pause, then, "Only two. Both on the twenty-eighth floor."

"How is the security up there?"

"Excuse me?"

"If a person had valuables, would they be safe leaving them in their room?"

Mike felt sickness churn in his middle, and he leaned slowly forward until his forehead rested against the cold metal trim of the phone cubicle. Valuables? Business? He gripped the receiver so tightly that he felt certain the plastic would snap, and he closed his eyes. He didn't need a great imagination to be able to figure out the direction of Alex's questions.

"Of course," the clerk said. "We at the Elysian have always prided ourselves on the security of our guests. We have a service for keeping things in our safe down here, and some suites have small safes themselves."

"That sounds good enough," she murmured. "Could you have the bellhop take my bag to my room? I want to look around a bit before going up."

"Of course."

Mike took a deep, unsteady breath, then chanced a look over his shoulder. Alex was standing with her back to the desk looking around, her sunglasses resting on top of her head and a single rose wrapped in white paper in one hand. Quickly, he turned and walked away from the front desk— and Alex. He headed in the direction of one of the casinos. He didn't really care where he was going; he just wanted to get out of sight. And he wanted to get the sight of the un-tourist-like speculation in Alex's dark eyes as she studied her surroundings out of his mind.

Chapter 4

Maybe it was just the Las Vegas attitude of "party and gamble 'til you drop," but the clerk didn't seem to think it was strange for Alex to choose to look around before going up to her room.

She twirled the rose between her fingers while she scanned the reception area with its overabundance of atmosphere; then she turned to her left. For an instant she thought she saw Mike heading into one of the casinos; then the man was gone and she wasn't sure. That was when she spotted a discreet sign near the bank of telephones. It pointed around a corner and read: SECURITY.

Alex hitched her purse higher on her shoulder, then casually walked past the telephones toward the sign. As she rounded the corner, she found a series of stairs that led downward. Skimming her fingers over the coolness of the brass handrail, she went down. At the foot of the steps she paused in front of a series of cigarette machines lining a marble-floored corridor.

Another sign for Security pointed to the left and down a side hallway lined with gold-hooded lamps on either side.

Alex was almost to the end before she saw what she was after, a door labeled Security Offices. She hesitated, then
stepped into a small room done in gold-flocked wallpaper
and deep brown carpet. The annoying tinkling music didn't
make its way down here, but the garishness did. Two prints
of almost-naked harem women lying under billowing gauze
adorned the wall above a desk that held a gold telephone
and a nameplate for a Mrs. Johnson. But no one was in
sight.

Through an arched doorway to the left was a short hallway with one door at the end. Alex headed for the door, saw
the brass tag with M. LINCOLN on it and knocked softly.

"Come on in," someone called, and Alex opened the
door.

She stepped into a dimly lit, smoke-hazy room where
heavy drapes lined the walls, making it impossible to even
guess where the windows were positioned. The glow from a
gooseneck desk lamp barely penetrated the shadows lingering in the corners of the twelve-by-twelve-foot space. As her
eyes adjusted, she saw a desk littered with papers and books
and two chairs facing it. Then she saw the high-backed
leather chair behind the desk, and the man in it swiveling
impatiently from side to side while he stared at her.

As she made eye contact with him, his chair stilled. Mr.
Lincoln wasn't anything like she'd expected. Portly, about
sixty, balding and dressed in black pants and a gray silk
shirt, he had narrow eyes with puffy bags under them. He
studied Alex through a cloud of smoke from a cigarette held
between his teeth. A mustache, trimmed precisely, looked as
if it had been penciled above a thin-lipped mouth.

"Mr. Lincoln?" she asked.

He nodded. "Alex Thomas?"

"Yes."

"Sorry I couldn't meet you at the airport, but something
came up here." He motioned toward a chair on the other
side of the desk and almost knocked a stack of papers over
in the process. "Please, close the door and have a seat."

Alex swung the door closed, then took a seat and watched Lincoln as he straightened the papers while smoke trickled into the air. So much for impressions over the telephone. "Thanks for the rose," she said for lack of anything better to start the conversation with.

"My pleasure. How was your flight?" he asked as he crushed out the cigarette in an amber glass ashtray near his elbow.

Alex shrugged and rested the rose on top of her purse in her lap. "Not bad."

"Good, good," he murmured and sat back in his chair as he studied Alex from under hooded lids. "I do apologize again for not being able to wait and drive you here, but this place makes a lot of demands on my time."

"I understand." Alex glanced around the room. "It's pretty dark in here, isn't it?"

"That's Las Vegas for you. They never want the customers to know if it's day or night. Create a fantasy and let the people buy it. That's their philosophy. Besides, people don't come here for healthy sunlight." He pulled a handkerchief out of his pocket and dabbed at his forehead. "I just can't stand the heat outside. But even with the coolness inside, I sweat no matter what." He folded the handkerchief into a small square, then pushed it back into his shirt pocket. "I'd offer to get you a drink, but I don't want to make this too long. I've got other things to take care of."

She wanted to get it over with, too. "All right."

He leaned toward her, folding his arms on the desktop, and gold flashed at his throat and on his wrist. He exhaled. "From what you told me on the telephone last night, you're exactly what I need for this job."

Alex nodded, without saying anything, while she tried to figure out why Lincoln made her uneasy. She seldom believed in hunches for the simple fact that hers were seldom accurate, but Lincoln didn't seem like a particularly nice man.

"I want you to find out if you can get into one of the suites in the tower."

Alex looked right at him. "Why?"

"We're going to be leasing some of the penthouses on a long-term basis, and we have to be able to promise complete security for our clients."

"I know the ins and outs of the system you said you use."

"Good. Then you know it's tight," Lincoln said. "Real tight."

"Do you have guards involved in the security for the tower area?"

He nodded. "On rotating shifts." He studied her. "I think that's as specific as I should be. It's up to you to work it out. After all, a thief wouldn't have been given the guards' schedule, would he?"

"You're right." Human beings were a bigger problem than any system might be. This would be a challenge.

"And if you're caught . . . ?"

Alex shrugged. "I won't be, but if things turn out badly, I'll have to give them my identification and have them contact you. But it will all be handled as discreetly as possible—I promise you that."

"Good enough." He sat forward and began to search the mess on the desk, then muttered, "No damned lighter." With a hissing sigh, he pushed his hand into the pocket of his slacks and took out a book of matches. He concentrated on lighting the cigarette with the last match in the packet, then looked up at Alex with narrowed eyes. "One more question?"

Alex rubbed her arms when they prickled in the cool clamminess of the air-conditioning. "What?"

"How did a little thing like you get into this business?" he asked through a haze of smoke.

The question reminded Alex of his "little lady" comment the previous night, and it was just as offensive. "I was captured by gypsies when I was little, and the only way I could get out of their caravan was to override their rudimentary, yet efficient security system."

He frowned at her as he took another drag on the cigarette. "None of my business, is that it, little lady?"

"Sorry," she murmured, swallowing the sarcasm before she said something that might cost her this job. "That's a bad habit of mine, coming back with a smart answer. Actually, I was in sales for an electronics firm that specialized in security systems. But I wasn't very good at selling.

"When I was on the verge of losing my job, something I certainly couldn't afford, I had an strange idea. I'd always been good at getting into places and making up stories to cover my trail, so I took a chance. I'd go into a place and show them my company's best system, and then I'd make a deal with them. If I could get in past their current system and take something from their premises, they'd buy mine. I started selling a lot of systems." She shrugged. "Ours wasn't perfect, but it was pretty difficult to break through."

Lincoln fingered the empty matchbook. "You finally struck out on your own?"

She nodded. "One of the companies I sold a system to contacted me privately. They had another store and wanted to know if that system was good or not. I agreed to do it for them when they offered me a fee that was double the commission I got on a sale. Then they recommended me to someone else. I quit my regular job and began to freelance." She made herself look away from his hands as he methodically opened and closed the empty matchbook. "I couldn't advertise, of course, but word-of-mouth business has kept me busy." She hated the way smoke curled in front of Lincoln's eyes, acting as a screen. "How did you find out about me?"

"Word-of-mouth. I know someone with Southern Lasers International." He spoke around the cigarette held between his teeth and twisted the matchbook around and around in his hand. "You did some work for them, and they were impressed."

"A satisfied customer," she murmured, remembering their job as simply getting past front-gate security and into their offices.

Lincoln stared at her for a long moment, then looked away as he tossed the matchbook at a wastebasket against the wall to the left of the desk. When the matchbook bounced off the back edge and fell behind the brown container, the man shrugged and looked back at Alex. "You seem to be a smart little thing," he said.

"Smart enough to do what I have to do," she said softly. "Now, let's get the details of the job straight. There are a few things I need to know."

Mike stopped just inside the broad archway that led to the casino, then turned and looked back, but Alex was gone. He waited another full minute, and when Alex didn't come back, he walked into the lobby and across to the registration desk. "I need a single room . . . preferably on the tenth floor," he said when the clerk looked up at him.

The slightly built man shook his head. "Sorry, sir. The lower rooms are pretty well booked up for the holiday." He looked down at the computer screen in front of him. "I've got one double on the sixth floor and a single on the fourteenth." He shrugged. "That's about it."

Mike hesitated, then asked, "How about the penthouse suites? Anything there?" That seemed to be an area that held Alex's interest.

The man smiled a bit more broadly. "On the twenty-eighth . . . a suite with two bedrooms, an entertainment area and a knockout view of the Strip."

If Mike couldn't be near Alex's room, the towers would do. Especially if that was where her "business" might possibly be taking place. "I'll take it."

Alex didn't get to go up to her room until half an hour later. Then she stayed in the red-and-cream room with its king-size bed only long enough to change into a simple yellow sundress and low sandals. She recombed her hair, caught it back in the clips again, then looped her purse strap over her shoulder and stepped out into the silent hallway. She headed for the four elevators that serviced her floor. It was time to see where she'd be doing the job.

When the mirrored doors of the nearest elevator slid open, she stepped inside, thankful to be completely alone in the car. She pressed the button for the highest floor in the main hotel—twenty-seven. When the car stopped, she got out and looked in both directions down a hall that was done all in reds and browns. Then she saw what she was looking for. Twenty feet to her left was another set of mirrored elevator doors.

She walked quickly down to the doors, then stopped. There was nothing but a round button with a key slot under it set in the brass plate marked TOWER. She looked right, then left, saw she was alone and reached into her purse. She took out a loop of bare copper wire about four inches long, pressed it together between her thumb and forefinger and carefully inserted the sharp loop into the lock. She slid it slowly back and forth, right and left, then twisted it upward and heard a very satisfactory click.

With a pleased smile, Alex saw her reflection in the doors disappear as the barriers silently slid open. She stepped into a car that had both the walls and ceiling lined with more mirrors and looked at the buttons on the control panel by the door. Five. One marked "27", then a second "28T," the next "29T," and the fourth labeled "30T." The last simply held a "P."

"Suite 2 on 30T is the one I'm interested in testing," Lincoln had told her during their meeting, so she pushed the button for the thirtieth floor.

The car started silently upward, and in less than half a minute, it stopped. The doors slid back with a soft, sighing sound. Alex looked out into an empty hallway with thick burgundy carpet and heavily framed paintings on gold paisley walls. A series of small crystal chandeliers cast soft light in both directions. With a deep breath, she stepped out into the hall. The door slid shut behind her, and a man's voice stopped her dead in her tracks.

"Evening, ma'am. Do you have a suite on this floor?"

Alex turned to her right and saw a heavyset man in uniform walking toward her. A security guard. She had no idea where he'd come from, and she needed to know. "Excuse me?" she asked while she got her thoughts collected.

He frowned at her. "Are you staying on this floor, ma'am?"

She went through the motions of looking up and down the hallway, then turned to him with feigned confusion. "Oh, I ... I'm sorry. This doesn't look like the floor I wanted." She gave the man her best "I'm hopeless" smile. "Where am I?"

"Thirtieth floor, ma'am." He came closer. "How did you get on this elevator?"

"It was open, and I walked on."

She looked past him and finally saw a little alcove to the right, a small area with a chair and a discarded newspaper on the floor. No one could get off the elevator without being seen. So much for that.

"Ma'am, this is a private floor," he said, getting her attention again. "You got on the wrong elevator." He pressed the elevator button, and when the doors opened again, he leaned inside and pushed a button. "This'll take you down three floors, then get on one of the four elevators that go to the main part of the hotel." He held the door open for her.

She flashed him another smile before she got on the car. "Thanks. I feel so silly."

"Nonsense. Just a mistake. Evening, ma'am," he said and touched his cap as the door slid shut.

And you never even asked for my name or any sort of identification, Alex thought as the car started down. She didn't dare stop at another floor in case the guard was watching the indicator, so she went all the way down and got off. But she didn't go toward the other set of elevators. Following a hunch, she walked along the hallway, around a corner and spotted a door marked "Stairs." She went to it and pushed it open.

There were no barriers here to keep anyone from going up or down, so she started walking up the stairs. By the time she got to the thirtieth floor again, she was a bit breathless from the climb. She took a few minutes to get her breathing back to a normal level, then pressed her ear to the door. She couldn't hear a thing.

Cautiously, she pulled the door back until she could see out into the hall. It seemed that the doors for the stairs were around the corner from the elevator up here, too. From what Alex could see, there was no guard at this door, and no place for him to be hiding. The walls were flat, with no alcoves. Carefully, she stepped out into the hall and quietly walked to the corner. Inch by inch she moved forward until she could see around the corner and get a clear view of the elevator and the guard.

The chair the guard used was empty. Alex stepped back quickly. This area was completely out of the guard's view when he was at his station, but she had no idea where he was now. A quick look showed no remote cameras. Four doors led off the hall, but the suite Lincoln had targeted wasn't there. If the numbers kept on in order, Suite 2 would be the first one on the far side of the elevator doors—right across from the guard.

Alex slipped back down the hall, into the stairwell and went slowly down to the next floor. Lincoln was making this difficult, but not impossible. In fact, it was intriguing her more and more. She stepped out into the hallway of the twenty-ninth floor as if she belonged there, headed for the elevators, rounded the corner and nodded to a couple heading to their room. She kept going to the mirrored doors for the elevator.

She needed to know one more thing: could she put the elevator out of commission for a few minutes if she needed to? With no key needed once you got into the tower section, she had only to push the button and step through the opening doors. As they slid shut, the car started to move down before Alex could press a floor button. Before she knew what was going on, the light for 28T flashed on, the car stopped, and the doors slid open again.

Alex looked out and barely stopped a groan. The same guard stood in the entrance, feet spread, his face grim.

* * *

Mike knew that Stanley wouldn't question the expense of a suite and, as suites went, this one was more than adequate. He looked around the spacious, two-level living area, elegant with its subtle tones of beige and brown and accents of clear yellow. If he ignored the mural on one wall of a desert and racing Arabian stallions, it looked good. It was meant for entertaining, with a small grand piano, a full bar and a sweeping view of the city.

But Mike didn't feel like partying. Instead he felt distinctly uncomfortable. For several minutes he sat on the linen sectional facing the sliding doors that opened onto a balcony overlooking the Strip, just thinking. Finally he did what he had to do—put in a call to the number in Paris.

Less than two minutes passed before Stanley called back.

"Why didn't you call when you were supposed to?"

"I ran into some problems."

"What's happening, Mike?"

"You tell me what's going on with this Thomas woman," he demanded. "What is she to you?"

"A necessity," Stanley said cryptically, then added, "A life-and-death necessity."

"Well, your 'life-and-death necessity' took off for Las Vegas first thing this morning."

"You didn't let her get away from you, did you?" It made Mike uneasy to hear very real panic in Stanley's usually controlled voice.

"No. I'm with her. At least, I'm in the same hotel."

"What's she doing there?"

"That's what I was going to ask you."

"How would I know?" Now he sounded annoyed and impatient, and Mike wished that he had a face to put with the man's voice.

"You're the one who wants her. You sent me after her and told me to stay with her."

"Yes, I realize that." Mike could hear Stanley's deep breath, even over the long-distance line. "I did."

"Stanley?"

"Yes?"

"Who is she? What is she?"

"That's what I'm paying you to find out."

"You paid me to find her, then to keep her in sight."

"But you must have found out more about her by now, such as why she isn't in jail."

Mike let his head rest against the cushions of the couch and closed his eyes. "She says they let her go, that the deal about stealing the bracelet was a joke, that she was in with the owner's wife on it. She took off for Las Vegas this morning, and she says she's here on business."

"What business?"

"Don't ask me. I don't know." He had an idea, but he couldn't prove it, and until he could, he didn't see any point in repeating it to Stanley. "She's an enigma. Nothing adds up." He stopped his words. "What do you want me to do now?"

"I need to know if she's worth bringing over here."

"What would make her *'worth'* that?"

"It all depends what you find out."

Mike sat forward. "Damn it, Stanley, you know that I find people. I don't get involved past that. It's not my business."

"All right. You don't have to get involved. Just stay with her a bit longer. I'll put someone else on her from this end. Give me everything you know, all the information, then I can pass it on."

It took almost five minutes for Mike to read the notes he'd kept in a small notebook, then answer whatever questions Stanley had. When he finished, he sank back down on the couch. "What now?"

"Keep with her until I know if she's what I need. Whatever you do, don't lose her, Mike."

That intensity in the man's voice set Mike's nerves on edge. Stanley had a bigger stake in this job than "work" would account for. "You don't have to get involved," he'd said to Mike.

But Mike knew it was too late for that. "How much longer do you think this will take?" he finally asked.

"Another day. Two, tops. I'm on a tight schedule."

"All right."

"Mike?"

"Yes?"

"What's your gut instinct on this?"

He closed his eyes, then exhaled. "I told you, I'm not a regular private investigator. I find people. That's it."

"But you must have some idea about the woman."

There wasn't much sense in offering Stanley false hope. "If you're looking for an honest, upright person, I've got a feeling Alexandria Thomas won't be worth what it takes for you to bus her across the street—let alone to Paris. But that depends on what you want from her, doesn't it?"

"Get back to me at this number if things change. If not, I'll contact you when I know what I'm going to do," Stanley said abruptly and hung up.

"Sure," Mike said into the dead line; then he hung up.

He sat staring out the window; then, finally, he stood. If he was going to keep Alex in sight, he'd better go and find her. If he got close enough, got to talk to her more, got her to trust him ... That thought died of its own accord. "And maybe horses can grow feathers," he muttered.

Without bothering to change, he grabbed his key and left his suite. As he stepped into the hall and closed the door, he heard raised voices. Then he recognized Alex yelling, "You can't treat me this way!"

He looked right and caught a glimpse of a guard in uniform blocking the elevator doors, then hurried down the hallway as he called out, "Hey, what's going on?"

The guard turned, and that was when Mike saw Alex in the elevator, looking tiny and almost delicate in a pale yellow dress. But there was nothing delicate about her expression. She looked furious, with high color staining her cheeks and her eyes flashing with anger.

She saw Mike, did a double take, then breathed, "Mike."

"What's going on?" he asked again.

The guard took a step back, but kept his hand on the door to keep it open. "You know this lady?"

"Why?"

"I caught her on another floor, and she didn't belong there. Now she's down here where she shouldn't be."

Mike stepped past the guard and into the car with Alex. The confined area seemed touched by her scent, a delicate floral perfume, and he didn't have to think twice before reaching for her. He put his arm around her shoulders, pulled her to him and felt her overwhelming softness against him before he turned to look at the guard. A lie came before he even thought about it. "She was coming to see me."

Alex pressed her head against his shoulder, and he felt her hand at his waist. Slowly her hand moved along his back just below his belt, and if he wasn't mistaken, she was heading toward his back pocket. "I got lost," she said in a small voice. "You know how I am, Mike. I'm such a scatterbrain. Then this man started yelling at me."

The guard looked from Mike to Alex, then back to Mike. "She never said you were on this floor, sir. She never showed me a key or anything."

So, that was what she was after. Mike moved his free hand, which held his key, casually behind him, and handed the brass key to her.

"Alex, show the man the key that I gave you to get up here," he said squeezing her shoulder.

"I never had to use it at all." She let go of Mike, but he kept his arm around her while she tugged her purse up in front of her and pushed her closed hand into the leather pouch. Then, with a flourish, she pulled her hand out of her purse, opened it palm up and showed the man the flat brass key.

"Why didn't you say you wanted to see this?" she demanded of the guard. "You just started yelling at me and got me all confused."

The guard had the decency to look taken back as he touched his cap. "Sorry, ma'am, but you never said you had it."

Alex handed the key to Mike, and when he took it, he felt the heat of her touch mingled with his in the metal. "I'm not a mind reader, you know,'' Alex muttered. ''You never asked.''

''I'm real sorry for yelling at you, ma'am.'' He backed up, letting go of the doors. ''Real sorry, but I've got a job to do. Mr. Lincoln's real particular about security up here.''

''Forget it,'' Mike murmured, and he looked down at Alex. ''No harm done, is there, love?''

''No, none,'' she echoed.

Mike stooped, intent on giving her a fleeting kiss for the benefit of the guard. But he couldn't fool himself. As soon as he tasted her softly parted lips, he knew he was doing it for his own benefit, too. He'd wanted to do it from the first time he had laid eyes on her.

He felt Alex tremble at the contact, then lift her tiny hand and spread it against his chest. He didn't see the guard turn and walk off, or the doors shut. He was too busy wondering why the taste of Alex seemed to be filling his whole being.

And Alex was too busy wondering if she'd ever been kissed like this before in her life.

Chapter 5

As the elevator slid silently upward, Alex realized one heartbeat too late that she was literally molding herself to the man kissing her. Not only was she allowing him to kiss her, she was actually offering up her lips with a familiarity that should have come only with a man she cared about—a lot.

That sliver of sanity gave her the impetus to break free and press herself back against the wall. She could feel coolness from the mirrors through her sundress and against the flushed skin of her bare shoulders and upper arms. When she looked up, multiple images of Mike bombarded her from the mirrored walls and ceiling, and for a moment she couldn't figure out which one was the reality. Then she did, and he was standing not more than a foot away from her.

She could have sworn he looked as surprised and unsteady as she did before he managed to block his expression. She hugged herself tightly to control her unsteadiness and wondered if she should give in to her impulse to slap him. No, that probably wouldn't make her feel any better, not when she didn't even know how she could get rid of his taste on her lips.

"Why did you do that?" she whispered, her words echoing in the stillness, her fingers holding her upper arms so tightly that her skin tingled.

Mike shrugged abruptly, his lashes lowering to partially veil the green depths of his eyes. "It seemed like a good idea at the time," he murmured at the same time that the elevator stopped and the door opened on the top floor.

Alex glanced at the door and moved back at the same time Mike did to let four people board—a young couple, tanned and blond, and a middle-aged man dressed all in white accompanied by a girl young enough to be his daughter. None of the newcomers gave them more than a cursory glance as they effectively separated Mike and Alex with their bodies.

The middle-aged gentleman pressed the bottom button, then moved back to put his arm around the girl who was wearing a bright red jumpsuit. As the car started down again, Alex began to feel that she was getting back some control. Then the young girl pressed more closely against the man in white and began to nibble on his ear while she draped her arms around his neck. Alex felt her own face flame.

What if she'd been kissing Mike when the doors had opened and these people had walked in on it? She looked away from the embracing couple, only to meet Mike's gaze. He lifted one eyebrow, then slowly winked at her.

Mike thought the display was funny, a joke. But it only deepened the burning embarrassment in Alex. Mike was probably letting her know that their kiss had been a joke, too. The fact that it had been far from that for her only made her feel worse. But as the elevator softly stopped at the twenty-seventh floor, she knew that keeping it light would probably be the best way to handle everything. Smile, nod, then leave the elevator and get away from the man.

The two couples filed off first, the girl and the man in white so close that daylight couldn't be seen between them. Before Alex could force a smile and make her escape with the others, Mike reached in front of her and pressed the "door closed" button. "Which floor are we going to now?" he asked.

"*We* aren't going anywhere. This has been a nice diversion, but *I'm* getting off," Alex said and reached for the "door open" button.

But Mike had her hand before she could do more than barely brush a cool brass button with the tip of one finger. "Just a minute."

She looked at his hand on hers, at darkly tanned skin making hers seem almost pale, then up into his eyes. "Let me go," she breathed.

A soft chime sounded, and the light at the top floor lit up as the elevator started upward. Mike took one look at the lighted floor number, then casually pressed the "emergency stop" button with his free hand. As the car jolted to a standstill somewhere between 29 and 30, Mike looked at Alex. "Now we have complete privacy for a few minutes. Tell me where you were going when that guard caught you."

While the constant tinkling background music filled the stillness, Alex stared at Mike. "You can't just stop the car—"

"But I did," he said evenly. "Where were you going?"

She touched her tongue to her lips and wondered why his hold on her hand had become the focal point of her entire being. "I . . . I was looking around."

"And?"

"I got lost."

His fingers tightened on her hand. "And?"

"And nothing," she muttered as she jerked and freed herself of his hold so easily that she stumbled back a bit. She clasped her hands tightly in front of her, her purse pinned to her side by her elbow. "Nothing," she repeated with emphasis.

Mike seemed unfazed, and Alex knew then that she had only managed to free herself because he'd chosen to let her go. The knowledge didn't make her feel any better. Neither did the multiple images of Mike in the mirrors that surrounded her.

"I just want to know where you were going," he said softly, determinedly.

Alex took an unsteady breath, then wished she hadn't when she inhaled the inviting mixture of after-shave and male essence that permeated the air. The elevator seemed to be diminishing in size as rapidly as Mike's presence seemed to be expanding. Slowly, cautiously, she began to inch toward the back wall, away from him. She didn't care if he knew what she was doing. She needed more distance between herself and this man. "None of your business," she breathed.

"You made it my business by getting me involved," he said, but he stayed by the door—and the buttons.

"*I* got *you* involved?" Alex asked from the corner.

"What would you call it when you try to pick my pocket to get my key?" He didn't make a move to get closer.

Alex knew that her face must be the color of flame, but she didn't back down. "You gave me your key."

"I thought I'd make things easier for you. I didn't want you to add pickpocketing to your list of...talents."

She sank back with a sigh. "Please, just open the door and let me get out."

He regarded her intently; then spoke words that set her back on her heels. "What kind of trouble are you in now?"

She closed her eyes for a moment, anything to make it easier for her to think. Trouble? She was beginning to realize that *he* was her trouble, a disturbing revelation that made it hard for her to open her eyes and look right at him again. But she did. "I wasn't in any trouble until you came along," she said in a fairly calm voice. But when he simply stared at her, as if he were waiting for her to bare her soul, she found herself striking out. "*You* almost ruined what I was doing at Aria's. Then you hijacked me in this damned elevator. *You*, Mr. Conti, are my trouble." Oh, God, she hadn't meant to say that, but since she couldn't take it back, she forced herself to keep eye contact. "If you won't let me out of this car, I'm going to..."

"What are you going to do?" Mike asked softly.

She glared at him.

"What are you going to do?" he repeated. "What do you weigh? A hundred pounds? I weigh a hundred and seventy. You're about five feet two inches tall, I'd guess. I'm five feet ten, so I've got you by at least eight inches. As far as screaming goes..."

She stood straighter. She couldn't believe she was having this conversation with a man who'd been in prison. That thought made her stomach clench. She only had his word that he'd been pardoned. Quickly, she said, "Stop it. Just let me out of here."

"I'll let you out when you tell me what's wrong," he persisted, his voice never rising.

"Nothing is wrong. Read my lips. Absolutely nothing!"

"Then why are you in this elevator?"

"Because you're crazy and won't believe me!"

"What business are you in?" he asked. "I'll believe the truth."

She took a deep breath. The truth? Damn the truth! Why should it be so hard lying to this man, anyway? She didn't really know him, and she wasn't at all certain that she even liked him. Slowly, enunciating every word carefully, she spun her story for him. "My business is just that—my business. And as for being here in this elevator, I got lost. I got on the wrong elevator. I got caught by the guard, and you showed up. Period." She took a deep breath. "Why do you care at all?"

Mike stared at her for so long she wondered if he was ever going to talk again, and when he did, he didn't answer the question, but asked his own. "How about our drinks?"

"You won't give up, will you?"

"You said you'd have drinks with me. Now's a good time for me. The casinos don't know if it's night or day. Or, if the casinos aren't your cup of tea, there's a great supply of any kind of liquor you could possibly want in the bar in my suite. I've even got a piano. How about coming in for a drink and some music?"

Drinks and music? Her throat felt dry at the images she could conjure up from those words. "No, I really can't."

"Alex..."

She knew right then that she wasn't going to have drinks with him in the casino, or, heaven forbid, alone with him in his room. This closeness in the elevator was enough to drive her crazy. A basic man-and-woman thing? Raw sexual attraction was more like it, and that was something she didn't want to deal with right now.

She couldn't even keep her stories straight when he looked at her with those eyes. Worse yet, she had a niggling suspicion that he could tell when she was lying. There was something in his expression, something that almost stopped the words before they came out. And the bottom line was that this job could fall apart if she wasn't careful. "I can't. I've got work to do. Believe me." At least that was the truth.

A telephone rang, and Alex jumped. A telephone? Then she saw it to the right of Mike, set in the wall by the control panel, with a red light flashing above it. Mike didn't even glance at it. "You can't work all the time," he said. "So have a drink with me. I need an answer before they send a rescue party down the shaft after us."

She knew the words to say, but the lies seem stuck in her throat. He couldn't tell if she lied. Common sense told her that he had no way of knowing the truth from the lies, but what if...? And why should she care if he knew or not? His opinion of her wasn't important.

Coughing softly as the phone rang again, she forced the words past the tightness. "All right, I'll have a drink with you, but not just now. I'm waiting for a business call."

"We can go down to your room and wait for your call, then go out for drinks."

"Listen, Mr. Conti..."

He held up both hands, ignoring the still-ringing phone. "Mike, I told you to call me Mike, and can't your partner take the call?"

Partner? Had she told him she had a partner? She didn't think she had, but she couldn't remember. So she took a chance. "I don't have a partner." When he didn't disagree, she felt a degree of relief. "I . . . I need to wait for the phone call alone." She swallowed hard and added a lie on top of lies. "Then I can call you, and we can go out for drinks."

"Promise?"

Please, not that. "Do you want me to cross my heart and hope to die?" she asked with what she hoped was enough humor to dissipate her own uneasiness. "Or spit in a snake's eye?"

"Yes."

She blinked at him. "What?"

"Promise me that you'll call."

Why was he doing this to her? She didn't want to promise, or swear, or take a blood oath. A lie should come out easily and be gone before you knew it, before it could be either enjoyed or regretted. "Okay, I'll call," she muttered and motioned to the phone. "Please, answer that."

Mike reached for the phone. "Yes?" He looked back at Alex, his green eyes never blinking. "We're fine. No problems. I must have leaned back against the stop button by accident." He listened to the person on the other end of the phone, but his gaze on Alex was so intense that she had to force herself not to close her eyes. "Just two of us. I'm sorry for the problems. I'll try the buttons again. We'll be down to the twenty-seventh floor in a moment." He replaced the receiver, then leaned against the closed the door. But he didn't reach for the buttons. Instead, he crossed his arms on his chest. "What's your room number?"

She hesitated, then knew that she had no choice. "Ten fifty-eight."

He studied her for another very long, very intense moment before nodding. "Good." With that he turned and pushed the lowest button on the panel. Immediately, the car lurched and started downward.

Mike stared at Alex, not saying a word until the car stopped softly. "I'll be waiting for your call," he said.

"All right," she breathed, and as he stepped back, the door slid open.

Another security guard faced them from the hall. "What the hell happened up there?"

"I pushed the wrong button," Mike said and moved to one side as Alex took a step toward the door and freedom. But just as she got into the doorway, Mike spoke up. "Alex?"

She turned less than a foot from him. "What?"

"Don't you want to know what my room number is?"

The doors started to close, but the guard reached to catch them. Alex stood very still, and she knew she had to play out the charade, then make her escape. It didn't help that she couldn't shake the sinking feeling that Mike didn't believe any of her lies. "What is it?"

"Twenty-eight T, suite 2."

She nodded, then turned and stepped out into the hallway, brushing quickly past the guard. She was almost to the other set of elevators before she realized that Mike's suite was in the same location as the one Lincoln wanted her to get into, only two floors down.

When Mike got back to his suite, he settled on the couch, then made a phone call to his partner in Santa Barbara. "Dan, I need some help," he said as soon as the burly, blond-haired man answered.

"You need help, Mike? Since when?" Dan asked with a touch of humor.

Mike exhaled and sank deeper into the softness of the couch. "Listen, I'm in Las Vegas."

That got Dan's attention. "What happened to L.A.?"

"The person Stanley wanted me to find was in L.A., then decided to come to Vegas."

"It's a good thing this job's for Stanley. At least we know he'll be paying his bill," Dan said. "Not like the last one. We ended up two thousand in the hole on that one."

"That much, eh?"

"That much."

"Well, everything works out. And you're right. Stanley always pays, and he pays well. What I need you to do is find out all you can on Stanley himself."

"What?"

"I think now's the time to find out who he is, and who he works for."

Dan was silent for a moment, then spoke softly, "Are you sure? I don't think we should mess with a good thing."

"I'm damned sure, Dan. It's important."

"Why?"

Why couldn't Dan have been the kind of partner who accepted requests without having to dissect them? "It's this case. Something isn't right about it. And I've got a feeling that getting to know Jack Stanley a bit better won't hurt. I don't even know what the man looks like."

"You found the woman for him, didn't you?"

"I told you, I followed her here."

"And?"

"Stanley's got me tailing her for a day or so. Dan, just do the favor for me." Mike heard the edge of impatience in his own voice, and he added quickly, "Call it a sixth sense, a hunch. This case is off center, and I don't know why."

"All right. Whatever you want. But the way I always understood it, we don't even have an address for the man— just a post-office box in New York."

"I've got a phone number now." He repeated the number Stanley had given him. "It's overseas—Paris. It's a place to start. Whoever answers that phone can get in touch with Stanley within minutes."

"Anything else?"

"I need to know as soon as possible, Dan."

He could almost feel Dan hesitating, needing to say something else, but discretion prevailed. "Sure thing," his partner said and hung up.

Mike hoped that if he found out about Stanley, he would get a clue to understanding Alex. He knew she had no intention of calling him or having drinks with him. He wasn't stupid enough, or gullible enough, to believe otherwise. He also knew that whatever she was up to involved the Towers in some way. The thought knotted his middle but didn't break his resolve. Alexandria Thomas *was* going to see him again. She didn't have a choice.

He rested his head on the back of the couch and pressed his fingers to his temples, kneading in slow, circular motions. The motion of his hands stopped when, for a fleeting instant, Mike wondered if he might be the one who didn't have a choice.

Alex was thankful for the full elevator as she rode down to her room. Just as thankful as she was to get inside and close the door so Mike couldn't show up at her back and demand to come in and talk.

With a sigh of relief, she kicked off her sandals and watched them land softly on the thick beige carpeting by the glass doors to the balcony. She needed to see one of the tower suites, to see the layout. One thing she felt certain of, hotels like this usually duplicated floors. Each floor imitated the one above and below it, even in the expensive section. The only variation would be on the penthouse level. Still, Suite 2 was probably the same on all the tower floors. And Mike had Suite 2.

But right now she didn't want to talk to Mike. She crossed to the phone on the bedside table and called down to the desk to tell them not to put through any calls unless they came from Mr. Dunn.

One of the last things she and Lincoln had talked about was his contacting her with the go ahead for the job. "I'll use the name Dunn if I have to call or leave a message," he'd said. She'd thought he had been getting into the intrigue of the situation a bit too much, but hadn't argued. She played her games. He played his.

Right now, Lincoln was the only one she wanted to talk to. She certainly didn't want to lift the receiver and hear Mike's deep voice on the other end of the line.

She sank into the easy chair by the balcony doors and propped her stocking feet on the red quilted spread on the bed. When had life stopped being simple? she wondered. At Aria's, she conceded almost immediately, right at the moment when Michael Conti had walked in and all but set her on her ear.

She closed her eyes to the panoramic view of the sun-bathed city and the distant desert and determinedly thought about the job. She went over what she'd found out about access to the thirtieth level, about what glitches she'd found in the security picture. The first guard she'd encountered had been reading the paper when she showed up. Most men in that sort of occupation found ways to kill the time between walking rounds.

Too bad she hadn't been able to observe the other guards. She didn't even know how many were in the rotation. Too bad Lincoln had decided not to give her the information. She could probably call the man down at the desk and ask. People were always more than willing to act knowledge-able. If she just pretended to be worried about security, they could reassure her.

She laughed softly. People liked to reassure nervous guests. The second guard had certainly bought the story that she and Mike were lovers. Mike. The thought of him pushed everything else aside until all she could visualize was him looking at her as if he could see right into her soul.

Maybe he could. She didn't think he'd believed her, yet he'd finally let her off the hook. Except for the promise to have drinks. Now she was beginning to think that might not be such a bad idea. She could control the contact, go to his suite, get a sense of the layout, then get out of there and get the job done.

She snuggled down farther in the softness of the chair, the low hum of the air-conditioning monotonous, yet soothing. Drinks. Maybe she shouldn't have any drinks, though. She wasn't a very good drinker. Or maybe her tolerance was incredibly low. Sister Elizabeth had told her that over and over again.

"Alexandria, you are not a drinker. Besides, alcohol only alters your consciousness. It distorts the truth." Alex chuckled. No, she wasn't a drinker, not even when she was back at the St. Thomas Home.

An image of the home came vividly to her mind—the two-story gray-brick building by the old church, the children in their tunics, rows of little people in green and white going back to their rooms after morning chapel or evening vespers.

Gradually, memories of the past enfolded Alex, until she realized she'd passed remembering and gone into a dream. But as an observer, as the one looking down, watching the scene unfold gently. An omniscient presence.

She could see herself fifteen years ago...Santa Barbara...sometime around Christmas...the dormitory room...seven beds...her looking at herself in the mottled mirror on the dull green wall.

She watched herself, a petite twelve-year-old with ebony hair confined in two tight braids who wrinkled her nose at her reflection. The deep green tunic had been annoyingly flat in the chest area. "I was hoping when I got to be a real teenager I'd get a real figure, Sister Elizabeth," she was saying.

The nun was there just as Alex remembered her, her habit gray and flowing around her, her tiny hands smoothing back the pale green chenille spread on Alex's bed. "You're not thirteen yet, child." Her round face flushed as she spoke softly. "And some girls just develop more slowly than others."

The young Alex watched the nun in the mirror, the total picture as crystal clear as if it were all happening right now. "I'll just die if I stay so...so flat."

"I can assure you, child, you *won't* die from that." Sister Elizabeth patted the pillow and stood straight. "Believe me, there are more important things in life than the size of one's bosom."

"There sure are." The child bit her lip, then blurted out, "I finally figured out who my father is. Really. I mean it, this time. I finally figured it out."

The nun turned, her hands pressed to the small of her back, her fingers massaging and kneading the aches and kinks there. "What did you say, child?"

"You heard me," the tiny girl said as she turned away from the mirror to look right at the nun. "I found out who *he* is."

Elizabeth frowned at the girl and shook her head. "Isn't it enough to know that your parents loved you enough to make sure you were taken care of?"

"No," the child said without having to think about it. "No, it's not enough. I figured out—"

"Enough of your stories," the nun interrupted. "I thought we'd talked this over and that you would stop these lies. Truth is its own reward, Alexandria."

The scene shifted, filtered and soft, with the child in bed, the covers pulled up to her chin. Long prayers had been flitted over, and Sister Elizabeth smiled down, smoothing the child's ebony curls where they spread darkly on the pillow.

"I know how you feel, with no family, but that doesn't excuse lying, child."

The ache in the girl began to make itself felt in the woman dreaming. "You have a family. How can you understand what—"

"Now, now. I have a brother, that's true. But you have people. You have me, and the sisters and Mother Superior, and the girls who live here."

Loneliness invaded the dream. "That's not enough," the girl said with aching truthfulness. "It's not enough."

In a flash, Sister Elizabeth was gone, and Alex stood in a place of cool dimness with cold stone flooring under her bare feet. The child was gone, too. Alex, the woman, was the center of the dream now, standing alone in a long, arched corridor. She recognized the way to Mother Superior's office.

"Where are you going?" someone called, but she didn't know who.

Without turning, she headed for the office door. "I'm going to talk to Mother Superior, then I'll know who I am," she called back over her shoulder.

Then, so suddenly it all but took her breath away, Mike stood directly in front of her, blocking her way. She didn't know where the knowledge came from, but she suddenly understood that he knew the truth about her.

She looked up at him, seeing him clearly despite the dimness of the hallway. "Mike, why are you here?"

He studied her intently; then a fire grew in the green depths of his eyes, a fire that began to warm Alex from the soles of her feet upward. Slowly he shook his head, and his voice flowed around her, gentle and soft and as all-encompassing as a summer breeze. "I'm here for you."

She shook her head sharply. "No, not you...." This was all wrong, so very wrong.

"Yes, me. I've been looking for you for a long time, and I'm not going to let you go."

She moved closer to him, and the dark chill of the stone walls gave way to the brilliance of the mirrors in the elevator. "No, not you," she whispered again, the sound echoing all around them, bouncing off the myriad images that floated on all sides.

"Yes, me, Alex. It was me all along."

"Why?"

"That's my secret," he said softly, his eyes unreadable. Then he reached out, cupping her upturned face, his hands warm, their touch incredibly welcome. "I can't tell you my secret until you tell me yours."

"I don't have any secrets," she said, but she knew that her whole life had been built on secrets. "You have to tell me," she said. "Please."

"No, Alex. I can't tell you until you tell me why you let me kiss you in the elevator."

She stared at him. "Because I wanted you to," she said simply, and knew it was the truth. Now she expected him to tell her why he had come for her. But he didn't. Instead, he drew her closer, and the kiss came again.

His mouth touched hers, the contact as consuming as a flame, yet as comforting as a caress. His taste was hers, his touch gentle, yet demanding—the touch of a lover. Then his hands tangled in her hair, capturing her, keeping her from drawing back. And every angle of him fit against her; every nuance of the man became real to her. She felt him everywhere, her shoulders, her breasts, her hips, her thighs.

She knew a completeness then, as frightening as summer lightning ripping the heavens apart, yet as sweet and smooth as honey flooding through her. His tongue thrust into her mouth, an invasion that held such intimacy that she felt as if she would cry from it. She felt filled and whole, safe and wanted.

Wanted. God, she wanted him. And she wanted him to want her the same way. Suddenly her response to his kiss went out of control, just as the dream itself began to do the same. The elevator started to descend, faster, faster, as frantic in its plummet downward as the kiss was becoming. This couldn't happen in real life. It couldn't, yet that didn't stop the swirling that only made Alex hold more tightly to Mike.

His mouth plundered hers, while everything mixed and tumbled together, and the ache of not knowing who she was was replaced with another ache. But this throbbing deep in her being had nothing to do with her past. It came from the present—from Mike. And it centered at her core, making her heavy with wanting.

He would come for her. He would protect her. That was all that mattered. He would come and she would be safe—finally. Downward, downward. Safe? No, she didn't even know him. She hadn't been waiting for him. Not him. And he was anything but safe. But that didn't stop her from holding to him as if he were her lifeline.

She moaned, shuddering, and she held more tightly to Mike, almost willing herself to fuse with him, to be part of him, to never be alone again. But the more intensely she held to him, the less substantial he became. Her arms were going through him, coming back to her own middle. Then she lost his taste, the sense of his heat against her. And at the same moment that she knew she was totally alone, the elevator hit bottom.

But there was no crash, no pain. Just a sudden jolting stop to the dream. Her breathing echoed all around her, and her heart beat furiously in her chest. She sat very still in the chair, keeping her eyes closed, willing the dream to go away, to fade into forgetfulness and take the ache of frustration with it.

Then she heard something above the pounding of her heart. A sliding rattle, and she jerked upright in the chair and turned to stare at the door. From across the room, she could see the handle slowly move. Someone was trying to get into her room.

Chapter 6

Alex scrambled to her feet and hurried to the door. Stopping two feet from the barrier, she stared at the handle rotating slowly to the left. She had no time to react before the door swung open.

For an instant all she saw was the blurred shape of a man. Mike? Breaking into her room? Then, as her still sleep-filled eyes focused, she realized how wrong she was. Mr. Lincoln stood in the doorway, staring at her, a key dangling from his fingers.

She exhaled a breath she hadn't even been aware of holding and had all she could do not to scream at the man. "You scared me to death!" she gasped.

"Sorry, little lady," he said, but he didn't sound sorry at all. He just sounded out of breath. "I knocked, but you didn't answer." Alex watched as he came into the room, swung the door shut and, without another word, went directly to the bed. With a sigh, he dropped down on the edge, then looked at Alex, who stood her ground by the door. "Sit. We need to talk."

She felt off balance from the remnants of the dream that still clung to her mind, and she was also aware of a growing anger at this man's high-handed attitude. She didn't know what to do, so she did what Lincoln said. She crossed the room, sank back down into the chair and gripped the arms tightly. "What did you think you were doing by letting yourself into my room?" she asked in what she considered an amazingly calm voice.

"I didn't think you were here. I was coming in to wait," the fat man said without blinking.

She fought for control while shock, anger and confusion mingled uneasily in her. It made her skin crawl to think about this man coming in here while she slept. She stared at him, at the perspiration stains at the underarms and neck of the gray shirt. Moisture even spotted the material at the man's bulging waist, where a belt rode low over his belly. "You had no right to—"

He held up one hand. "I don't have time to go over personal rights." He quirked one eyebrow at her. "Suffice it to say that I wasn't going to wait around in the hallway until you came back."

Her hair felt damp and clinging on her forehead, but she thought better of brushing at it when she realized how badly her hands might shake. She didn't let go of the chair arms. "What couldn't wait until later?"

He took a handkerchief out of his shirt pocket, unfurled it and began to wipe at his face. "Damned air-conditioning. You'd think they could get it so it felt natural, wouldn't you?"

"What's wrong?" Alex asked, impatient to get this man out of her room.

"Didn't say anything was wrong, little lady." He wiped his upper lip, one side, then the other, neatly smoothing the mustache in the process. "I'm just confirming a 'go' for tomorrow evening. Everything will be in place by then."

She looked down at the floor and saw her stocking feet only inches from his white suede loafers. "Is there anything else I need to know?"

"I feel I should tell you that the suite won't be set up to fool you. It'll be just like it is when a guest is in residence."

"That's best." Alex fingered the nubby fabric under her hands and looked back at Lincoln. "Did you decide what you want me to bring out for proof?"

"Something small, easily hidden—and taken." He was neatly folding the handkerchief, concentrating on the process until the damp piece of linen was a small square of white. He stared at the material in his hand. "A simple wooden box about four inches by six inches sealed with a brass strap around it. A small star's been burned into one corner on the top of the lid."

"Will it be in a safe?"

He looked back at Alex from under his eyebrows. "I think I'd call its hiding place more of a security spot." He stood, and her relief at seeing him getting ready to go died when he paused to look down at her. "One more thing."

"What's that?"

He tucked the hankie back in his shirt pocket and took out a package of cigarettes. Alex wanted to tell him that she minded if he smoked, but when he didn't ask, she let it go. He crossed to the small table by the sliding doors, took a pack of matches out of the ashtray, then took his time lighting his cigarette. He tossed the burned match into the ashtray, along with the pack, then pushed the cigarettes into his shirt pocket as he crossed back to Alex. He looked back at her through the curling smoke as he exhaled. "Who else do you know here?"

"No one."

"Then why did you block all your incoming calls unless they came from me?"

The hair at the back of her neck prickled. "And how did you know I did that?"

He took another long drag on his cigarette, then let the smoke trickle out. "I know everything that goes on at the Elysian."

She didn't see any reason to lie to Lincoln, yet she didn't feel she owed him an explanation about Mike, so she settled for a selective truth. "I met a man who's been a nuisance, and I didn't want him to get through to me. So I left the message."

Lincoln chuckled, a hoarse sound that shook his ample middle. "Can't say as I blame him, little lady. A guy's got to try. But that was a smart move, putting him off. Best to keep a low profile while you're here."

"I wasn't planning on spending my time at the gambling tables trying to get rich."

"Just as well. The best bets in Vegas aren't at the tables."

"Oh?"

"Real estate's the best. Buying up things, waiting for them to appreciate, then going in for the kill." He wasn't smiling now. "That's gambling, little lady. Laying everything on the table and coming out on top—one way or another. It's a real rush." He stopped, then exhaled on a hiss. "Gotta go. Just remember, you offered me discretion, and I believed you."

"I won't do anything to compromise this job."

"It's both our necks if you do," he said, then smiled to soften the implied threat. It didn't quite work. "I'll be in touch."

"If I need you . . . ?"

"Call the number I gave you and tell the person who answers that you're returning Mr. Dunn's call. I'll get back to you." With that, he turned and crossed to the door.

When he had his hand on the knob, Alex called after him, "Can I ask *you* one more thing?"

He looked at her and nodded.

"Are the floor plans for the suites in the tower all the same?"

"No. Each one's different."

"But is each floor the same as the others, the same suites, the same floor plans in the suite?"

He frowned at her. "I guess so. I never thought about it, but yet, that's probably right, except for the top level. The penthouse suites are all unique. Why?"

"Just asking."

He looked at her for a long moment, then left without saying anything else.

When the door clicked shut behind Lincoln, Alex hurried across and threw the safety bolt. Lesson number one—secure the room from the inside. With a sigh, she leaned against the door and pressed a hand to her stomach. Vague sickness churned just below the surface. Anticipation of the job she had in front of her. First-night jitters. Or maybe it was the dream.

Daydreams were what she usually remembered, dreams that she orchestrated and envisioned. Not those visions that came in sleep. She didn't want to remember *those* dreams. Not when they were so distorted and upsetting.

She crossed to the windows. The very idea of Mike invading her dreams was as crazy as the notion that he'd come here for her. It didn't make sense. She touched her lips. Her fleeting feeling of belonging when he'd said those words made even less sense. She reached out to the glass and spread her hands flat on its coolness.

She knew right then that if her stay in Las Vegas included being around Michael Conti, it could only be on her terms. That decision had been made for her even before Lincoln had reminded her about the need for anonymity. It had probably been made when she'd let Mike kiss her on the elevator, or maybe when she'd realized that his green eyes could see right through her.

As Mike walked down the hallway on the tenth floor, he saw a heavyset man dressed in gray and smoking a cigarette walk off in the opposite direction. The man had disappeared into the stairwell before Mike got to room 1058. He stared at the gold numbers for a long time before he finally knocked softly on the white wood.

There was a minute of silence; then a bolt clicked and the door opened. "Did you forget...?" Alex asked, but when she saw it was him, her question trailed off and her eyes grew wide. "You?"

She was expecting someone. *Was* there a partner? Or a
lover? That thought caught his middle in a vise. He'd never
thought of her having anyone here, but how did he know she
didn't? Maybe it was the same person she did "business"
with. "Do you always greet people like that?" Mike asked,
his light tone at odds with the oppression he felt inside.
Nothing added up about this woman. Then he caught the
smell of cigarette smoke and didn't know if it came from the
hall or her room.

Scattered ideas ran through his mind; then everything
settled as he realized how searing his reactions to Alex were.

She stood barefoot in front of him, her hair vaguely
mussed, her mouth free of lipstick. The vulnerability he
recognized in her expression wrenched at something so basic
in him that he couldn't begin to name it.

Mike looked away from Alex and decided to jump into
the situation with both feet, figuratively *and* literally.
Without asking, he stepped past her and into the room. An
empty room. Something in him relaxed just a bit.

When he turned, he saw Alex still by the door, bright dots
of color on her cheeks.

"Excuse me, Mr. Conti," she said in that vaguely husky
voice that ran riotously over his nerves. "I didn't ask you to
come into my room." Her chin lifted just a bit.

"But you were just going to, weren't you?" he countered, then glanced at the telephone before she could respond. "Did your call come through?"

"No . . . yes. One did, but I'm expecting another one."

He moved closer to her, but pushed his hands in his
pockets so he wouldn't act on impulse and reach out to
touch her. "Please, close the door. I need to talk to you for
a minute. We don't have to go for drinks, but we need to
talk."

"Why?"

She wasn't going to be easy, or make it any easier on him.
"Humor me, please."

She hesitated, then slowly closed the door. At the same
time that she looked up at him, she leaned back against the

door and crossed her arms over her breasts. Mike hoped that the person Stanley had looking into Alex's background found some answers to the riddle of the person standing in front of him.

Alex stared at Mike, so cool-looking in his white cotton shirt with its rolled-up sleeves and his faded Levi's, and she knew that she couldn't begin to match his control. But if she stayed this far away from him, maybe she could at least think straight.

He hooked his thumbs in the belt loops of his Levi's and spoke softly. "I know I'm just about a stranger to you. And we've been thrown together in strange circumstances, but..." He took a breath. "You're in trouble." A statement, not a question. "And I want to help."

His voice all but drew her to him the way it had in the dream, into some invisible circle where she knew he *could* help with anything. A knight in shining armor? A knight with green eyes and hair spun with rich highlights and flecked with just a touch of gray? An Italian knight? Get a hold on yourself, Alexandria, she admonished herself. But that didn't stop the idea from ending with the fact that *if* she were really in trouble, she would want this determined man to help.

But she wasn't in trouble. And as much as she hated to concede the point to Lincoln about secrecy, as a rule of thumb, the more people who knew what was going on, the more the chance for exposure and failure. She didn't need another near-fiasco like Aria's.

She looked at Mike, wishing she wouldn't notice the inviting way his lips lifted at the corners, or the thickness of the dark lashes that shaded his eyes. The memory of the kiss in the elevator overlapped with the kiss in the dream, and she had no idea where reality fell away and fantasy began. "I...I thought we talked about this before," she managed. "You don't have any reason to be concerned about me."

"You said you're here on business."

She detected a subtle edge of challenge in the simple statement, and she stood straighter. "Yes." The best defense was a good offense. So she took the offensive. "Why are *you* here in Las Vegas? You never really said."

He came closer, so close that she could catch his scent in the air, pleasantly subtle after the acrid odor of cigarette smoke. If she didn't breathe too deeply, maybe it wouldn't affect her this time.

"I came here to get away from things, to enjoy what the city has to offer. But what if I said part of that enjoyment was to meet a beautiful woman?" he asked in a low voice.

The words brought heat to her cheeks and a tightness to her chest. "Listen, if that's what this is all about . . ."

He held up one hand. "Just a minute. I won't tell you the thought hasn't crossed my mind. I'm not a good liar." His hand dropped to his side. "I'm really going about this all wrong. I came here to offer my help, to see if there was anything I could do to stop . . . to help. That's all."

Alex stared at Mike, trying to figure out why she should feel such ridiculous excitement because he'd even suggested that he might just be trying to get her into his bed. She swallowed hard. The idea of making love with Michael Conti was a very disturbing fantasy. "I appreciate the offer. I really do, believe me," she said quickly, a bit breathlessly. "But I never said that I needed any help."

"If you did, could you get your family to help?"

She swallowed hard. How did this stranger know all the right buttons to push to keep her off balance? "Sure...yes. *If* I needed help, I could ask them."

He crossed his arms on his chest. "Where are they?"

"They?"

"Your family."

She shrugged and held more tightly to herself. "Here and there. Spread out." She wasn't about to start telling the stories she usually did when people asked about her family. "They live all over the country now."

"So you have a large family?"

Alex thought of the girls she'd shared her space with in the dormitory. "Very large."

"Lots of brothers and sisters?"

"Just sisters."

"I'm one of seven children, myself. A big Irish-Italian family. The O'Briens and the Contis."

A real family. That brought remnants of the dream back to Alex, that nudging ache. She didn't really have anyone. Certainly not Mike. She moved abruptly to break off this line of talk by turning to the door. She wanted to be alone. "Now that you know I don't need help . . ."

When she would have opened the door, Mike's hand, warm and controlled on her shoulder, stopped her. She stood very still and kept her eyes on her own hand on the doorknob.

"Alexandria?"

The way he said her name made every nerve in her body jump. "What?" she asked, not daring to move under his touch.

"Can we start all over again? Can we go back to square one and forget what's past?"

She nodded. Anything to get her world back on an even keel.

"Thank you." The words came softly, as if Mike really was grateful that she'd agreed to start over. "Will you have drinks with me?"

She stared at her hand, at her fingers clutching the knob so tightly that her knuckles were white. The logical decision she'd made to see his suite to get information on the one on the thirtieth floor seemed less logical now. It was out of the question, actually. Being alone with Mike wasn't something she could deal with. If she was going to start over, she had to put her job first; then she could figure out what this thing with Mike was all about.

Before she could answer, his fingers moved slightly in an almost indiscernible soothing motion, just enough to keep her refusal from becoming reality. "Just an hour," he said.

"We can go anywhere you'd like for one hour, and I promise not to bring up the words 'help' or 'trouble' again."

One hour. Then she could get on with Lincoln's job without worrying about Mike looking over her shoulder. And if they went to another one of the hotels on the Strip, she could see what kind of systems *they* used. Maybe later she could get another job here.

"All right, but not here at the Elysian," she said.

"Anywhere. You pick the place. God knows, there are enough casinos and restaurants up and down the Strip."

She closed her eyes for one brief moment. "All right." Then she asked, "When?"

"Now."

Ian Hall watched the nurse leave, and he didn't relax until the door swung shut behind the white-clad woman. As he sank back onto the pillows, he realized how much he hated being dependent on strangers for his survival. He hated it almost as much as he hated this insidious weakness. The simple act of getting up and going to the window to look out at a city he'd loved since his first glimpse years ago was beyond him.

"Four more days and things will be on the right track," Stanhope had told him just before he'd left to make a phone call.

Stanhope had never been an optimist of any sort. The stocky man had always been a stark realist—an asset in their trade. And Ian knew Stanhope was too old and too set in his ways to change now. All of his encouraging smiles and words over the past week had rung false. But Ian did know that the man was on edge.

"We're going to die," Stanhope had said once, years ago in the Sudan, a statement of what had seemed obvious, since they were both facing the wrong end of a gun. But neither man had died that day.

I was saved for this? Ian thought. To die not with a bang, but a whimper... and all alone?

Alone. The last word stuck in his gut. *Alone.* His life had always been solitary, mostly by choice, but he'd never felt lonely. He'd been the only child of an army career officer and a mother who gave up on life after her husband had been killed. Ian had gone into the army when he was old enough, and he hadn't thought twice about joining the Agency when he'd been approached by Stanhope after the Korean conflict.

He'd only felt lonely after being with Meg. A flashing memory came to him. That hot July day in Egypt when Margaret Robertson had swept into his life and exposed every hidden void and chasm in his being. He closed his eyes, startled by the unfamiliar tears that burned in them. Weak and helpless. Damn it all.

Meg.

He lay motionless on the bed, the idea of fighting the past nonexistent now. He simply had no strength to hide from the past any longer. And he didn't want to.

Meg. Tiny, dark, with amazing blue eyes the color of cornflowers. The past came in flashes, in bits and pieces, broken frames of remembrances of things buried for so long and so deeply that they shocked him when they reappeared.

He'd been out in the brilliance of the sun that baked the land on the outskirts of Alexandria, the shimmering panorama of desert on one side, civilization on the other. He'd cursed the heat and discomfort that day until he'd turned and seen Meg step out of the shade of the awnings of the bazaar. His world had been brought to a halt by a woman who had barely come up to his chin even when she stood on tiptoes.

His assignment had been pushed aside, and for the first time in his life, everything of value had been encompassed in another person—a person he hadn't known existed until that moment. He couldn't quite remember how he'd crossed to Meg, how he'd first approached her, but he remembered the smile. More brilliant than the sun. And the way she had of looking right at him from under ridiculously long lashes.

They'd talked as one American to another, then as a man to a woman.

He shifted in the bed, wondering if this was his life passing before his eyes, fleeting images, yet so clear that they could have been cut from crystal. Maybe his life had only consisted of those three weeks with Meg, and the rest had been an illusion.

"Meg." He said her name softly, letting it sound in his ears in the silence of the room. Its familiarity started a growing pain in his chest that had nothing to do with his ailing heart.

He'd found Meg, the other half of himself, and he'd possessed her, loving her more deeply than he'd thought humanly possible.

And only Stanhope had known. His partner had called it insanity, and it had been, but he hadn't seen it for himself until death had come too close to the job he was supposed to be doing. Ian had awakened the next morning physically sick from the knowledge that he couldn't stay with Meg. His job wasn't nine-to-five, safe and secure. And Meg could have been used against him; she could have paid for his excesses, his risks. He shouldn't have gotten involved, yet he'd loved and been loved. And he'd never thought of leaving the Agency. Not right then.

Instead, he'd torn a part of his heart from his chest and walked away from Meg at the airport when she'd gone back to Los Angeles.

"I'll write, and I'll come later," he'd said, knowing the bitterness of lies even before the words had been uttered.

His existence had been a blur of time for a full year before he'd admitted to himself that nothing was right. He was marking time, wasting his life on a job that had ceased to be the center of his world. He'd needed Meg. He'd wanted her, and, on impulse, from his hotel in Athens, he'd called the number she had given him in Los Angeles. Disconnected and no forwarding number. So he took a new assignment, tried to go on, but finally admitted he couldn't exist without Meg.

But he'd been tied up with the assignment. He couldn't walk away to find Meg himself, so he'd turned to the one person who would understand, the only person in the Agency who had known about Meg—Stanhope.

He sighed, and his body shuddered under the cool cotton sheet.

Whiskey had become his only friend for a long time after Stanhope had come back to tell him, "Sorry, Ian, she's gone. Killed in an automobile accident a month ago. Died instantly. Gone."

And he'd cried in his whiskey, the only tears he'd known until now. Gradually, he'd gone on with his life, but hardly with living. Maybe his heart giving out physically was simply the practical way of ending a life that had been over for a very long time.

Completely alone.

The silence in the sterile room was deafening.

The noise in the multitiered casino was deafening. When Mike touched Alex's arm to get her attention across the leather-topped table of the booth they shared, she jumped as if she'd been burned.

Her deep brown eyes widened, startled for a moment, as if she were surprised he was still sitting there. "Yes?"

"Your drink," he said, raising his voice as he motioned to the barmaid hovering over their booth.

"Oh, thank you," she said, taking the cool glass and cradling it on the tabletop between her hands.

Since they'd left her room, she'd seemed edgy and preoccupied. He hadn't missed the distance she'd maintained between them while they rode down in the elevator, or the nervous glances around the lobby when they crossed to the entrance of the Elysian.

Then they'd stepped out into twilight and heat, the noise of cars and the bustle of pedestrians. He'd asked her where she wanted to go, and she'd motioned farther down the Strip, where hotels and casinos framed the sidewalks as far as the eye could see.

So they'd walked, together yet separate, down the sidewalk. With the clear desert sky overhead almost obliterated by the flashing lights and signs up and down the wide street, and the heat of the day tempered only slightly by the coming night, it had seemed to Mike as if he'd stepped into another world. A strange world of ribbons of car lights, streams of pedestrians crowding the cement, and a strange sense of electricity that almost radiated from the city itself.

Alex had shaken her head at the first casino they'd come to. "Too small," she'd murmured and kept walking.

Mike had hurried after her, aware of the fact that her head barely topped his shoulder. She twisted the strap of the purse hooked over her shoulder and never looked at Mike. He'd begun to wonder if she even remembered he was with her until she'd finally stopped outside this casino, one of the largest on the Strip.

"This one looks good," Alex had said, and he'd agreed with her. Right then he would have agreed to anything that offered a seat and a cold drink.

Now, in one of the booths of the bar on the balcony ringing the casino on the floor below, Mike never took his eyes off Alex. The flashing brilliance of the multicolored overhead lights shot her dark hair with highlights—red, blue, yellow, white and green. Colors danced all around them, gleaming off her full bottom lip, touching her cheeks with streaks of scarlet and gold.

Mike tossed part of his drink to the back of his throat. Beautiful. She was really beautiful. And she hadn't stopped scanning the room since they'd been seated. He followed her gaze to the area below as she intently watched the changing of the dealers, then the guards taking the money from the tables to put it in the safe. Abruptly, she looked up, her gaze skimming the walls, stopping only at a closed-circuit camera or wide-angled mirror. She'd spent the last few minutes looking at a windowed room way above the crowd—an office, probably, but with tinted windows that couldn't be seen through.

The speculation that narrowed her dark eyes was easy to read. Mike couldn't get away from the idea that he'd been watching her case the place. That sounded melodramatic, but was it possible? Was she capable of pulling off a robbery? Then the answer came. She was—if she had a partner.

He looked away from Alex, scanning the surrounding tables and wondering if one of the people sitting there sipping drinks could be her partner. Anything was possible. Anything at all. A sickness welled up in him, and he took another drink of Scotch before he looked back to Alex. He had to raise his voice to be heard over the jazz band on the upper level, the conversation and the incessant ringing of the slot machines. "Alex?"

She didn't respond until he repeated her name; then she turned abruptly to him. He more read her lips than actually heard her response. "Pardon me?"

"What do you think of all this?" he asked, motioning to the different levels filled to overflowing.

"Very impressive."

He glanced at the red and green vinyl that covered the seats, then down at the same colors twined in a painfully busy pattern on a carpet that seemed to flow everywhere. "Actually, I was thinking of the word garish," he muttered and sipped more Scotch. He motioned to her untouched drink. "Not thirsty?"

She looked down at the glass cradled in her hands, then dutifully took a drink, only to grimace horribly. "What is this?" she gasped.

He sat forward, resting his arms on the cool tabletop. "Scotch."

She shook her head, the colors from the overhead lights dancing crazily in her hair. "I don't usually drink hard liquor," she said, and he saw her swallow hard.

He wanted to say, *I said I was ordering Scotch,* but he knew it wouldn't do any good. She'd barely heard anything he'd said for the past half hour. "What *do* you want to drink?"

She took another, more tentative, sip of the amber liquid. "This...this is fine," she pronounced as she set the glass down.

Another lie, if the distaste in her expression was any clue. "I can order anything you'd like."

"No, I'm fine."

"Well, I need another one," he said and motioned to the waitress. He held up one finger, and in less than a minute, the girl brought him another Scotch. He handed her money, then sat back holding the cool drink between his hands. This wasn't what he wanted at all. He was doing what Stanley wanted, not letting her get out of his sight, but this was too hard.

Besides, if he was any good at reading people, Alex was going to ask to go back to the Elysian any minute now. Once there, there was no way he could stay with her short of camping out in her room. Duplicity wasn't his strongest trait, but he had to figure out some way to keep them together, some way so that she wouldn't have the option of leaving until Stanley said what he wanted to have done with her.

"Alex?"

She looked up at him. "Yes?"

He watched her waiting for him to say something; then he decided what to do. A simple plan, if it worked. More importantly, if he could carry it off. All he needed was a little information, and he knew where to get it. "Why don't we get out of here?"

Chapter 7

Excuse me?" Alex asked.

"We can go for a drive. See the desert." He waved one hand in the general direction of the noisy space around them. "Anyone can see the casinos and the shows. How about a drive at twilight in the desert?"

She took another sip of her drink, and he didn't miss the vague unsteadiness in her hands. She took her time swallowing, then licking the liquor off her lips, an action that he found precariously close to being endearing. "I don't know. I need to get back to work, and I . . ."

Was her partner waiting for her to make contact? He glanced at his watch, then set a smile on his lips. But the false expression wasn't easily maintained when he looked back at Alex. "We've still got a half hour. Can't you forget business for a bit longer?"

"Where can we drive in a half hour?"

She had him there. So he smiled more broadly. "Can we call this last half hour a preliminary test, then start the hour when I get a car from the rental agency at the hotel?"

Alex looked away from his smile and wished that the simple expression didn't have the power to draw up every nerve in her body. Quickly she drank the last of her Scotch, a bit shocked that it didn't taste quite so bad now and that the heat seemed to be steadying something deep inside her.

She'd found out what she'd wanted to in here. Their security seemed complex and tight, but she knew the system and that its effectiveness hinged on one simple part. And that part was the weak link. If she had the time and resources, she thought she might be able to get around it. Maybe she could approach the manager later on and make him a deal.

She kept her eyes on her empty glass, wondering if she should make Mike a deal. She would agree to go with him for a while if he'd respect her privacy and leave her alone until her work for Lincoln was done. "I'm here on business, but if I—"

He didn't let her finish before he interrupted, something that she noticed he was doing more and more. "No one comes to Las Vegas purely for business reasons, not unless they're up to something."

Those words brought her head up sharply, and for a minute she caught a glimpse of an intense look deep in his eyes. But before she could read more than that, the smile came again, and its brilliance rocked the foundations of her reasoning process. "Excuse me?" she asked.

"Professional gamblers," he said, and she had the distinct feeling that he hadn't meant that at all. That brought a flash of uneasiness, reawakening the same suspicion she'd had before, that Mike could tell when she was lying. She hadn't had that feeling since Sister Elizabeth. And she hated it now. It left her uncertain of what to say and how to say it, and feeling vulnerable.

Mike spoke without waiting for her to respond. "I'll make you a deal," he said.

She pushed her glass away. "What kind of deal?"

"Come with me for an hour, so we can take a nice drive. We can talk, or we don't have to say anything. Whatever way you want it. Then I'll bring you back to the Elysian, and I promise I won't bother you again until your business is done.''

His "deal" made her breath catch for a second in her chest. Could he read her mind, too? Out of self-protection, she almost refused, a bit afraid to be alone with this man in a car. Then she knew she was protesting too much, and if she wasn't careful, Mike would realize that. "It's a deal.''

"It won't hurt to put off your business for an hour or so, will it?''

"It can wait.''

Mike stood and held out his hand to her. "Let's go.''

Alex ignored the offered hand and stood, pausing just a moment to let a sudden rush of light-headedness from the Scotch settle. Then she looked at Mike. "Where to?''

He nodded and led the way out of the casino, back down the street and into the lobby of the Elysian. He crossed to the car-rental desk, and Alex hung back while he talked to the clerk. Then Mike was at her side, his hand on her arm, leading her back to the front doors and out into the softness of the night.

They waited silently in the heat until a red Camaro pulled up to the curb in front of them and an attendant got out. "Mr. Conti?'' the boy, wearing a white shirt and black pants, asked.

Mike nodded. "That's me.''

The boy motioned to the idling car. "She's all yours. The air conditioner is going full blast, and the tank's full.''

Mike tipped the boy, helped Alex in, then went around to get in and put the car in gear.

Alex settled back in the comfort of the bucket seat and let the cool air rush over her face and shoulders. She looked out the side window, at the hotels and restaurants on the Strip. Then the establishments began to thin, and she saw two or three new structures going up. More hotels and casinos, she gathered from the signs posted on the partially constructed buildings.

"A building boom," she murmured. "Just what Las Vegas needs. More hotels and casinos."

"There must be a demand for them," Mike said.

Several minutes passed before Alex finally turned from the window and looked at Mike, a shadowy man just inches from her. "Where are we going?"

Mike shrugged. "North. The clerk at the car-rental desk told me about a nice ride that's off the beaten track."

Alex looked back to the window to see that the city lights were pretty much behind them, and that the desert, bathed in the deepening shadows of night, was ahead of them on both sides of the four-lane freeway.

When she looked at Mike, his profile was as blurred as the land around them. If he wanted to talk, there was something she would like to hear about. "How did someone like you ever get arrested?" she asked.

Mike glanced at her, then took a breath. "It's a long story."

"I've got almost an hour."

"I'll make you another deal. You tell me a story about you and I'll tell you a story about me."

Alex swallowed hard. This was like the dream—*tell me a secret, and I'll tell you one.* But this wasn't a dream. "What kind of story?" she managed.

"Anything about your past."

"There isn't much interesting about my past." She shifted a bit closer to the door and realized she still felt just a bit fuzzy from the Scotch. "I was never arrested."

"Never?"

"Not even close...until you..." She realized her slip and tried to cover it up. "I mean...I never did..."

He reached out and touched her hand, patting it softly where it rested on top of her purse in her lap. But he didn't pull back. Instead, his hand stayed there and stayed very still. "That's okay. I know you've never been in prison. Tell me something about when you were little."

She nibbled on her bottom lip and found the lingering taste of the liquor there. Not an unpleasant taste now. "Why don't you go first? I'm finding it hard to believe you were ever arrested," she admitted. "You don't look like someone who's been in jail."

"Prison. There's a vast difference between that and jail. Jail's for little things, like unpaid traffic tickets, or a place to visit while you're being processed to be sent someplace else. Or the place where they kept you during a trial. Jails are tucked into police stations." He inhaled deeply. "A prison is a penitentiary. It's off in some miserable place, far away from decent people. It's cold and hard, and it's a world unto itself. It's the ultimate punishment, except for the death penalty. The end of the line."

Mike turned onto the freeway off-ramp, then drove back under the freeway overpass and headed north on a two-lane highway. Only a scattering of cars passed them now, and the lights of businesses and houses began to get fewer and farther between. The desert seemed vast on both sides of the road. "Why was someone like you in a place like that?" Alex asked, really wanting to know, sensing something so upright in this man that the idea of him being arrested seemed absurd.

"Someone like me? Someone who doesn't look like an ex-con? Someone who doesn't have tattoos over most of his body? No bulge under his jacket from a hidden gun?"

Someone who's gentle and caring, she wanted to say, but she kept the words to herself. In some way she knew that saying those words out loud would change things. And she couldn't afford for that to happen—not yet. "You seem so decent. You're always trying to help."

He laughed at that. "That's one of my flaws. I'll help someone even if it kills them."

"You don't take no for an answer, do you?" Alex countered, feeling a smile playing at the corners of her mouth. "Really stubborn."

"If I listed my character traits, I'm afraid stubbornness would be right up there in the top three."

"What are the other two?"

"Loyalty and honesty." He chuckled softly. "That makes me sound like a damned Boy Scout, doesn't it?"

"No, stubbornness sort of puts you out of the running for that."

"Touché."

"Did being stubborn get you sent to prison?"

"You're not going to give up on that, are you?"

"I guess I'm stubborn, too," she conceded, and she knew it was true. That was why she had never given up trying to figure out who she was. "Tell me the story."

He stared straight ahead into the night. A car came from the opposite direction, and its lights burst across Mike's face for barely a second. But Alex could see the way his jaw worked, the way his eyes were narrowed. "Once upon a time..." he began.

"No fairy tales," she said quickly. "No make-believe. Just the truth."

"Then you'll need a bit of background." The soft beauty of the desert night couldn't take the raw edges off memories that still held the power to tear at him. But for a flashing moment, it seemed as if someone else had lived through the past; that the real Mike was here touching the softness of Alex's hand, a sensation that seemed to be sinking into his soul.

Yet as the memories came more and more clearly, he found himself resenting the lies. And resenting Alex just a bit with each memory. He drew away from her and held tightly to the wheel. It made it easier to talk if he didn't have any physical connection with her.

"When I was growing up, I was always looking for my identity, for who I was."

"What?"

"Who I was. What I was. Why I was on this earth. Oh, I knew I was the youngest son of Rose and Gino Conti—Michael Allan Conti. Half Irish, half Italian. With green eyes from my mother's mother. I was the kid brother of Gino Junior, Thomas, Marco, Anthony, Angelica and Rosie, but I never knew who *I* was. I didn't realize this until much later in my life, but my search for that niche in the world, that reason for existing, was the reason I got into a lot trouble growing up. I gave my parents a pile of grief, and I've had a lot to make up to them.''

He exhaled, wondering if he could ever, even after all these years, make it up to his mother and father for those visits to the prison. He'd hated seeing them there, sitting in the visiting room with the others. They hadn't belonged there any more than he had. ''That's not an excuse,'' he said quickly. ''Just an explanation. I grew up in a pretty poor neighborhood, seven kids in a two-bedroom house, and an easy escape seemed to be hanging out with gangs, nothing like today's gangs, but they were all trouble.

''My reputation as the worst kind of pain in the neck was well deserved by the time I was in my teens, believe me. I barely squeaked through high school without being thrown out. The local police knew all about me, and I knew most of them on a first-name basis.

''Then something happened. There wasn't any great flash of insight, but I knew that I wanted to do something with my life, to make a difference, not add to the problems. I swear, I was going to look into job counseling and maybe college. The problem was, I was a bit too late.

''Out of nowhere, the police showed up at my place. I couldn't figure out why they'd be there. Then they told me a gas station nearby had been burglarized and a car had been stolen out of the garage bay. They said that the owner, who had been working late, identified me as the one who did it.

''I'd done a lot of things, but nothing like that. I wasn't into doing real damage.'' He held more tightly to the steering wheel. ''But my past gave them no reason to take my word for my innocence or believe my alibi.''

''What was your alibi?''

''When the robbery took place, I was out walking, just thinking. But the guy at the station insisted I was the one. I went in there all the time, and I'd given him a hard time before, so he knew me.

"With my reputation and my past with the station owner, the police didn't look for anyone else. And no one else showed up and said, 'I did it.'"

"But you didn't do it, did you?"

"No, I didn't. I thought the station manager made a real mistake, but a mistake. That he'd been scared and angry, and that any teenager with long hair would have looked like any other one."

"How did you ever get out of prison?"

"The insurance company that covered the station investigated, and they made a settlement with the owner. Then, over a year later, the car turned up in another state, altered, but they could tell from the serial numbers that it was the one that had been stolen. The guy who had it swore he'd bought it legally, and when they looked into it, the man he'd bought it from looked just like the station owner. The owner eventually admitted he'd done it himself for the insurance, and he'd thought I was under eighteen and wouldn't serve any time. That they'd just scare me. When he found out I was eighteen and that I'd go to prison, he was in too far to back out."

"Why would he do that to you?"

Mike shrugged and swallowed hard. "Who knows? The guy needed money, and he figured the insurance was one way to do it. He collected on money that was supposedly taken and on a car that he'd been able to sell."

"You must have been angry."

"Angry?" That didn't begin to cover the feelings he'd had after losing over two years of his life, after seeing his family dragged through the gutter. "A lie cost me two years of my life, and it cost my family, too."

"What happened to the station owner?"

"I don't know. I never wanted to know, actually." He pushed the memories away. "It's over and done. And I've made a life for myself."

"And what did you do with your life?"

He glanced at Alex, at her shadow two feet away from him. "What?"

"Now. What do you do? What's your job?"

"Public relations," he murmured, then pointed out the front window. "Look at that moon." Huge and orange, it hung above the desert, yet strangely didn't give off much of a glow. "I never really knew what a liar's moon was, but I always thought that type of moon had to be one. It looks like it could light the whole world, but it hardly gives off any light. It's a lie."

"You're wrong," she said softly.

"What?"

"A liar's moon is nothing like that."

"And how do you know?"

"I had someone tell me a long time ago that a liar's moon is the kind of moon that's all misty and haloed with shadows. Clouds smear across the front of it." She shifted in the seat. "It's a liar's moon because you don't know what it is, what it's meant to be. You can't see past the illusion of the night to the moon."

He glanced at Alex. Was that the truth, or one of her stories? He felt his hands tighten on the wheel again. He would do what he had to do, then leave this all behind.

He looked out the front window and saw an orange sign to the right of the road, a faint glow reaching into the sky from the lights underneath it. He couldn't see the source, but he knew, from what the car-rental clerk had told him, that he'd found what he was looking for.

He hit the gas pedal, then eased off and felt the car jerk and falter. "Damn it," he muttered, then looked at Alex again. "Do you know anything about cars?"

"No, not a thing."

At least it had worked out this far. "Neither do I. That's something they overlooked when I supposedly stole the car from the gas station. I didn't have the vaguest idea how to hot-wire a car." He made the car jerk again. "Something is wrong with this one," he said and drove onto the side of the road.

"What can we do?" Alex asked as the car coasted over the gravel.

"I could take a look at it, but I'd probably do more harm than good under the hood."

"It was running just fine before." She sat forward, her hands on the dash. "Is it out of gas?"

"There's plenty of gas." Mike kept driving toward the orange sign, but made sure that the car slowed more and more. "It's not hot."

"Then why's it acting like this?"

"I wish I knew," Mike breathed, wondering why he didn't choke on such a blatant lie. "I just hope we can get to that light up there."

Alex stared into the night. She knew she shouldn't have come on this drive. She should never have left Las Vegas until the job was completed. She saw a huge orange gas sign down the road; then, as the car got closer, she could make out some buildings huddled in the glow cast by the sign. Then she saw the sign above the middle building—HANK'S OASIS.

"I hope Hank knows something about cars," she muttered with sarcasm, but meaning it, too. Someone here had to know something about cars.

As the car limped into the gravel parking area, Alex felt her hopes plummet. To the right was a small gas station with two pumps, but no garage, and it was locked up tight. To the left was a series of small cabins strung together by the roofs of carports situated between each unit. Right ahead was a low-roofed, glass-fronted restaurant and bar. Two huge diesel trucks were idling in front, and two cars were alongside them.

Mike coasted the car the final hundred feet, fitting it between one of the trucks and a car. Then he turned off the motor. "Lets go inside and see what they can do for us."

"All I need is a telephone," Alex said, getting out into heat that she'd completely forgotten about in the air-conditioned car.

"I'm sure they have one. But who are you going to call?" Mike asked.

"A taxi." She headed to the door, the pieces of gravel pressing into her feet through the leather soles of her sandals.

"It'll cost a fortune to get a cab to come out here," Mike said, stepping up behind her as she reached the door.

Alex turned and swiped at a moth that fluttered by her face as she looked up at him. "I need to get back to Las Vegas. I've got business to take care of, in case you don't remember, and I can't be gone for hours."

"Then I'll call the rental place and have them send out another car. They'll do that, and it won't cost anyone."

Alex considered that. It made sense. "Okay." And she pushed back the door.

The sounds of a jukebox and the smell of smoky air greeted Alex as she stepped inside. But at least it was cooler than outside, with its air stirred by slowly rotating fans overhead. The long, narrow room, with a bar on the left with stools in front of it, and a long string of booths on the other side, was far from full, with maybe six or seven customers scattered around the room.

No one looked up when Alex and Mike went in, except for a totally bald man behind the bar. His full face was as clean-shaven as his head, and his green T-shirt was emblazoned with the orange logo of HANK'S OASIS done against a background of palm trees.

"Evening, folks," he said and came down the bar toward the door. "What can I get for you?"

Alex went to the bar and slid up on a stool. "Do you have anyone around here who fixes cars?"

The man shook his gleaming head. "Sorry. No one until tomorrow. Dudley comes in then and takes care of the gas and things. He can do little repairs, belts and hoses and things."

Mike came up behind Alex and spoke to the man. "My rental car quit on me. Can I use your phone?"

The man motioned to the far end of the room. "Back there. There's a pay phone by the men's room."

Mike thanked him, then headed to the back of the building. Alex only waited a second before following him. When he got to the phones, he turned to her. "I'll call." He motioned to a booth nearby. "You sit down, and I'll find out what can be done."

Alex went to the second booth from the back, then dropped down on the tufted plastic seat. On the knotty pine wall to the right were a small slot machine and, above that, a wall lamp that barely gave off enough of a glow to show the fake wood grain on the tabletop.

Alex watched Mike putting coins in the slot, then watched him talking to someone. He shook his head, waited, then shook it again. Finally, he nodded, said something else and hung up.

He came back and slipped into the booth. "They'll send out another car, just as I thought. But it might take a little while."

"What's a little while?" she asked.

"An hour or so. Maybe more."

She sat back in the seat. "Another hour?"

"Sorry," Mike said and unexpectedly reached across the table to pat her hand. "I'm really sorry. I hope this doesn't mess up your business plans."

Alex shook her head. "No, I can handle it. But I need to call someone."

Mike hesitated, then motioned to the phone. "Do you have change?"

Alex looked in her purse. "Not a bit."

Mike pushed his hand in his pocket and came out with some coins that he handed to her. "Here. It's not a local call to Las Vegas. That's where you wanted to call, wasn't it?"

"Yes." She took the money, very conscious of his body heat trapped in the metal. "I'll be right back."

She went to the phone and called Lincoln's number. "Yes?" a man said.

"Dunn?" she asked, using the code name she'd been given.

"No."

"Can I talk to him?"

"Sorry. I'll take a message."

"All right. Tell him Mrs. Gray won't be in her room for a few hours. If he's got anything she needs to know, he can contact her after..." She looked at the bar and saw a clock over it. Nine o'clock. "...midnight." That gave her plenty of time to get back to the city.

"After midnight," the man repeated. "Anything else?"

"No."

A click sounded on the line, and Alex hung up.

She stared at the phone for a minute, then turned and went back to the table. "Done."

"I didn't know you knew anyone in Las Vegas."

"Just my business contact," she hedged. "I wanted him to know I'd be gone for a few hours."

Mike looked at her for a long moment, then asked, "Do you want something cold to drink?"

"Yes, that sounds good." She sighed as she settled on the plastic seat.

Mike motioned to the bar, and the bald man came over to the table. "What can I do for you? The kitchen's closed, but we got sandwiches already made—tuna, chicken and bologna."

"I'm not hungry," Mike said. "But I'll have a beer." He looked at Alex. "How about you?"

Alex realized she hadn't eaten all day. "A tuna sandwich and a Coke."

"Sorry, our soda machine's broken down."

"What else do you have that's cold?"

"Beer, wine, any kind of drink you want."

"Iced tea?"

"Sorry. But we got wine coolers. They're sort of like soda pop. Real mild."

"A wine cooler sounds fine," Alex finally said.

The man left; then Mike looked across the table at Alex. "Your business associate wasn't angry about the delay?"

"No, not at all. What did the rental agency say about their car breaking down?"

"Just that they'd send someone out, and they'll repay us for any expenses we're out because of the problem."

"Expenses?"

"I guess if it turned out we were stranded and needed to spend the night ..."

"What?"

"I'm just supposing."

The man returned right then and set a beer in front of Mike, and a glass with pale liquid and ice cubes in it in front of Alex. A sandwich still wrapped in plastic was on a small plate beside the glass. "Enjoy your stuff," the man said and went back to the bar.

Alex looked down at the sandwich. "Will they repay us for this?"

Mike chuckled softly. "Maybe you'll get a bonus if you can eat the whole thing."

Alex undid the plastic, then took one bite. Stale bread and crumbly tuna were a terrible combination. She chewed slowly, then reached for her glass to wash it down. The wine cooler tasted sweet and refreshing. It wasn't soda, but it tasted good to her. She drank half the glass before setting it down, not realizing how thirsty she had become; then she pushed the sandwich plate toward Mike. "Do you want some?"

"No, thanks."

She stared at the sandwich, then took another drink of her cooler. Not bad at all.

"Your turn," he said.

She looked up at him. "My turn for what?"

"A story."

Chapter 8

Alex drained the last of her cooler and looked at the ice cubes in the bottom of the glass. Maybe another one would help if Mike really expected her to tell him a story. "I'm still thirsty."

Mike got up and crossed to the bar. When he came back, he had four bottles in his hands. All coolers, all different flavors—peach, raspberry, orange and some exotic red one. "I didn't know what flavor you wanted, so I brought you a choice."

Alex took the closest bottle, one with a ripe peach on the label, and opened it. She poured it over the ice, watching the pinkish-yellow liquid swirl around the cubes. After she tested it and found it as delicious as the first one, she sat back with the glass in her hand. "They're good. I've never tried them before, but they're really good."

"You've never had wine before?"

"Oh, sure, I have. But I always thought it tasted a bit like fruity vinegar."

Mike smiled at her. "Just what kind of wine have you been drinking?"

"I don't know. Whatever a restaurant serves."

"Not a connoisseur?"

"Far from it. I usually order by color, not by label. It's usually safe to order white wine. In fact, it's the thing to order now, isn't it?"

"Just a minute. This isn't your story, is it? Because if it is, you're not playing fair. I told you about the biggest mistake I ever made, and you're telling me about the colors of the wines you've tasted."

Alex sat forward, resting her elbows on the tabletop. She fingered the condensation on the sides of her glass. "All right. How about if I tell you about the first time I tasted wine? Would that qualify as a story?"

"It all depends on how old you were and how much trouble you got in."

"Trouble? Oh, I got in trouble all right." Alex smiled, the memory still there after all these years. "I was eight, and I ended up wishing I could die before it was over. How's that for a story?"

"I'd say that qualifies," Mike murmured and sat back, his fingers clasped loosely around his glass of untouched beer.

"I was with a friend, Joanie, at this...this boarding school I went to a long time ago." That was a good name for the home. "She and I stuck together...for a while, until she got..." She bit her lip. She wasn't about to talk about Joanie getting adopted. "Until she got to go home."

"What sort of boarding school was this?"

"A very strict one that was run by the church," she said honestly.

"A convent school?"

"Uh-huh." That sounded right to her. She took a long drink of the cooler, then licked her lips. "On this particular night, it was really late, around midnight, and Joanie and I couldn't sleep. We told stories in the dark, then she got this idea that it would be romantic to drink some wine. And she said she knew some wine was kept in Mother Superior's office." She took a sip of her drink, then looked back at Mike.

"You have to understand that Mother Superior's office was in this stone building, all gray and dark at night. Really spooky. The entry hall was really long and had big tapestries in it. When you walked, your footsteps echoed all around."

She'd never told anyone this before, and it felt good to remember, to be able to tell about memories from her past as if that past had been normal.

"You went there at midnight?"

She nodded and took another drink. "Right at midnight. Joanie and I sneaked out of our room and decided that going barefoot was the best thing, so no one would be able to hear us. So we left the dormitory and headed across the lawn. It was really damp, and we only wore our white nightgowns. All the girls wore these long cotton gowns in the summer and flannel gowns in the winter." She looked at her glass, and she didn't understand why it was empty.

She kept talking as she reached for the next cooler in line, the raspberry one, and poured it over the remnants of the ice cubes in her glass. "Our feet were freezing by the time we got to the office, even though it must have been June. It was before my birthday, I remember that. And we had to go down this hall that only had one light on. I never knew how, but those tapestries always seemed to move back and forth, maybe from a breeze or something. The place always seemed cold.

"Joanie and I looked at those moving tapestries, then at the shadowy hall, and we grabbed each other's hand and we ran as hard as we could for Mother Superior's office, way down at the end of the passageway."

She tried the raspberry cooler and vaguely wondered how it could taste so much better than the peach had. "Anyway, we got there, and the door was unlocked. I don't think it was ever locked. So we went inside, but we couldn't find any wine anywhere. Then we went back into a big walk-in closet filled with freshly pressed nuns' habits. Way up on the top shelf we found a decanter, a really pretty bottle, all sort of cut crystal, with a big round ball lid and really heavy."

"I take it there was wine in it?"

"Uh-huh," Alex murmured as she drank more cooler.

"What kind?"

She took another drink, then answered. "Red. I told you, I don't know more than that. Joanie went out and found some glasses in the office. Then we sat in the closet with just a flashlight that we'd brought with us for light, both of us on the stone floor with the decanter between us. She dared me to taste the wine first. A dare's a dare, so I did, and it was putrid. I mean, it was like vinegar that someone had added fruit to. It wasn't anything like this," she said, holding up the almost empty glass. "This is really good." She stared at the remaining deep red liquid with tiny chips of ice floating on the surface. "That stuff with Joanie was the worst."

"And that's your story?"

"I'm not done yet." She drank the last of the cooler, then put the glass on the table. "This is the good part," she said and heard herself giggle. She put a hand over her mouth and stared at Mike, liking it when he smiled at her the way he was now. "You know, you have a wonderful smile." Surely it wouldn't hurt to tell him that. "A really nice smile."

"Thank you," he said, that wonderful smile exposing a dimple that had suddenly appeared on his left cheek. "The story..."

"Oh, yeah." She'd almost lost her thread of thought concentrating on Mike's smile. "Well, Joanie and I drank a lot of the wine. And the next thing I know Sister Elizabeth was—"

"Who's Sister Elizabeth?"

"The best person ever, and the very best teacher ever. She was my friend. She found Joanie and me almost passed out in the Mother Superior's closet, and she took us both up to bed. Luckily I got up there before I got sick." She grimaced. "Then she nursed me through the worst hangover ever. She even made an excuse for Joanie and me not to go to class the next day."

"She sounds like quite the lady," Mike murmured.

"She...she was," Alex said, shocked at the stinging of
tears behind her eyes. "She sat with me and told me all
about the merits of temperance. But she was great."

"Did you keep in touch with her?"

"She died." Alex swiped at her eyes quickly, then went to
take another drink. She'd completely forgotten the glass was
empty. She held out the glass to Mike. "There's no ice left."

He must have gotten up and filled her glass with ice, because the next thing she knew, he was handing her a glass
loaded with ice cubes.

She reached for the next cooler, but found she couldn't
undo the lid. "Could you do this?" she asked Mike as he
settled across from her.

He took it, twisted the lid, then handed her the open bottle.

"Th...thanks," she said and poured the pulpy liquid over
the ice.

"Are you sure you want that one?" he asked.

She looked at the berry-colored drink in her glass, then up
at Mike. "Yes, I want it." She took a swallow of the cool,
sweet liquid and rotated her head slowly from side to side,
trying to ease the tension she could feel in her neck and
shoulders.

"Tell me some more about Sister Elizabeth."

She looked at him from under lowered lashes and shook
her head. "No. Not now." Not even for Mike. She couldn't.

"Then tell me about the school."

She drank some more, hoping to ease the liquid past a
growing tightness in her throat. "It was a school. I had to
live there. It wasn't all bad, because they really cared about
you." She tasted the drink once more and thought how some
memories could still hurt years later. "They really cared."

"Alex?"

She looked up at Mike, hoping that he couldn't tell how
close to tears she felt. "What?"

"Who cares about you now?"

That brought the tears back fresh. "No...no one."

"No boyfriends?"

"No." She drank more cooler. "I almost got married...once. Three years ago. I didn't date a lot, not really. I mean, I was brought up around all these girls, and when I met Rick, he seemed so...so nice. He wanted to get married and live happily ever after, but I realized he was too nice. That was it. I broke the engagement, and hated myself for a long time." She blinked rapidly when she remembered the loneliness after Rick, the few dates, the men who weren't special enough to see more than a few times. Rick. She thought hard, trying to get a mental picture of him. "I can't really remember what he looked like now, but he was really..."

"...nice?" Mike finished for her.

She laughed unsteadily. "What a terrible word." She narrowed her eyes, wondering if it was the bad light or the threatening tears, or maybe the smoke in the room, but Mike seemed a bit blurry. "But you're nice. And it's nice that you're nice."

Mike reached across the booth and touched her hand on the tabletop. "Alex, no one's really nice. Everyone's got their dark side, their crazies and their ghosts."

"What ghosts do you have?"

"I told you about my misspent youth."

"No other ghosts?"

"I guess my marriage."

"You...you said you were divorsh..." She stopped, wondering why she couldn't pronounce such a simple word as "divorced."

"I *am* divorced." He obviously understood her scrambled words. "But failure haunts me. I hate giving up on anything."

"Boy, you can say that again," Alex muttered and turned her hand over so her fingers tangled with his. "You're really stubborn, Mr. Conti," she said, liking the way his hand, dark against her fingers, held hers. "You're so safe. So very safe."

"I'm what?"

"Safe. Didn't you know that? I knew that the first time..." She hesitated. "No, maybe the second time I saw you...in the taxi cab from the airport. I thought 'He's safe.' I really did."

His fingers kept the contact with hers. "That makes me sound boring."

Boring? This man? He was crazy. He was anything but boring. And what he did to her was anything but boring. "I liked you right away, you know. Even when you were messing up my thing at Aria's." She licked her lips, the sweetness of fruit still there. "I liked you even then. Oh, I didn't know it, exactly, but I do now. You were different, and your eyes..." She couldn't believe what she was saying, but she didn't seem to be able to stop. "...they're so green. And you're Italian. I always thought Italians had brown eyes like mine. I ush...used to think I might be Italian." That stopped her dead. I don't know what I am.

Mike had watched with fascination as her guard dropped, as she told him about the home, about Sister Elizabeth. Then about Aria's. But now she sat looking at him, the fingers of her free hand nervously smoothing the dampness on the glass while he held to her other hand. She didn't even know her heritage. "What difference does it make?" he asked and wished he could take back the words as soon as he saw her reaction to them.

She didn't move for a full minute; then she closed her eyes so tightly it drew two lines between them. He could feel her tremble under his touch; then she looked at him, her lashes damp with tears. "That's just it. It does. I...don't...don't know," she said unsteadily.

Then two huge tears rolled down her cheeks, but she didn't make a move to wipe them away. "It doesn't matter," he said, wanting to comfort her, but saying the wrong thing again. "It doesn't matter at all about a person's past."

"It doesn't to...to you, because you're Michael Allan Conti. And you've got family. I bet you've even got a birthday."

"Sure. November second."

"See. I told you. I knew you'd have a birth...birthday."

"Everyone has a birthday, Alex. When's yours?"

She drew back from his touch and lifted her glass with both hands to her unsteady lips. She gulped the last of the drink, then put down the glass and swiped awkwardly at her eyes. "How does July Fourth sound to you?"

He knew the coolers were having an effect on her; he could hear the slurring in her words, see the flush on her cheeks. But he didn't understand the bitterness in her voice. "Your birthday's July Fourth?"

"Probably."

"What?" He didn't understand.

"It sounds like it sh...should be, but..." She gulped hard and lifted a delicate necklace she wore with the yellow dress. But before he could see it clearly, she let it fall free, and it slipped under the neckline of her dress again. "The Fourth of July." She spun her glass around and around, but her hands were shaking, and her eyes were bright with more tears. "Fireworks...and sh...shows. It shooo...should..." The glass hit the table with a cracking sound; then Alex pushed it away and dropped her head to her clenched hands on the tabletop.

Mike moved immediately, without giving himself time to think about anything beyond helping Alex. He was beside her on the seat, pulling her into his arms, feeling her trembling and the silent sobs racking her body. But she didn't make a sound. He kneaded her bare shoulder slowly, and he felt helpless and stupid. He hated his own lies and what his questions had done to her. He'd never realized how alone she must feel. God, he wished he understood so he would know what to do for her.

The bartender came over to the table and looked down at Alex and Mike with a frown. "You got problems here, buddy?"

Mike stroked Alex's head pressed into his chest, smoothing the silky hair. "She's upset." Alex trembled in his arms. "Some people have a low tolerance for alcohol," he said, knowing hers must be incredibly low.

"I don't want the other customers upset. You understand what I mean, buddy?"

"Sure, of course."

The man shrugged. "If you need a place to be private, I can help you out."

Sometime during the talk, Mike had decided to take Alex back, to abandon his idea of forcing a situation where she had no alternative but to stay with him. The call to the rental agency had been a fake. But now he considered the idea of staying with her longer. What if he could get her to open up to him? What if he could help her? "What did you have in mind?" he asked the bald-headed man.

"I got some cottages available, if you want one. Forty bucks a night, with air-conditioning and clean sheets."

Mike hesitated, then nodded. "I'll take your nicest cottage."

"Follow me," the man said and headed back past the men's room.

Carefully, Mike stood and drew Alex to her feet. But she didn't let go of him, and he knew it would be impossible to walk with her against him this way. So he swept her up into his arms, his heart lurching when he realized how light she was. She clung to him, her arms wrapped around his neck, her head pressed into his chest. Vulnerable. It caught at something in him.

Carrying Alex easily, he followed the bald man down a short hall, then out a door and into the heat of the night. They crossed the gravel area and passed three of the cottages; then the man went up the three steps to the door of the next unit. They looked all the same, wood-framed buildings with chalky paint that reflected back the orange glow from the overhead sign. The man unlocked the door, then stood back to let Mike pass.

"That'll be forty dollars up front," he said as he flipped on the lights.

Mike took a cursory glance at the room, wondering how anyone could get away with decorating in "early tacky" and get any customers. Then he realized that this place was

about the only one in the vicinity, and it was probably used
for various reasons besides as a sanctuary for weary travel-
ers.

The multistriped carpeting, the walls with dull-looking
murals of the desert, and a king-size bed covered with a
fuzzy spread, all looked pink. Then he realized that the pink
cast to everything came from the lights and was reflected
back from the mirrored ceiling.

"It's the bridal suite," the man said as Mike crossed to lay
Alex on the bed. He turned, took out his wallet and was a
bit surprised to see that the man was serious. The bridal
suite. He took out two twenties and handed them to the
man.

"Hope she sobers up," the man said and left, closing the
door behind him.

"Mike?"

He turned to find Alex sitting up in the middle of the bed.
The pink glow touched her skin, but where the tone had
cheapened the room, it only enhanced the beauty of the
woman on the bed.

"M . . . Mike, I need to get back. I . . ."

"We'll just stay for a while, until you get on your feet.
Those wine coolers weren't soda pop, Alex."

She tugged her legs up until she was sitting Indian fashion, then smoothed her skirt over her knees. "Am I
drunk?"

"I think that's a pretty good bet," he said as he locked the
door, then crossed to the bed. "We'll just sit and talk until
you feel better. Okay?"

Her head dropped until her chin rested on her chest, and
she muttered something. When Mike asked her what she'd
said, she repeated it, just as incoherently as the first time.

Mike moved closer, getting on the bed in front of her.
Then she looked up at him with those huge brown eyes.
"Mike, I feel strange." She started to sway, and he moved
quickly to grab her and hold her to him.

"So do I," he murmured against her hair. But he knew
exactly why he did. Just holding her, feeling her soft curves

and the heat of her breath against his chest, he began to feel things he didn't want to. Not now.

Alex looked up at him and whispered, "Thanks for being so nice." She stretched to touch her lips to his, and he sat very still. Then she had her arms around his neck, her mouth against his, and he could feel her breasts against his chest. With a low groan, he twisted until they fell back on the bed together.

"You're really nice," she whispered against his mouth. Her tongue touched his, tentatively, tasting of fruit, and Mike felt his whole body leap to life. It had been so long, so very long, since he wanted a woman as much as he wanted Alex. No, he doubted that he'd ever wanted a woman this much.

She moaned softly and twisted until her body was alongside his, each curve fitting neatly into his, and her hands framed his face. "You ... you even taste nice," she said unsteadily.

Mike knew that Alex was a liar, maybe a thief, but she also touched his heart so unerringly that it was almost painful. He placed the tips of his fingers to her lips, then trailed them along the line of her jaw to her ear. "Alex ..." He bent to taste her again, to see if he'd been right, if her taste was really as unique as her personality. "Alex," he groaned, and his tongue invaded her welcoming mouth. He explored and tasted, and he felt his whole world begin to center on the woman in his arms.

Slowly, afraid to move too quickly, he touched her throat, then her shoulder, and gently pushed aside the thin strap of her dress. He felt the locket on its fine chain under his fingers; then he dipped his mouth lower and tasted the silken heat of her throat. He felt the rapid beating of her pulse in the tiny hollow there; then the swell of her breast was under his lips.

With small whimpering sounds, Alex strained toward his touch while her hands tugged at his shirt and finally got under the fabric to the bare skin. Her touch was cool, yet her hands felt as if they could burn him—brand him.

Oh, God, he wanted her. He needed her. Whatever reason told him, it held no validity in this bed. When her hands trailed around to spread across his back, he pushed her dress lower until her breasts were free. They were perfect, as perfect as their owner, and the locket, a heart, lay between them. Then he felt her silken skin under his hand, swelling and pulsing with life.

His lips followed, tasting her, feeling her nipple tighten; then he heard her shuddering moan. He found her mouth again, but his hand stayed over her heart while he kissed her, needing more, demanding more. His tongue loved her taste, his hand her textures, and he was so lost in the glory of what he'd found with her that he didn't realize for a minute that she had become very still.

Moving back to look down into her face, he exhaled, a low, shuddering sound. Alex had either passed out or fallen asleep. Her eyes were closed, her dark lashes lying like delicate fans on her flushed cheeks. Her lips were softly parted, bare of lipstick and slightly swollen from kissing, and her breathing was deep and regular. With real regret, Mike drew her dress back over her breasts and adjusted the straps.

Propped on one elbow looking down at her, he saw the locket again. Hating the unsteadiness in his hands, he almost picked it up, but he realized that would mean he would touch the flushed skin at the cleavage of her breasts. Very carefully, he caught the chain at her throat, then drew the necklace up until the locket was in his hand. *Alexandria, July 4th,* read the delicate script on the back. Her birthday. Her name. He still didn't understand the bitterness.

He let the delicate jewelry fall from his fingers, watching it rest lightly on her silky skin; then he sank back on the bed with a groan. His body ached from the denial of what he could have had with Alex, but when he would have gotten up to take a shower, she turned to him. Still asleep, she snuggled trustingly into his side like a kitten. Her arm went around his waist, and she buried her face in his shoulder. With a satisfied sigh, she settled against him.

Mike closed his eyes tightly for a minute, then put his arms around her and looked up at their images reflected in the overhead mirrors. She looked peaceful, sleeping like a baby. But when he looked at his own reflection, he didn't have to look too carefully to see how very *unpeaceful* he was.

Yet he was beginning to feel a strange sense of relief. He'd been stopped before he could make a mistake, before he could get so involved that there would be no letting go of Alex. He should be thankful that she'd passed out. Things had worked out so that he'd be with her for the night and keep her in sight. But that thought added to his frustration.

With a low oath, he closed his eyes to shut out the sight of just how treacherously his body displayed how much he wanted Alex.

Alex opened her eyes, and the first thing she saw was her own image floating high above her. And she was all pink. She blinked and would have sat up, but her head felt as if a ton of lead was lying on it, and her mouth tasted as if someone had put a wad of cotton in it and left it there for a very long time.

Closing her eyes, she took two deep breaths, then looked above her again. Finally she could see that she was looking into a mirror of some sort.

A mirror? On the ceiling? And she was lying on a horrible, fuzzy pink bedspread. Carefully she looked left, then right, at a room that all but glowed with horrendous pink tones. Awkwardly, she pushed herself up, biting her lip to stop a gasp when her head felt as if it was going to explode, then began to pound in time with her heartbeat.

She heard water running, so she looked toward an open door to the right and saw another mirror, a bathroom mirror. And reflected in it was Mike, no shirt, washing his face.

Mike? Then she remembered, but just snatches, and she sank back down on the bed. The wine coolers, crying, him carrying her. Then kisses, kisses like she'd never experienced before, and feelings that seemed new and explosive. His touch on her, his hand on her breast, his mouth, then...

"Oh, no," she groaned, the rest of what had happened lost in a black void. She stared at the mirrors above her. She was still dressed, but her skirt was up around her thighs, her shoulder straps were both down her arms, and her hair spilled out of the clips on the pink-toned spread. She couldn't remember anything after Mike kissed her breast. Or maybe it had been a dream. The other dream had been so real, but she'd known it had been a dream. This time...

"Alex?"

She turned her head, but didn't get up. Mike stood in the doorway, his chest bare, an intriguing chest with smooth skin, yet overlaid with dark hair that formed the most intriguing T pattern. It crossed at his dark nipples, then ran down. The view stopped at the waistband of his jeans, and Alex literally had to drag her eyes away from the sight.

"What's going on?" she asked, her voice a croak.

"Just waiting for you to wake up. We need to talk about what happened last night."

She wished she knew what that was. "I drank too many coolers." She struggled to her knees on the bed. "This place...what is it?"

"It's the bridal suite, or that's what the bartender called it."

That explanation didn't help Alex at all. It only added to the discomfort in her middle and head. "Why...why are we here?"

"Since you weren't in any condition to move, I took it for the night."

"The night?" Her throat contracted. "All night?"

"All night." He reached for his shirt, which had been lying on the dull brown dresser near the bathroom door. "The car's ready whenever you are," he said as he shrugged into the shirt.

"Mike, I..." She sat up and scooted to the edge of the bed. Without taking her time, she stood, and for a minute she felt as if she would topple backward and her head would fall off. Then she steadied herself by pressing the flats of her hands to her temples and taking a deep breath. She swallowed hard, then looked at Mike. "What did we...?" She licked her lips. "I mean, how long were we...?" She tried again. "What time is it?"

He looked at his watch. "It's nine o'clock."

She closed her eyes. "Morning or night?" she asked, almost not wanting to know.

He leaned back against the doorjamb. "Morning."

"Tomorrow?" she gasped.

"Today," he corrected with a trace of a smile playing around the corners of his mouth.

"Oh, no." Cautiously, she let go of her head, waited, then, as the room settled, tugged at the straps of her dress until they were over her shoulders. Nervously, she tried to smooth her tangled hair. The whole night was lost to her. Her one comfort was the fact that she'd been dressed when she woke up. "I need to get back to Las Vegas," she muttered, being very careful not to look at the tumbled bed as she hurried past Mike and into the bathroom.

"Dudley fixed the car, so I'm ready to go whenever you are," he called after her just before she closed the door.

Alex crossed to the sink in the tiny room, turned on the water and drank a glass as quickly as she could. When she'd finished her second glass of tepid water, she put the glass down and stared at the mirror over the sink.

Mirrors. She hated them. Mirrors over the bed. She swallowed, certain she was going to be sick. Then she remembered Mike touching her, his exploring hand on her breast, and the sickness changed into a heaviness deep in her belly. *Then what happened?* she wanted to ask her reflection, but all her memory held was blackness. If only the blackness had come before she remembered offering herself to Mike. She groaned, cupped the running water in her hands and splashed it on her face.

She'd told Lincoln she'd be back by midnight. *That* she remembered. She grabbed a towel and wiped off her face. Maybe if she called Lincoln? No, she needed to get back, and Mike said the car was working. She just needed to get back, to return things to the right track. Get the job done.

She gave up trying to remember what might have happened between herself and Mike, and finished cleaning up. Leaving her hair loose, she went back into the bedroom. At first she thought there were no windows. Then she saw them, but realized they'd been blocked out by heavy curtains that matched the wall.

Mike was nowhere to be seen, and she hurried past the huge bed without looking at it and crossed to the dresser to grab her purse. Then she went to the door and opened it. For a minute she was blinded by the brilliance and inundated by the scorching heat. Her head settled into a steady pounding. She fumbled in her bag for her sunglasses, then put them on and focused on the Camaro idling not more than five feet away on the gravel. No one was in it.

"Alex?" Mike called, and she turned. He was jogging toward her from the direction of the restaurant, a paper bag in his hand. "Ready?" he asked as he stopped by the cottage steps.

She looked down at him, cringing inside at how fresh and attractive he looked even though he was wearing the same clothes he'd had on yesterday. She felt rumpled and sticky, and her dress hung limply around her bare legs. "I'm ready," she said and went down the steps, past Mike to the car. She got in, thankful it was idling and the air conditioner had already cooled the interior.

When Mike got in, he settled in the seat, then turned and held out his closed hand to her. "Here, you'll need these," he said and dropped two aspirin on her palm. "I thought they might help," he said as he rummaged in the paper bag and took out a covered paper cup. He peeled back the lid and held it out to her. "You had a pretty rough night."

She took the cup and looked down into it. "What's this?" she asked, swallowing hard.

"The best combination in the world for a hangover—tomato juice with a twist of lemon and two aspirin."

"I don't . . ."

"Trust me," Mike said softly.

Anything seemed preferable to the pounding in her head and the knots in her stomach, so she finally put the two pills in her mouth and washed them down with the surprisingly pleasant, tart-tasting tomato juice. She sank back in the seat. "Thank you."

Mike took the cup, crushed it and tossed it into the sack, then put everything into the back seat. "Ready?" he asked, and when she nodded, he put the car in gear and drove out onto the highway in the direction of the city.

Alex kept her eyes closed and her head back against the headrest for most of the drive. Then she opened her eyes just a bit and saw the new construction on the outskirts of Las Vegas. She swallowed hard. With her headache beginning to ease, she knew she had to find out exactly what had happened between them last night. The direct approach seemed the best and least complicated. "Mike, last night I—"

"You're awake. I thought you'd sleep until we got to the hotel."

"No, I'm not sleeping. I've been thinking about last night, and I—"

"Don't worry. You don't need to apologize. Some people have a problem holding liquor. They have a low tolerance for alcohol. Look at it this way, you found out wine coolers aren't soda pop."

Was there something she needed to apologize for? She pressed a hand to her stomach. "I hope I wasn't too...too obnoxious."

"Obnoxious?" He chuckled softly, a sound that made Alex's heart sink. "Far from it."

"I didn't...bore you all night with stories, did I?"

"No, you weren't boring at all." He reached over and let his hand rest on hers. "Not at all."

With each word he uttered, her heart sank further. Surely she would remember if she and Mike had made love. She wasn't that experienced, but making love with someone wasn't something she would forget. She was overwhelmingly aware of his hand still on hers. If he'd touched her, and held her, and loved her, there would be something there, there would have to be.

"Alex?"

"Yes?" she asked in a small voice.

"You passed out."

She sat up straighter and turned to look at him squarely. "I what?"

"You passed out."

He hadn't kissed her and touched her? It had been a dream? Nothing but a dream? "Nothing happened?" she asked, her voice tight and strange in her own ears.

He squeezed her hand slightly, then drew back and gripped the steering wheel tightly. "Nothing," he echoed, looking straight ahead.

"I knew that," she lied. "I just didn't want to feel as if I'd embarrassed you."

"You didn't. Not at all," he said.

A part of her collapsed inside. A dream. She'd ached because of it, tasted a frustration that still lingered deep inside her, yet she'd never experienced his caress, his touch, exploring, demanding.... No, she hadn't. She felt strange and foolish, and more than a bit disappointed. But she didn't try to figure out her feelings. Instead she let an unreasonable anger surface. She moved closer to the door. It was so much simpler being mad at Mike. "I told you I had business, that I had to get back to Las Vegas."

"I didn't force you to drink those coolers."

His simple logic infuriated her. "I know, but I just hope this . . . this didn't cost me the job."

"Could you lose it that easily?" he asked, his voice tighter now.

"No, I guess not." She turned to the side window and saw they were on the Strip now. "But this really fouls up my plans."

"Mine, too," he muttered, then sank into his own silence.

The Elysian looked just the same as they drove up to it. It seemed that only Alex was different. She felt off center, out of control, and caught between anger and frustration.

Silently, she went inside with Mike, through the lobby and to the elevators. The doors for the closest car were open, and it was half-full when they stepped inside. There were several stops before her floor, letting people off, and by the time the car stopped at the tenth floor, Alex and Mike were alone.

The doors slid back, and she looked up, anxious to get away from him, yet she didn't make a move to get out. She stared through the open doors and straight down the hall. Lincoln, all dressed in black, was coming out of her room.

Chapter 9

Alex saw him pull the door to her room shut and swipe at his face with his hanky; then, as he looked up, she stepped quickly into the corner of the car and out of sight.

"I just remembered I don't have my key," she said, not about to let Lincoln see her with Mike. The last thing she wanted was to have to explain one to the other. Her job was precarious enough right now. "I'll have to go back downstairs and get one from the desk clerk." As the doors slid shut, she leaned back against the coolness of the mirrored wall.

Mike looked at her hard, then pushed the button for the twenty-seventh floor. "You can call down from my suite. They'll send someone up."

That wasn't what she wanted at all. "No, I . . ."

But the car had already started up, and she couldn't take the chance of going right back down in the same car. She didn't want to have the doors open on the tenth floor and find herself facing Lincoln. So she kept silent and waited.

When the car stopped, Mike got out and turned to Alex. "Coming?"

"Yes," she murmured and followed him to the other elevator. As he inserted his brass passkey, she looked at the doors and faced their dual images in the mirrors. She was a splash of yellow with a riot of dark hair loose around her face. Her hands twisted the strap of her purse over her shoulder, and she didn't have to look too closely to see the tension in her eyes and mouth. Conversely, Mike seemed cool, almost neutral, yet strikingly good-looking, with his hair brushed back from his tanned face. He put the key in his shirt pocket; then his green eyes suddenly met hers in the mirror.

Alex felt her breath catch as a jolt of awareness coursed through her. She looked away quickly to hide her reaction, thankful that the doors opened right then. She stepped into the empty car and avoided looking at the mirrors all around. Just the idea of all those reflections made her stomach churn. She'd never thought she would react to mirrors this way, and she closed her eyes while the car moved up.

When it stopped, she felt Mike touch her arm, and she jerked back. Quickly, she got out and headed down the hall toward his suite.

Mike reached past her at the door and unlocked the room, then motioned her inside. The curtains had been pulled open, and the fragrance of brewing coffee filled the air. "Part of the service," Mike said. "Coffee and rolls. Do you want some?"

Alex stood by the door, not wanting to go any farther into the luxury suite. "Just coffee, thanks."

"You call the desk while I get us both some coffee. I think we need it."

I know I do, Alex thought as she watched him go to the right and disappear around the corner. She waited for a minute, took several settling breaths, then ignored the phone. She had to follow through on the lie of not having a key with her, yet this lie might not be a total waste. She could at least see what the suite looked like, especially if it was identical to the one on the thirtieth floor.

She would give Lincoln time to get out of the way before she told Mike she was going to meet a security man with a key at her room. Ten minutes would be plenty of time. She studied the space in front of her, making herself concentrate on its layout. The design of the suite seemed simple enough. Three levels. One for conversation, one for eating and entertaining, and one for sleeping, up some stairs and out of sight to the left. But where would they hide a security box?

"Alex?"

She turned at the sound of her name and found Mike holding out a mug to her. "Oh, thanks," she said and reached for it. When her fingers brushed his, she stiffened, then took the mug and looked down into the dark liquid. "Sorry."

"Cream or sugar?"

"No, black's fine," she said and took a tentative sip.

"What did the desk say?"

She looked back at Mike. "They'll send someone up in ten minutes to unlock the room for me."

"How's the head?"

She shrugged, her fingers tightening on the mug. "It's still there. But the aspirins helped. Thanks for getting them for me."

"The bartender was very helpful," he said, a smile touching the corners of his mouth.

Alex looked away from Mike before the smile grew. "Where is the . . . the rest room?"

"Up the stairs. On the right and through the bedroom."

Without looking back at Mike, Alex crossed to the stairs and went up into the hallway, glad to be alone for a minute. Along with the vague pounding still going on in her temples, her nerves were raw, and she was having trouble concentrating on the layout. Mike's presence was playing havoc with her, and she was forgetting to look for the most elemental things, such as lock types and light positions.

Enough of that. She had to take advantage of this opportunity and look around as much as she could. She took a deep breath, then opened the door to her right and stepped into the bedroom. Straight across the huge, white-carpeted room was a wall of glass that overlooked the Strip. Gold and white seemed to be everywhere, from the gold curtains that framed the windows to the white enameled furniture, from a bank of golden throw pillows leaning against the gold headboard of the huge bed to her left to the white velvet bedspread and gold leafing at the corners of the high ceiling. A heavy mirror with a gold frame hung over the bed.

As she studied the silent room, she decided that in its way it was tasteful in a way the hotel itself wasn't. Slowly, Alex walked around, her feet pressing into the thick carpet as she looked for places that could hide a safe. The huge dresser. The nightstands. A shelf on the far wall with silk plants and a brass clock. She turned and looked at two huge pictures hung on either side of the bed, matching paintings of massive white stallions running across the desert. Symbolism? she wondered with a touch of welcome humor as she glanced back to the bed.

Then she thought of Mike in this bed, then of Mike in the bed with her at the motel, and the smile fled. Her breathing sped up, and she quickly took a sip of the hot coffee she'd all but forgotten she was holding. As its heat spread through her, she crossed to the bathroom, a large room that echoed the color of the bedroom—all white, from the carpeted floor to the tiled walls to the ceiling. A sunken tub sat in front of the frosted window, and golden fixtures shaped like swans' heads curved gracefully over it.

She looked in the bank of drawers in the marble vanity, then stepped into the walk-in closet that went through to the bedroom on the opposite wall. It only held a few shirts and pairs of pants on hangers. Brown moccasins were on the floor. No drawers in here, not even any containers. The floor was carpeted. She walked through the closet into the bedroom, still cradling the mug between her hands.

A safe place? A secure place? She looked at the pictures again and crossed to them. Carefully, she eased the heavy print nearest the door away from the wall. No safe there, just blank white wall.

"Lose something?"

The painting hit the wall with a thud, and Alex looked to her left to see Mike standing in the doorway. "No, just admiring the paintings," she said quickly.

"Those?" he asked, raising one dark eyebrow.

"You have to admit that they fit the atmosphere," she said as she adjusted the frame until it sat absolutely level.

"They certainly do that," he said softly.

She looked back to Mike, and when he smiled at her, she knew it was time to go. Every time she looked at him, she thought about pink-toned rooms and dreams of gentle hands and exploratory kisses. About dreams and not about her job. "I think I'll head down to my room. The security man should be there with the key by now."

She put her mug down on the nightstand, then smoothed her dress over her hips. "Thanks for the coffee." Then she thought of one other thing she needed to know. "Is there only one bedroom in this suite?"

He laughed, a low, rough sound, and his smile deepened. "How many can I use?"

She felt heat stain her face, and she forced a smile, the same way she had to force herself to look right at him. Any smart reply she could have thought up died, killed by the intensity in the depths of his eyes.

"I don't know." she murmured.

"I don't know, either," he said softly. "But there is another bedroom. A small one." He motioned behind him at the hallway. "Want to see it?"

"No," she muttered and left the room, making a wide circle as she went past him and out the door.

Mike watched Alex hurrying away from him, and he knew he needed to be alone as much as she seemed to need to get on with her business. That brought a knot to his stomach. Business. Yet he knew that no matter how much he stayed with her, he couldn't stop her from doing what she seemed bent on doing.

That brought him up short. That was what he'd been trying to do. Oh, he'd gone about it under the guise of "staying with her" for Stanley, but he'd really been trying to save her from herself. *Protector of the world.*

He followed her down the stairs to the door and watched her as she reached for the knob. She looked back at him, her dark eyes partially veiled by improbably long lashes, and then she was gone without a word. Mike stood very still until the door clicked shut behind her; then he crossed and sank down in the nearest chair.

He ran a hand over his face. Save her from herself? Make her see the light? He wasn't equipped to do either. The ringing of the phone broke into his thoughts, and he reached for the receiver.

"Yes?"

"Mike? Dan."

He sat up and leaned forward, his elbows resting on his knees. "What did you find out?"

"You aren't going to like this, but there is no Jack Stanley."

"Come on, Dan. I'm not in any mood—"

"No joke. I checked out the post-office box in New York. It's rented to Jack Stanley, but they can't seem to find an address or a telephone number. They slip a bill in the box once a year, and they find an envelope with a cashier's check in there to pay the rent."

"The Paris number?"

"I called it and got a man, and he hung up on me when I asked about Stanley. When I finally found a way to get through to the Paris phone company, they said that number is a private residence and they don't give out addresses or names. They'd only tell me it was in central Paris. If I want to know any more, I have to go to Paris and fill out forms and show identification and pay money for the service. I don't suppose we're going to pay for a trip to Paris?"

"You suppose right, Dan. When you called the number, what did the man who answered sound like?"

"American, a deep voice, well educated."

"No accent at all?"

"None."

That sounded like the man Mike had had contact with before.

"What now?" Dan asked.

"I don't know." Mike sighed. "I don't know. Just hold on, and I'll get back to you as soon as I can figure out my next step."

Stanhope looked down at Ian sleeping in the bed. Did his friend look paler today, or was it just his imagination? He didn't know. He turned away and crossed to the window. He hated waiting. He always had.

"Excuse me, Monsieur Stanhope?"

He turned to see a nurse looking around the door, a pretty dark-haired woman who had been very helpful since Ian had been brought in. "Yes."

"A phone call for you. Do you wish to take it in here, or where you have answered the others?"

He crossed the room and stepped out into the hall with her. "In the office."

He followed her down the green-tiled corridor and into a tiny office near the pay telephones. She pointed to a phone with a blinking red light on it that sat on a small metal desk by a single window. "There it is. Press '1.'"

He nodded, then waited until she was gone and the door shut before he picked it up and pressed the button. "Yes?"

"You got a call here."

"Conti?"

"No, but I think it was someone calling for him."

"What are you talking about?"

"I got a call from this guy asking for you. He said that he was with some insurance company and they needed to contact you about some premiums. I got him off the phone, then called our contact at the phone company and had the call traced. It came from Santa Barbara, California, from Conti's office number. Why would Michael Conti be trying to figure out who you are?"

Stanhope sank down in the chair behind the desk. "That's it? He didn't try to call again?"

"No. Is there something I should know about this?"

"I'll get back to you," he said and put down the receiver.

He sat for several minutes, then picked up the phone again. Using the telephone credit card he had in the name of Jack Stanley, he put in a call to Michael Conti's number in Las Vegas.

After Mike showered and changed into fresh Levi's and a short-sleeved white cotton shirt, he slipped on his running shoes and left his suite. He'd only taken two steps toward the elevator when he heard his phone ringing. He turned and hurried back, got his key out of his pocket and let himself into the suite. But when he picked up the receiver, all he heard was a click, then the dial tone. He dropped the receiver back in place and waited, staring down at the phone.

When it didn't ring again, he finally left his suite and took the elevator to the twenty-seventh floor, where he switched, then rode down to the tenth floor. When he stepped into the hallway, he made sure Alex wasn't in sight, then walked toward her room.

At her door, he stopped and, since he was alone in the corridor, leaned toward the door to listen. He could hear someone talking behind the barrier, but the words were muffled. The only thing he knew for sure was that the person speaking was a man.

"I'm glad you finally got back here and called me, little lady," Lincoln said, his back to the door. "I was just about ready to write this whole thing off."

"I told you on the phone that I was looking over other hotels and casinos to see if I could offer my services to them." Alex didn't offer Lincoln a seat, so they stood facing each other, and she had the most uncomfortable feeling that they were squaring off for battle.

"That took you all night?" he asked, eyeing the white terry robe she'd put on after she'd stripped off her dress.

"No, I've been in and out," she lied easily, resisting the urge to tug the lapels of her robe more tightly closed.

"I was here at midnight, but you weren't here." He pointed to a chair by the bed. "I sat there for two hours before I left. Then I was back here about ten this morning, and you still weren't here."

She thought of offering the lie that she'd probably just missed him both times, but the bed was still turned down perfectly from the night before. "You know how it is in Las Vegas. Night and day get all mixed up."

"Sure do," Lincoln muttered.

"What did you want?"

"I needed to make sure you knew not to try and get into the suite until after ten tonight. From then on, it's open to you." He smiled at his choice of words. "So to speak."

"All right."

"Listen, little lady, I'm not trying to ride you or anything, but this job is important to me. It's my career on the line, you know. I just want to make sure that I'm not going to end up with my butt in a sling."

"It's important to me, too." Maybe mine will be in a sling, but not yours, she thought. "I'll do my very best."

"Good enough. What are you going to do now?"

"Get to work. I've got a lot of figuring to do before I try to get into that suite."

"Can I ask you how you're planning on doing that?" he asked.

"No, not until it's done. Then I'll tell you everything. You'll either be very pleased that I couldn't get in, or you'll be happy to know how to keep someone else from getting in in the future. You'll be completely satisfied, I can guarantee you that." She wished he would leave so she could take a long, hot bath, then get on with things. "Now, if there's nothing else..."

A sharp knocking on the door stopped her words. She saw Lincoln tense and cast her a sharply questioning look. She stood where she was and called out, "Yes?"

"It's me. Mike."

Lincoln frowned at her and mouthed the name. "Mike?"

She shrugged. "The man I told you was annoying me," she whispered. "He's staying here at the hotel."

"Great. Get rid of him."

She nodded, and as Lincoln moved to his left to one side of the door, she walked over and reached for the knob. She opened the door a crack and found herself bracing as she looked out at Mike in the hall. "What do you want?" she asked.

He'd changed clothes, and the moisture from a recent shower still showed at the damp ends of his hair clinging at his neck. "I was on my way down to get something to eat and stopped by to see how you're feeling."

Very aware of Lincoln standing just out of sight behind the door, she weighed her words before she said them. "I'll feel better after I get cleaned up. I was just about to step into the shower."

He glanced into the room, then back to her. "How about lunch? I bet you could use something solid in your stomach."

"No, I don't think so. I'll order room service later. I've got work to do."

"Dinner?" he persisted.

"Sorry. I'm busy," she said and started to close the door. "Thanks for coming by." She had a final glimpse of his dark frown before she shut the door firmly, and she just prayed that his stubbornness wouldn't make him knock again. Leaning back against the closed door for support, she turned to Lincoln. "I'm sorry about the interruption."

The man studied Alex, then wiped at his face with a white handkerchief. "Real smooth, little lady. You can take care of yourself, I see."

She wasn't about to thank him for the compliment, so she got the subject away from Mike and back to business. "Was there anything else you needed to tell me?"

"No. You won't be seeing me again until this is done."

Good, Alex thought, but simply asked, "Where do we meet so I can hand you the box?"

"How long will it take you to get in there and get out with it?"

"If I can't go in until after ten, I should be done by midnight."

He lifted one brow. "All right. Meet me outside the door at the very bottom level of the stairwell. I'll be by the Dumpster in the staff parking lot. The door's always kept unlocked. Fire regulations."

When she nodded, he unexpectedly reached out and flicked her chin with clammy fingers. "Take care, little lady, and let's see how you earn that money." He motioned to the door. "My staff thinks I'm on my lunch break. I wouldn't want them to think I'm spending the time with a beautiful guest in her room. Fraternizing with the clients is definitely against hotel policy. Do me a favor and take a look out there and make sure no one's around."

Alex wasn't certain she wouldn't be facing Mike when she opened the door, but when she looked out, no one was in sight. "It's clear," she said as she stood back for Lincoln to leave.

Mike waited in a small alcove halfway between Alex's room and the elevators, where the ice and soda machines were kept. He leaned against the wall, and when he heard a door open, he peeked around the corner. He barely ducked back out of sight in time to avoid Alex when she looked out of her room into the hall. Then he heard muffled voices and footsteps.

Mike chanced another look and saw a man heading off in the opposite direction—the heavyset man he'd seen yesterday. The man went to the stairwell door again, about fifteen feet from Alex's room, and disappeared through it. The door swung shut behind him with a solid thump.

Mike stood very still as an answer to one of his questions about Alex clicked into place. Was she doing her "business" alone? No, she had a partner.

His first instinct was to follow the fat man, but that idea died quickly. Alex was the one he didn't want to lose sight of, the one he didn't want to disappear. So he drew back into the alcove, his whole being tightening in the most unpleasant way. Slowly he sank down on a bench opposite the machines. A partner. And he instinctively knew something else. Something was going to happen, and happen soon; something he wished he had the power to stop.

He ran his hands roughly over his face and sat forward, then buried his face in his hands, his elbows on his knees. You wanted answers, Conti, he told himself. Be man enough to take them when they come along. They just shouldn't hurt this much.

And they only hurt because of the past twenty-four hours, the time he'd spent with Alex. He tried to push the memories of the night just past out of his mind. He didn't want to relive those long hours when Alex had slept by his side and he'd stared at the mirrors above them. He'd watched her reflection, the gentle expression, her body lifting ever so slightly with each breath, the way her hand had lain trustingly on his chest, and the dress riding up on her thigh as she settled with her leg draped over his. And he'd heard the soft sounds of sleep, the sighs, the murmurs.

He stood abruptly and began to pace the tiny space. Memories could tie him in knots, but answers should set him free. And he *did* want answers. Until they came, all he had to do was make sure Alex didn't leave her room without him seeing her go.

Alex called down to the desk for something to eat, hoping that would take care of her unsettled stomach. While she munched on a ham sandwich and chips, she studied the colored brochure about the Elysian that she'd found in the dresser. As she washed the sandwich down with coolly soothing milk, she spotted what she was looking for, a section of the brochure with the heading "Courtesies for Guests."

At no extra expense to our guests, valuables may be kept in the hotel safe. In addition, some of the rooms in the towers are equipped with security boxes. The Elysian has the best interests of the guest in mind and takes extra effort to make their stay secure and dependable.

Security boxes? But where? She felt certain she could get up to the room and get past the locks, but finding the security box wouldn't be so easy.

She thought about Mike's suite and closed her eyes, making it easier to reconstruct the layout in her mind. After several minutes she knew that wasn't good enough.

Getting up, she searched through the drawers of the table by the bed and found a pad of hotel paper and a pen. She sat at the table by the windows and carefully sketched the layout of the suite as she remembered it. Logic told her that the box wouldn't be too well hidden. The safest spots weren't always the hardest to find. They were places that you could look at and think nothing of, then go looking someplace else.

Alex stared at the layout of the rooms, every so often sketching in another detail as she remembered it. The company that had installed the system was an older, well-established security-systems outfit, and she knew their general policies. One thing she knew for certain was that they always gave recommendations for the types, positions and locations of any safes. They favored the old standbys: setting a safe in the wall behind a picture, or behind a set of false books on shelves. But she hadn't seen any books in the suite, and there hadn't been anything behind the one print. Maybe behind the other one, but she doubted it. They fit too snugly against the wall.

If only she'd had time to look more carefully. She sat back and stared out the window, past the array of buildings to the desert in the distance, then the hills rising from the desert floor. Actually, she was surprised that she remembered so much about the suite. At the time it had seemed that Mike had been a terrible distraction.

She looked at the clock by the bed. One o'clock. Nine hours for her to figure out what she was going to do.

Mike stayed in the alcove, never leaving, drinking Cokes and munching on stale potato chips from the vending machines. At least Alex had better food, he thought, remembering the delivery that had been taken to her room.

Mike sat on the bench, rested his head back against the wall and closed his eyes. It had been a long, hard night. While Alex had slept like a baby, he'd been restless and awake most of the time. With her that close, he hadn't been able to relax at all. And he felt exhausted now.

He would just close his eyes for a minute, regroup and let his body rest. He would be sure to hear her door open if she went anywhere.

He was snatched out of a sleep so deep that it was like being lost in a black hole. He sat very still, blinking, trying to figure out what had awakened him so abruptly; then he knew. Screaming.

"Drop dead!"

The shrill voice tore across his nerves, and he scrambled to his feet and looked out into the hall. Two children were down by the elevators, taking turns yelling at each other.

"I won't do what you say, smarty pants!" a red-haired boy yelled. "You're a jerk. A real jerk!"

A blond girl about ten years old, wearing a bright pink sunsuit, faced him down, her hands on her hips. "You will so, Daniel John Warren! I'm in charge, and I'll tell you exactly what to do!"

"Oh, dry up, Susan, you're being a jerk. A jerk. A jerk. A jerk," the boy chanted, and he didn't stop even when they got on the elevator. Finally the doors slid shut and peace returned to the hallway.

Mike ran a hand over his face and took a deep breath, then glanced down at his watch. Five o'clock! The last thing he knew, it had been just about one o'clock. Damn! Thank God he'd been in the corner and not easily seen from the hallway. At least, he hoped he hadn't been easy to spot while he slept. Quickly, he looked up and down the hall, and he killed an urge to go to the right. He picked up the phone and asked for Alex's room number, and his heart plunged when the phone rang six times without being answered.

Chapter 10

Alex had fallen asleep at the table, her head resting on her crossed arms, and when the telephone rang, she had a terrible time waking up. By the time she'd roused enough to get up and go to the phone, it had stopped ringing. With a sigh, she'd stretched out on the bed and gone back to sleep.

She finally stirred around six o'clock. While she showered, she decided where to get some of the answers she needed. A half hour later, she'd found the kitchens in the basement of the Elysian and been taken on a guided tour of the facilities from a tiny, gray-haired woman wearing a bright orange work tunic, Marlis Woolery, the head supervisor for food preparation.

When they finally got back to the main entrance, Alex paused by the swinging metal doors that led out into the passageway. She'd worn a pink-and-blue spatter-print T-shirt and white walking shorts, pulled her hair up into a high ponytail and been accepted as a tourist by Mrs. Woolery— a tourist who happened to own a hotel and wanted to look at the Elysian's food preparation. "It's amazing," she'd said as she surveyed the milling workers preparing, cooking and serving the food. "And this goes on all day and all night?"

Mrs. Woolery nodded. "It never stops." She looked at Alex. "Where did you say you come from, Miss Schuster?"

"Oh, near San Diego, east, in the mountains. Our hotel is very small." She motioned to the scene in front of her. "While I was here, I just couldn't resist asking to see how you manage all these guests. It's staggering. I don't know how you do it."

"Schedules. Make them and keep them," the lady said. "The head chef was brought all the way from Paris two years ago, and he makes up the menus. Then I make sure there's enough of everything to make his dishes and enough people to do the work. It's not easy, but it's never dull."

Alex shook her head, genuinely in awe of this lady who seemed to control the heart of the hotel. "My kitchen at our hotel would fit in your pantry," she said, remembering the hotel's three pantries, all twenty-by-twenty-foot rooms. "I could never do this."

"Few can," the lady said. "Now, can I answer any questions you might have?"

Just what I wanted you to ask. "I don't know where to start."

"If you have time tomorrow or the next day, I could show you the other kitchens."

"There's more than one kitchen?"

"Two more, so there's hot food, lots of it, and good wine any place in the hotel. A winning combination."

She couldn't wait another day or two to find out about the other kitchens' schedules. "What area does this kitchen serve?" she asked.

"The casino restaurant, and the main restaurant and bar. All of the prep—cutting up vegetables, making sauces and pastries—is done here, too. The other two kitchens serve the main part of the hotel and the Towers."

"Each area gets its own food?"

The lady nodded. "That's right. The Towers get pretty fancy stuff. They want good food with very few calories. The richer some get, the thinner they want to be. Chicken and fish go big up there, and fresh fruit, and they order at all hours."

She knew the right question to ask now. "Where does the help eat?"

"They have vouchers for food up to a certain amount, but they can't eat in any facility that services our guests. So there are rooms in each kitchen where they can go and eat. Mostly the ones who eat in the hotel are on tight schedules."

This is it, she thought in triumph. "Schedules?"

"Like some of the dealers or the security people."

"The guards?"

"Yeah, they go into the kitchen in their own areas. They only get fifteen-minute breaks during their shifts instead of a full hour off for lunch or dinner."

"That's pretty tight, isn't it?"

"Sure is. Just fifteen minutes here, fifteen minutes there. Especially in the Towers. They've got three men up there and shift them around all the time."

"It must get confusing," Alex said as she fingered the leather strap of her purse.

"Oh, it's simple. There's only three of them, but it's not really such a big area to cover, you know. One walks all over, while one sits on the top floor and reads or whatever, and one sits on the lowest floor. Then the first one sits, and the next one walks. Then, at fifteen minutes to the hour, every hour, one gets a break and the others walk. When I'm up there, those guards come into the kitchen fifteen minutes to the hour like clockwork."

"Where is the kitchen up there?"

"It's on the twenty-eighth floor, and there's a nice service elevator that goes up to it from here."

"This has been absolutely unbelievable," Alex said. "And I want to thank you for being so kind." She held out her hand and shook the other woman's hand. "I need to get back to change for this evening. But I couldn't miss looking in here. Thanks for showing me around."

Mrs. Woolery smiled and pushed her hands in the pockets of her bright tunic. "Anytime, my dear. We're very proud of our facilities at the Elysian."

"You have every right to feel proud," Alex said and left.

Out in the hall, she looked down the corridor toward the casino area, then thought better of it and headed toward the service doors at the back of the building. She pushed back the warm metal doors and stepped out into the unrelenting heat. Even though twilight was washing the city in brilliant colors, the heat was as oppressive as ever.

She considered going right back inside, then decided against it. She stood on a steep ramp that ran down into a huge parking lot filled with the workers' cars. A piece of moon, not yet at its full brilliance, hung low in the eastern sky where there wasn't a trace of a cloud. No liar's moon tonight, she thought, then looked away from the skies to the sea of cars in front of her.

Finally she knew what she was going to do, how she'd get past the guards with the least amount of risk. A schedule was a stupid thing to have when it involved security. You should always keep the unexpected a possibility. The locks wouldn't be a problem for her. And once she was in the suite, she knew she could find the hiding place. She would have ten minutes to look around, or else she would have to wait for the next guard's break. If there was a safe there, she would find it.

She looked to her left, then spotted what she'd hoped to see. Dumpsters. A whole row of them about a hundred feet farther down, by another ramp that led up to a set of black metal doors. She walked down to the parking lot level, then turned and looked at the far doors. She could see writing on them in huge block letters: Emergency Exit. In smaller letters, Keep clear. Fire regulations.

The final piece of the puzzle fell into place. Now she knew where she was going to meet Lincoln. She checked her watch. Eight o'clock. She'd meet the man in about four hours and be done with this job.

All day, while she'd been trying to get this plan set, she'd had to deliberately try not to let thoughts of Mike intrude. They were disruptive and distracting. And she couldn't afford that yet. Yet? That qualifier stopped her dead.

Suddenly a thought slipped into her consciousness. As soon as this job was done, she really wanted to look Mike up and talk to him. Maybe she couldn't explain the details of this job. Maybe she couldn't bare her soul and tell him everything, but she would be free to tell him what she did for a living, that she hadn't been stealing at Aria's. That she worked honestly and worked hard. And just maybe he'd want to spend some time with her.

That idea was very appealing.

Mike finally went back to his room and, without turning on any lights, threw himself down in the chair nearest the balcony. "Damn, damn, damn," he muttered into the shadows. He'd been all over the Elysian, and he hadn't found Alex anywhere. And he hadn't spotted the fat man, either.

Three solid hours of walking and asking questions. He'd been right when he'd told Stanley he wasn't a real P.I. Hell, he wasn't even close.

He ran a hand over his face and let out a hissing breath. It made him feel strange to recognize the fact that the only reality he'd experienced in the past twenty-four hours had been Alex, being with her, talking to her, touching her.

His low groan echoed in the stillness of the darkened room. Touching her. That brought back sensations that hit him in the pit of the stomach. Skin so soft he could hardly believe it, her smell, her taste, her low moans. Oh, God. He stood abruptly.

He shouldn't even like the woman, yet he came precariously close to caring for her in a way he'd never thought he would care for another human being. Caring? An inadequate word at best to describe what he felt when he just thought of her. A liar, a thief—a woman who could endear herself to him with the smallest expression.

The telephone rang sharply, and Mike hurried across to answer it. Anything to get Alex out of his mind.

"Yes?"

"What are you up to, Mike?"

He recognized Stanley's voice, and the harsh directness in it made him stiffen. "Stanley?"

He didn't answer that. "Why are you trying to find out about me, Mike?"

So Dan had raised a little dust with his inquiries. "What are you talking about?" Mike hedged.

"No games, Mike. I can't handle them now. Just give me a straight answer. What difference does it make who Jack Stanley is?"

"It doesn't matter to me a bit," Mike said evenly. "What matters is who Alex is. You're after her. The fact that she's probably a crook matters to you."

"What happened to professional confidentiality?" Stanley demanded.

"Nothing I find out is going any farther than me, believe me, but I'm at a point where I need to know, Stanley, and I need to know now."

"But *I* don't know. I really don't."

"You don't know *what*?" Mike all but yelled into the phone, the frustrations of the past three hours making his nerves raw. "Give me a break! You wanted her found. I found her. Damn it, Stanley, who is she?"

The open line buzzed in his ears; then Stanley said in a flat voice, "The daughter of a business partner, a friend of mine. He ... my friend may be dying, and I wanted the girl found for his sake."

Mike sank down in the chair by the phone; nothing had prepared him for this revelation. "What?"

"If she's what you think she is, she isn't any good to him."

"She's got a father?"

"At least for the next few days."

"But she was in that damned orphanage! She's an orphan."

"She was taken care of wonderfully, provided for and educated," Stanley countered a bit tightly. "My own sister was a nun there, and she took good care of the girl, very good care of her."

"Elizabeth?" Mike asked softly.

"How did you know?"

Mike didn't bother answering that question. "All this time, Alex has had someone, hasn't she?"

"Yes."

The ache in him came from nowhere and became all-encompassing. He remembered Alex's pain last night, the revelations she'd allowed to slip out past her barriers. And all the time she had a father. "What kind of father...?"

"A father who never knew she existed. That was my choice a long time ago. And now it's my choice that he'll never know if she's trash. He needs the will to live, something to make life important to him again, not a daughter who's a liar and a thief."

Mike closed his eyes and exhaled harshly. "Maybe that choice should be up to him...and Alex."

"No." The single word sliced over the line. "Keep your mouth closed to the girl. *I'm* your client. *I* make the rules."

"It seems you've been making the rules for a long time," Mike bit out, his sarcasm deep and cutting.

"That's none of your damned business. What counts is what *I* want, what *I* feel is best. The girl isn't to know a thing about my friend until I hear from the investigator I've got working on her background. And then only if she's exonerated. Only then," he repeated intensely.

The pain Mike felt for Alex was excruciating, and when he was finally able to speak, his voice sounded tight and unnatural. "Who do you have on it?"

Stanley said a name that Mike recognized, a good investigator from Los Angeles with a good reputation. "He'll get you the facts, all right."

"Until then, just don't let her get out of your sight. If she's what my friend needs, everything will work out. If she's not, she'll never have to know anything. And you can just walk away and forget you ever heard of her."

"Sure," Mike said, not about to tell Stanley that he had no idea where she was right now. Or that he doubted he could ever walk away from her. One thing he knew for certain—he could never forget Alex.

Alex stepped into the main casino of the Elysian at nine o'clock, pausing at the huge, arched entry to scan the room. Filled with gamblers, it was alive with the sounds of conversations, music, machine noises and the clinking of glass on glass. Not more than a square foot here or there was empty, and a perpetual haze of cigarette smoke rose and haloed the huge gold lanterns suspended from the muraled ceiling.

The cacophony of sounds set Alex's nerves on edge, but at the same time she welcomed it. It made her acutely aware of everything. And she needed that awareness tonight. She would spend a half hour down here, then go up to her room, change and get the things she needed to do the job.

"Alex?"

She spun around at the sound of her name and found herself with not more than two feet of deep red carpet between herself and Mike. Black and white—black, leanly cut slacks and a white shirt with the sleeves rolled up to expose the strength of his forearms. And his eyes... Even across the open space between them in the noisy, smoke-filled room, the look in those green depths stunned her.

There was surprise, and maybe relief. Relief?

"You," she whispered as she tried to coax air into her lungs.

"There you go again," he said with a smile that was her final undoing. "I was just going to dinner. Won't you join me?"

She wondered if she could move, let alone eat. She could barely absorb the stunning awareness she felt for this man.

How long had she known him? Twenty-four hours, maybe a bit longer, yet she felt as if she had known him for more than a lifetime.

"I...I...wasn't..." she began, but stopped when she realized she was stammering. Pull yourself together, she ordered herself. You aren't some teenager at a prom. So why did she feel that way? Tongue-tied, overwhelmed, excited. Then she remembered her reasons for being here—and they didn't include being taken over by Mike.

"Alex." He moved closer, so close that she could see flecks of brown in the green depths of his eyes. "Dinner. Let's have a bite to eat. I promised I'd leave you alone so you could do business, and I haven't seen you for hours. But everyone needs to eat, and I suspect you're hungry, so why not have something with me, then I'll fade off into the night?"

She didn't want him to fade off into the night, not at all. But she supposed that he'd better—just until the job was over. "Could we get together later?"

He studied her from under lowered lashes. "How much later?"

"After midnight. I've got things I need to do."

"Business?"

"Yes, business. Then, when it's done, I'd like to have dinner with you."

Unexpectedly, Mike leaned toward Alex and kissed her, a fleeting caress on her lips; then he stood back. "Can I talk you out of doing business tonight?"

She didn't understand the intensity in his eyes, or the hint of what might have been sorrow. It didn't make sense. "I'm anxious to get this job over and done. Then I'll be here for a few days, and we can..."

"We can what?" he asked tightly.

She didn't understand. "Get to know each other."

"After your business is through?"

"Yes, after it's done."

He took her by the arm and pulled her with him toward the entry. "We need to talk," he muttered, taking her to a corner by the metal cages that contained the cashiers' stations. With her back against the curtain-covered wall, Alex looked at Mike, who had pinned her there without touching her. He pressed his hands flat on the wall on either side of her shoulders, and, with just inches between his body and hers, he stared down at her.

"What do you want to talk about?" she asked unsteadily.

But he didn't answer her. Instead he leaned forward and kissed her again. Not a fleeting or insubstantial contact this time.

His mouth slanted over hers, his lips claiming hers as his tongue found entrance to her mouth. If a person could be ravished with a single kiss, Alex knew that was exactly what Mike was doing to her. Completely and irrevocably, he was claiming her, drawing her to him, demanding, teasing her until she reluctantly put her arms around his neck and pressed against him.

Yet the moment she responded, he moved back, abruptly breaking the contact. His eyes were blazing with the same feelings she was experiencing, and he breathed hoarsely. "Come with me. Now. And we can finish what we began in that terrible motel."

It hadn't been a dream. It had been real. As real as the fact that every part of her wanted to be with him. Yet she stayed against the wall, just staring at Mike. So little time since they'd met in Aria's. Could someone start to fall in love that fast? Could another person become the focal point of her world in one day? She didn't have any answers. And she had to look away from Mike's eyes, so she stared at the knot in the tie at his throat.

"I can't," she whispered hoarsely. "Later...I will later, but I can't right now."

He caught her chin with his fingers and, none too gently, tilted her head until she had no choice but to look back into his eyes. "You won't?"

"I can't, Mike. Not until..."

"...you finish your business?"

She touched her lips with her tongue. "Yes, I have to…"

He let go of her abruptly. "I understand," he said. "I understand completely." And he left her.

Alex stared numbly after him as he made his way through the crowds, then disappeared from sight. She pressed a hand to her mouth and wished she understood what had just happened.

Mike kept walking and didn't stop until he was out of the casino, on the far side of the lobby and entering the bar of the main restaurant. He spotted an empty seat at the circular wood bar and crossed to it.

"A double Scotch," he said to the bartender; then, when the drink was put in front of him, he sat staring down into it without tasting it.

Why had he done that? Why had he challenged her. *Make a choice between me and stealing whatever you're out to steal!* He held the glass tightly. Why in heaven's name had he kissed her? And why had it hurt so much when she'd made her choice?

He washed the taste of her off his lips and out of his mouth by taking a gulp of the liquor; then he put the glass down. He waited until the fire dissipated in his stomach, then laid a bill on the bar and left. As he stepped back into the lobby, he automatically looked toward the casino on the far side, but he didn't see anyone. Anyone? He wasn't looking for just anyone. He didn't see Alex.

Stay with her, he told himself. Just keep her in sight. Then, when she does whatever it is she's going to do, tell Stanley and let it go.

He moved into the crowded lobby and glanced at the wall clock. Fifteen minutes to ten. Tension made his back and shoulders feel painfully tight. A lousy night and a day that had gone from bad to worse only increased the tension. "Here goes nothing," he muttered as he headed back toward the casino to find Alex.

* * *

Alex wandered around the huge casino area after Mike left, past the blackjack tables, to a bank of slot machines along the back wall. She waved away a waitress who was threading her way through the patrons offering free champagne. She didn't ever want to drink again, not when she'd found she couldn't remember what had happened, not to mention that she couldn't tell the difference between dreams and reality.

As the waitress walked away, Alex turned her back to the machines and looked at the vast room. With great concentration, she forced herself to do a security inventory of the space. It helped her forget what had just happened.

After several minutes she conceded that the security down here was tight, very tight indeed. The guards were plentiful, moving all the time, always watching. And the surveillance cameras overlapped in their scanning patterns. She looked up at the "crow's nest," a room high above the crowds, where a team of employees kept an eye on televisions that focused on each game in progress. Very tight.

She tried to find a clock, then spotted one near the door to the rest rooms. Almost ten o'clock. She would wait another fifteen minutes, then go upstairs and get started.

She set off again, walking slowly from table to table; then she spotted a man at one of the blackjack tables who seemed different from the other gamblers. Not in looks, but in personality. He seemed relaxed, not at all nervous, even when he pushed five thousand dollars in chips forward for his bet. He watched the dealer, then picked up his cards, signaled for a hit, then stood pat.

In the end he turned over his cards and had twenty-one. Strangely, Alex had a feeling that he'd known what he would have, and that intrigued her. He wasn't cheating; she was almost certain of that, yet he was so secure in his bets. She had heard of people with systems that worked, and she wondered if this man was one of the few. She watched him go through another game, watched him win again, then followed him to the cashier's cages, where he cashed in most of his chips.

But as she got close to the cages, she had a vivid picture of Mike kissing her, of his request for her to forget everything and go with him. Averting her eyes from the spot where he'd trapped her with his body and arms, she headed for the exit.

Mike watched Alex from a distance and kept out of her way. She looked at the clock; then she went from table to table, watching the dealer for a few minutes, then moving on. The only time she seemed intrigued was when a man hit it big at blackjack. She stared at him, seemingly fascinated, inching closer each time he made a bet until she was within five feet of him. She watched every move; then, when he pulled out of the game, she followed him toward the cages.

Just before she got to the cages, she veered off and headed for the entrance. And Mike followed. In the lobby, she didn't hesitate before going to the elevators and getting in one. Mike approached and got into the one next to hers, thankful to find it empty; then, hoping he'd guessed right, he hit the button for the tenth floor.

When his car opened at ten, he looked out and saw Alex just starting down the hall. He waited, holding the door partly open; then, as she went into her room, he hurried forward to the alcove with the machines in it. He hoped he wouldn't have to wait there for too long.

His wait ended up being less than half an hour. Alex came out dressed in a deep blue T-shirt, well-worn Levi's and white jogging shoes. Her hair was still in the ponytail. She never even looked at the elevators. Instead, she went down the hall, stepped into the stairwell and shut the door firmly behind her.

As soon as the door closed, Mike jogged down the hall, waited just a few seconds, then cautiously pushed the door open. The landing was empty. He stepped into the stairwell and listened intently, but he couldn't hear a thing. He wondered only for a second which direction he should head in; then he decided which way to go—up.

* * *

By the time Alex was approaching the landing of the thirtieth floor, her heart was pounding from more than the strenuous climb. This nervousness had never arisen with any of her other jobs. She'd always stayed cool and calm until the job was done. But this time she felt nerves twisting inside her. Maybe it was because the past days had been so strange, so unsettling. Mike. He was the cause. But now she had to push thoughts of him aside and get this job done.

She checked her watch as she stepped onto the landing. Seventeen minutes to eleven. In two minutes, one guard would be on a break in the Towers' kitchen on the twenty-eighth floor, while the other two would be roaming the halls. That made everything simpler. She could hear someone walking, even on the carpet, and that would give her an edge.

There shouldn't be anyone by the elevators. She listened intently, then cracked the door open just enough to see into the hallway. A couple passed, then moved out of sight.

She stepped out into the hall and stopped at the corner. She looked around the edge of the wall and saw the couple get into the elevator. But when a guard stepped out and passed them with a nod, Alex retreated to the stairwell again. Careful to close the door silently, she stepped to the hinged side of the door and pressed her ear to the crack.

She heard whistling, a low, toneless sound that got closer and closer. Then the door handle turned, and she pressed herself back against the wall. The door latch clicked, and the door opened partway. She could see the shadow of a man with a cap on look into the stairwell. Then the door shut, and the whistling faded away.

But Alex didn't move. She waited; then, sure enough, the whistling came back to the stairwell area and went past. Finally she cracked the door open again. The guard was at the corner, going around it. From the sound of the whistling, he was walking in the direction of the elevator.

Alex looked both ways, then stepped out and hurried to the corner, peeked around and watched the guard pass the elevators and stroll on. Alex could hear his whistling get fainter and fainter; then, just as it was dying out, it began to get louder again. In a few seconds the guard was back at the elevators. He jabbed the button, the doors opened, and he stepped inside.

The doors closed, and Alex made her move. Keeping her eye on the elevator indicator and seeing it stopped on the twenty-seventh floor, she quickly went past the mirrored doors to Suite 2. She checked the elevator light one more time, saw that it was still on twenty-seven and took a piece of metal out of her pocket. It had uneven ridges on both sides. With any luck at all, one of those ridges would tickle the right spot in the lock itself and make the door open.

She pushed the metal into the slot up to the first toothed ridge, then lifted, pushed down, slid it from side to side, then pushed it on to the next ridge. She kept up the painstaking process, all the time keeping her eye on the elevator indicator and listening for anyone coming down the hall from either direction.

At the second to the last series of ridges, she pushed the metal up and heard it click. The door swung silently open. Quickly, Alex stepped into the darkened suite, closed the door and stopped to catch her breath. She hadn't been aware of holding it until now. While she drew in air, she looked into the shadows. For good measure she called out, "Hello, honey. I'm back."

She could explain getting into the wrong room if someone just happened to be here. She wouldn't be able to explain her presence if someone came upon her while she was working. When she heard nothing at all, she stepped forward into the heavy darkness.

Chapter 11

Mike hurried up the stairs, but even though he ran three mornings a week on the beach and worked out at a health club, he found that he was seriously out of breath when he got to the twenty-eighth floor. While he waited for his breathing to settle into a near-normal pattern, he leaned against the cold wall by the door and tried to think clearly.

He'd really only had one thought on his way up here, and that thought bothered him more and more all the time. He wanted to find Alex so he could stop her from doing what she was planning. God, he didn't even know for sure what it was, or how her partner was involved, but he couldn't let her go ahead and be hurt. *Protector of the world?* It seemed all he wanted to protect was one tiny, incredibly appealing woman.

Find her, then figure out what to do, he told himself, and decided to start looking for her from the top floor down. The trip up to the penthouse level was easier, and it was only a few minutes before he was carefully opening the access door. He looked out into a long, straight hallway with just three doors going off of it to the left, and two to the right,

with a set of mirrored elevator doors between them. Nowhere to hide there, and he couldn't hear a thing except
muffled music coming from behind the nearest door.

He ducked back inside the stairwell and listened intently.
If he could only hear footsteps—anything to let him know
where she was. But when he heard nothing, he started down
to the next floor. He got to thirty, opened the door and went
out into the silent corridor. After walking all the way down
it in both directions and finding nothing, he went back to
the stairs.

He did the same on the next floor, found nothing, then
went down to the twenty-eighth floor and opened the access door.

"Can I help you?" asked a guard standing dead in front
of him.

His jolt of surprise at the appearance of the man almost
made Mike gasp; then he focused on the quizzical expression on the guard's flushed face, dominated by thick glasses.

Mike stood still, hoping he didn't look too stupid, and
simply shook his head. "No, I was just walking up...for
exercise."

The man raised one eyebrow above his horn-rimmed bifocals at that explanation. "Oh?"

"Good for the lungs and the heart." Mike patted the spot
where his heart was thudding behind his ribs.

"You going down or up?"

"To my suite." Mike stepped past the man into the hallway. "A good walk," he said as he walked away from the
man, "is good for the heart. Very good."

"Sure is," the guard said, and Mike jumped when the
voice came from right behind him. He glanced over his
shoulder and saw the guard following him about a foot
away. "You have a good evening, sir."

"Sure," Mike muttered and kept walking to his suite. He
took out his key, put it in the lock, then stepped into the silent room. As he turned to close the door, he groaned in-
wardly when he saw the guard go to the small alcove by the
house phones to one side of the elevators. The man dropped

down on the chair, picked up a newspaper, then glanced up
to see Mike looking at him. "Just taking a bit of a
breather," he said. "Good evening to you, sir."

Mike nodded again and shut the door with a click.

Alex wondered if she could chance a light? No, not if the
suite wasn't occupied. The guard might come by and see the
light under the door. But she knew how she could get some
visibility. She waited for a few moments for her eyes to adjust to the dimness in the multilevel suite; then she silently
crossed to the windows. She pulled back the drapes, and a
multicolored glow flooded the room, light that came from
the collective voltage of all the signs on the Strip.

Alex checked her watch. Twelve minutes to eleven. She
had ten minutes, tops, to find the "safe place." She turned
to the room, now bathed in rainbow hues, and quickly went
to work. She'd made a mental list of possible sites for hiding the box Lincoln wanted, and it didn't take her more than
two minutes to rule out most of them. Not in the kitchen-
ette refrigerator, not in the closets, nor the bar.

She even checked the pictures in the bedroom, but nothing was behind either print. Lincoln had promised that the
suite wouldn't be specially equipped to fool her, but maybe
she'd fooled herself. She had expected the safe to be in a
traditional spot, and she had a feeling she'd underestimated the company that had designed the system.

Quickly, she went back to the entry door and dropped to
her knees. She froze when she heard the soft thudding of
footsteps out in the hall. Then they were gone, and she released a breath, only to catch it again when the footsteps
came back by the door. When they faded into the distance
and didn't return, she swiped at her face with an unsteady
hand, then got back to work.

Slowly she crawled on the carpet next to the baseboard to
the right. All the while she trailed her fingers along the
wooden molding at the base of the wall. Five feet from the
door, she felt what she'd hoped to find.

The staid old company that had put in the security system had gone very modern in this suite. They'd put something that needed wires. Something electronic. The thin wire was only as thick as heavy thread and almost invisible, its color blending with the background of the wallpaper and the paint on the baseboard. From the way it emerged from the wall, Alex knew it must have been threaded through from the corridor. Its power came from a central display that held the alarm somewhere else in the hotel. That meant an alarm was rigged at the safe itself.

She stayed on her knees, keeping her fingers on the wire. It jogged up the stairs, but only to the third step, where it went to the entertainment area with the piano and bar. Right there it slipped under the carpet. On a hunch, Alex felt on the far side, where the steps flowed into the second level, and she felt nothing. She scrambled to the nearest wall at the corner of the bar and sank back on her heels.

She'd checked the bar and found nothing at all. She scooted to the other end of the bar to double-check, but she didn't find any wire there. It never came out of the huge bottom cabinet that made up the lower half of the bar.

Maybe she'd been wrong about the wire. Then she brought herself up with a cold fact: she was running out of time, and the wire was her only hope. She tugged open the set of doors at the bottom of the bar, and the rainbow of lights flashed over bottles of mixers, an array of glasses and some folded linen on two heavy shelves. She couldn't see anything out of the ordinary.

As a last-ditch chance, she closed her eyes and began to run her fingers over the surfaces of the cabinet, the bottom, the sides, then the top. Nothing. She looked at her watch. Four more minutes and she would have to admit defeat. But she hadn't come this far just to give up. One by one she began to remove the bottles; then she found four of them all on a single tray. When she tried to pick one up, the whole tray lifted in her hands, bottles and all. And it barely weighed what one bottle should.

Ingenious, she conceded as she pulled the whole con-
glomeration out and set it on the carpet. Quickly, she took
a tiny flashlight out of her pocket and aimed it at the spot
where the fake bottles had been. A clearly defined square,
about six-by-ten, showed in the wooden bottom of the cabinet. Alex knew she'd found what she had been looking for.

She pushed down on one corner, and the adjacent corner
popped up. She lifted the lid and laid it by the fake bottles.
She looked inside and saw the safe. It consisted of what
looked like a metal safety-deposit box set into the floor. It
had a large ring on the top, making it easy to open—if not
for a very sophisticated digital alarm with a red light glowing above the number plate. That sort of alarm would go off
if the lid were shifted at all or the ring was lifted away from
the metal. A neat little setup, and a lot more difficult to get
past than she'd expected.

She shone the light on her watch. Three minutes. Then she
flashed the light on the code box. She'd never heard of a
hotel providing this sort of security for its guests, but the
Elysian obviously did. The thought niggled at her, but she
pushed it aside to concentrate on the box.

She played the light over it, then saw the pattern. The
same code had been in use for some time. The four digits
that were used were smeared slightly with dirt from someone's fingers. Quickly, she began trying combinations,
slipping from one number to the next, then doing the other
three in various orders. Ten times, then the eleventh, the
twelfth, and she could feel sweat trickling down her tem-
ple. On the thirteenth she heard a click and the red light
went out.

She aimed the small light at the lid, lifted the ring and
opened it. A box sat inside, and she took it out. A simple
wooden container, just as Lincoln had told her, and she
could feel the star burned in the corner. She put the metal
top carefully back on the safe, pushed the ring down to
touch the metal, then pressed the reset button for the alarm.
The alarm light flash back into life, and she put the wooden

square over it. When the fake bottles were back in place, Alex stood and tucked the wooden box under her arm.

She glanced at her watch. Less than two minutes to go before the guards went back to their usual rotation. Moving quickly, she tugged the drapes shut, then crossed to the door. Cautiously, she pulled it open a crack and stopped. A guard she'd never seen before was sitting in the chair by the elevator doors, intent on a paperback novel. She was trapped.

Mike had called Alex's room twice from his suite; then he went back to the door and cracked it enough to look out. The guard hadn't moved. But he was sitting lower in the chair, his book on his lap and his head low, with his chin resting on his chest. Mike suddenly realized that he wasn't a prisoner. He could leave any time he wanted to. As casually as possible, he stepped out into the corridor and walked quietly past the guard.

He kept walking down the hall, past the elevators, around the corner and out of the guard's sight. Without hesitating, he stepped into the stairwell. He paused, listened, couldn't hear a thing, then headed down to the tenth floor, hoping he would discover where Alex had gone.

Alex looked at her watch. Time was up. She pressed her ear to the door and thought she could hear someone talking. She cracked the door a bit and realized that someone was the guard.

"What are you talking about?" he asked.

Alex could see him, with his two-way radio close to his mouth, and heard another voice come over it. "I'm down on twenty-eight, and some guy's using the stairwell for exercise. Says it's for his heart. I didn't pay much attention to him at first, but I've been thinking about it, and it feels funny to me. Why don't you start down from your end, and I'll head up. I'll meet you halfway." The other man laughed over the radio. "Besides, I'm falling asleep up here. I need to move around."

Alex watched the guard speak into the radio. "Me, too. It's a slow night. See you in a minute." She saw him toss the book on the floor by the chair, tuck the walkie-talkie into a leather pouch on his belt, then head slowly down the hall. When he was out of sight beyond the curve, and the way was clear, she left. She heard the door lock catch, then went to the elevator.

God only knew who was in the stairwell, but she owed him one. He'd effectively taken the guards not only off this floor, but away from the floor where she had to change elevators. She just hoped she didn't get there at the same time that the guard who'd taken a break came back on duty. She pushed the down button, stepped into the elevator and hit the button for the lowest of the Tower floors.

As the mirrored car slid downward, she felt the box dig into her diaphragm. She'd done it. She'd succeeded. Now all she had to do was meet Lincoln, give him the box, get paid and tell him that she would write up a report as soon as she got back to Santa Monica.

She got off, passed three strangers waiting to go up, and switched elevators. She was alone for only one floor before six people boarded. By the time the elevator stopped at the fourth floor, the car was so crowded that Alex decided to get off and walk down the rest of the way to meet Lincoln.

She had forty-five minutes; then she would be free and could go find Mike. The idea made her smile, and she ended up hurrying down the stairs. At the bottom, she stepped into a narrow hall painted bright yellow, with huge black arrows pointing the way. She followed them, and as she rounded a corner, she saw metal doors marked Emergency Exit in huge black letters. She examined them for a long moment, then saw wires that had been painted over running along the wooden door frame, then turning right along the wall. They blended with the painted surface, just the way the small alarm box they led to did.

Alex glanced behind her, saw no one, then opened the metal box on the wall. A simple alarm to let the hotel know if someone was leaving by the fire exit. She got closer, saw the connections and simply undid the wires. Nothing happened.

She closed up the alarm and reached for the door handle. In a moment she stepped out into the heat of the desert night. She was at the top of a cement ramp overlooking a parking area where high vapor lights robbed everything of color. Grays, blacks, muddied neutral shades, all blended together in row upon row of cars. In the sky high above, the moon was clear and bright, but no stars showed at all. Alex leaned back against the stucco wall and inhaled the fresh air. Patiently, she waited for midnight to come.

Alex glanced at her watch. One minute past midnight.

"Miss Thomas?"

She turned and saw Lincoln emerging from the shadows by the trash Dumpsters. When they made eye contact, he motioned her over. She went down the ramp and over to the Dumpsters, stopping about five feet from the man. His face was half in shadow, the other half exposed by the pasty yellow of the vapor lamps.

"Does the Elysian need a new system, or did it foil you?" he asked in a low voice.

Without saying a word, Alex lifted her top just enough to take out the box, then held it out to Lincoln.

He motioned her closer, and she could see the way he was staring intently at the box. "Well, I'll be damned," he murmured. "You did it, little lady."

"This *is* what you wanted, isn't it?"

He took the box, then looked at her, his eyes dark holes in his heavy face. "Exactly what I wanted. How long did it take you to get in and find it?"

"Twelve and a half minutes."

"The system's that bad?"

"No, not really. It's pretty good, just a few flaws that need to be worked out."

"I want to know all about that later," he said, his thumb moving slowly over the star on the corner of the box. "Damn good work," he murmured again. "Damn good."

"And worth a bonus," Alex added.

He looked at her and didn't hesitate. "Well worth it." He reached into his back pocket with his free hand and took out an envelope. "We never settled on an amount beyond your fee, but I think you'll be pleased with what you'll find in there."

Alex took the envelope, lifted the flap and was surprised to see cash as opposed to a check. "Cash?"

"Don't people take that anymore?" he asked.

"Of course. No problem. The real problem is your guests thinking they're totally secure in those suites."

He smiled at her, a full, pleased smile. "But you'll tell me how to keep them secure, won't you?"

"That's what you're paying me for." She didn't bother counting the money before she folded the envelope in half and pushed it into her pocket. "How soon do you need a report?"

"A week. Send it to me here."

"All right."

"And Miss Thomas . . . ?"

"Yes."

"A damned good job." He held out his hand to her, and she took it. His handshake was clammy, but firm and brisk. "If you ever need it, be assured that I'll be glad to give you a very good recommendation."

"Thank you. I might take you up on that," she said, thinking about the other casinos she might approach before she left for home.

He nodded, then turned and walked away into the shadows.

Done. Alex stood very still for a long moment, letting her freedom sink in. That was exactly how she felt. Free, as if a huge burden had been taken off her shoulders. She had her freedom, and she knew what she was going to do with it. She turned and went back inside. She would go and change, then find Mike. She wanted to explain things, at least as much as she could. She could let him know why she'd had to put off being with him until this job was done. She went back through the emergency doors, along the hall and up a single flight of stairs to the lobby level.

Once she reached the lobby, she made her way through the guests who were milling around, and she didn't stop until she got to the elevators and the mirrored doors slid open.

Mike had sat on the top step by the door to the tenth floor for over fifteen minutes. He'd heard vague, distant noises in the stairwell, but he hadn't been able to tell where they'd been coming from. Finally they'd stopped, and he had given up, deciding he needed to get himself a good, stiff drink.

He rode down to the lobby in the elevator, and when the doors opened, Alex stood in front of him. For one brief moment he was certain he'd fabricated her image; then she smiled, a brilliant, wonderful smile.

Without thinking or taking the time to measure his actions, he strode out of the elevator, ignoring the people all around, and reached out, pulled her to him and held her. She was here, not upstairs. "Where've you been?" he asked, his words muffled against her hair.

"Here—at least, outside." Her voice sounded soft and gentle, running across his nerves in the most delicious way. Then he inhaled unsteadily and caught the freshness of the night air clinging to the silky strands of her hair.

When someone bumped him from behind, Mike finally moved and held Alex back a bit, but he never let go of her shoulders. "I need to talk to you," he said.

"I need to talk to you," she said at the same time.

They both laughed unsteadily; then he nodded. "You first."

"I need to explain things."

"So do I." She felt so tiny and soft under his hands, and his body ached with awareness. "I've got something I need to tell you."

She touched his face, her fingers incredibly gentle against the line of his jaw. "Me, too. At least, I want to explain as much as I can."

"Good," he breathed. "But not here. I can barely hear myself think above this noise."

"No, someplace where we can be alone."

Mike looked down into Alex's dark eyes, eyes that seemed to glow with pleasure, and he knew that was exactly what he wanted—to be alone with her, to shut out the world for a while. "My suite?"

She never hesitated. "Yes."

Without a word, he reached out to take her hand.

She barely realized that they'd crossed to the elevator and gotten on until the car started upward. All she seemed aware of was Mike holding her hand, his fingers laced with hers, tight and warm. His touch wasn't intimate. It was almost casual, in fact, yet it seemed to link her irrevocably to this man. Held tightly by Mike, she felt strangely free. And, most of all, it felt right for her to be here.

Through the most unexpected turn of events, she knew she might have found the one person she'd been looking for in her life. She'd always thought she'd needed family, a mother or father, a sister or brother, but all the time it had been one person. The other men she'd dated faded into a blurred memory. They had all been flawed, lacking that certain something she needed.

She looked at Mike's profile, at the strength of his jaw, the fine lines at the corner of his eye, the way his hair swept back. He was special in a way she couldn't begin to fathom any more than she could fathom that sudden sense of coming home she'd felt when she'd looked up to see him coming off the elevator. She'd never experienced that before in her life, that feeling of comfort and excitement all at the same time, that familiarity that should come only with years of intimacy.

She couldn't think of a thing to say to the man at her side, yet there didn't seem to be a need for words. Their silence continued when they changed to the tower elevator, then went the last leg of the trip to Mike's suite. And he never let go of her until they were at his door, when he released her so he could unlock the door and motion her inside ahead of him.

She stepped into the dark, silent rooms and for a moment had a flashing vision of the matching suite two stories above. Then, as she turned to Mike, who looked at her through the soft shadows, that notion fled. Her job was in the past, gone as if it had never been. All the reality she could ever hope or wish for was here—Mike.

Without a word, he came closer and gently framed her face with his hands. "Alex, this is so strange. I'm a logical person, a person who needs reasons and motives for anything I do. Yet where you're concerned, I feel as if I'm in another dimension, experiencing something I've never experienced before."

She knew exactly what he was saying, yet she could only stare at him and nervously touch her tongue to her lips.

"You feel it, too, don't you?" he asked, his thumbs moving slowly back and forth on her cheeks.

"Yes . . ." Was that her voice?

In the darkened room, he pulled her to him. When his lips found hers, Alex couldn't move. She was overwhelmed by sensations, bombarded physically and emotionally. Could a person die from this need for another person? she wondered, then knew how foolish that thought was. She wasn't dying; she was being born again. She was being filled with wonder and a sense of rightness and needs so strong that they made her ache.

When Mike's mouth moved on hers and his tongue gently parted her lips, Alex wasn't prepared for her own response. Fiercely, swiftly, she reached out for Mike and never looked back. Frantic for contact, she tugged at his shirt, lifting the soft material so she could feel the heat of his skin under her hands. And his reaction was just as fierce.

It was as if they'd been lovers before, then parted for a long time. Urgency touched every action, drove every caress and exploring kiss. Her own needs all but drowned Alex. She pressed herself against Mike as hard as she could, wishing she could fuse with him, simply disappear deep inside him and know him from the inside out.

A part of her was shocked at her response to him, shocked at the way she helped him undo her top, the way she tugged her bra off to free her breasts for his touch. In novels people were overcome with passion. In movies they were frantic with desire, but this was neither, yet Alex was experiencing both extremes.

Letting herself go, she tasted Mike, felt the smoothness of his teeth with her tongue, stamped his taste into her soul. Freedom. Yes! This was a freedom she'd never known before, never. She felt powerful and strong, yet open and vulnerable. The combination stunned her.

"Now," Mike whispered. "Now." And then they were tangled together, falling backwards until they were lying on the floor, the thick pile of the carpet springy and soft underneath them.

Alex looked up at Mike, and she shuddered at the fire she could see in his eyes. She knew he wanted her, the strength of his arousal barely confined by his slacks. In a daring move, she drew her fingers over his chest, lower and lower, over his diaphragm; then she felt his breath catch when her hands found the fastener at his waist. Without ever taking her eyes off his, she undid his pants, then pushed aside the cotton fabric of his underwear. Yes, he wanted her. She could feel his need in her hands, and she could hear it in the words he uttered as his head dropped toward her.

Then his mouth was on her, his hands working their wonder on her body, and her own urgency grew even stronger. In one swift motion Mike was on his feet, shedding the last of his clothes; then he was back with her. She helped him take off her remaining clothing, lifting her hips to free herself of her Levi's and lacy underpants.

For a brief second Mike simply looked down at her, his eyes trailing from her throbbing breasts to her navel to her hips, which automatically thrust toward him as if he'd touched her physically.

She was dimly aware of lights everywhere, colors and shadows playing over silky skin; then Mike was above her again. "I want you," he whispered, his hot breath on her face sending chills along her spine. "Now."

"Yes," she responded. And that yes included everything, from needing, to wanting, to loving. The last thought flitted into her mind but didn't have a chance to stop and grow before Mike had his legs between hers. He tasted her breasts, drawing first one nipple, then the other into hard peaks. His knees moved farther apart, widening her legs; then she felt him touch her. He hesitated for only a fleeting moment before his thrust met her arching hips, and Alex realized what the phrase "when two become one" really meant.

Tears burned her eyes, blurring Mike's image over her; then she closed her eyes and gave in to the feelings that exploded in her when Mike began to move. Urgent, demanding, his thrusts drove her on, higher and higher, compelling her to feel things she'd never even dreamed of before. Just when she felt certain she couldn't survive any more, a deep quivering grew in her. It came out of nowhere, strong, almost painful; then, as it came to fruition, the glory and joy were unspeakable.

She heard a groan echoing around her, though she couldn't be certain whether it was hers or Mike's, then felt as if she was being shattered into a million shards of pleasure. She entered a world of joy where there was only her and Mike, no one else. And then Mike brought her back together, holding her, stroking her, murmuring words that she was too dazed to understand.

As she began to focus again, she held to him, snuggling into the angle of his body. She covered his hand, which rested on her tingling breast, with hers and closed her eyes.

Gentle grayness surrounded her, mingling with sleek body heat, and she smiled to herself. This wasn't a dream. It was better than any dream she'd ever had, better than any story she'd ever made up.

Mike. She could feel his heat at her back, her body fitting into the curve of his. His leg was heavy over her thigh. Not a dream. Reality. She lay there, afraid to move, not wanting to break whatever spell this man had woven around them; then she felt his breath warmly caress her neck the split second before his lips did.

"Awake?" he whispered by her ear.

"Mmmmmm," she sighed.

He nibbled on her earlobe, sending shivers along her spine. "You taste wonderful . . . everywhere."

She turned in his arms until she felt the roughness of his chest hair tease her tender nipples. And she looked at him, the shadows softly muting the intensity in his gaze. "So do you." She touched her lips to his throat, felt the beating of the pulse there, then lightly ran the tip of her tongue over his vaguely salty skin. "Delicious."

She felt him tremble, and she moved closer, tasting his collarbone, then up to the hollow by his ear. "Mike . . . we never did talk. . . ."

"No," he breathed hoarsely. Then he moved abruptly. He got to his feet and in one easy motion lifted Alex high in his arms against his heart. "That floor's getting hard," he murmured as he carried her up the stairs and into the bedroom.

He set her on top of the bedspread, then he lay down beside her. "Come here," he whispered as his hands spanned her waist, and he lifted her over him and set her astride his hips. She gazed down at him, her hands flat on his chest to steady herself. She could feel the urgency in him, racing heart under her palms, and his growing response to her. And she bent lower, feeling her nipples graze his chest just before Mike circled her with his arms and pulled her down.

"No talking," he said hoarsely against her lips. "There are other things I want to do . . . now."

Chapter 12

When Alex woke the next morning, she knew instantly that Mike wasn't there. She was under the sheets, but she felt no heat beside her, and she turned to find the bed empty. Sunlight managed to penetrate the central closure of the heavy drapes, but the room was still shadowed and soft. And it smelled of Mike. Heat, maleness, a scent that Alex couldn't begin to place. But it was Mike, all Mike.

She pushed herself up and back against the headboard and heard the entry door to the suite open and close. Tugging the sheets up over her breasts, she leaned back and savored what had happened last night. It was as if every action, every response, every sensation, were engraved in her mind. And beyond that, the talking through the shadows, the glimpses Mike had given her of his past. She'd ached for his pain when he spoke about his time in prison. And she'd almost cried with happiness when he told her about the day he was released. She knew the memories would stay forever, overlaid with others, then others, and others.

She hesitated. Forever? A future? There hadn't been words of love last night, but surely there had been actions

of love, of caring, of belonging. She still felt a throbbing
deep in her being when she thought of him, and she hugged
herself tightly. One thing she'd learned at the home had been
to take one day at a time. That was exactly what she'd do
now.

She heard footsteps taking the stairs quickly, then moving softly in the hall. She turned, and each detail of the man
who stopped in the doorway seemed almost painfully clear,
from his shower-dampened hair to his bare chest to the jeans
unbuttoned at his waist. Seeing him as a lover made her
pulse race and her mouth go dry. It startled her that desire
could be born so quickly from just a simple glimpse.

But the desire faltered when she saw his features tighten
as if with pain and his eyes narrow with burning anger.

"Mike?" she asked uncertainly. "What's wrong?"

He moved abruptly into the room, crossing to the bed,
then she saw the newspaper in his hand. He tossed it onto
the mattress by her knee. "Read it," he bit out.

She felt lost, with no idea what was going on. With unsteady hands, she picked up the paper. The headline leaped
out at her.

ROBBERY AT ELYSIAN. Then, just below it in smaller
print, *Over a Million in Diamonds Stolen from Secured
Suite.*

A robbery? She looked up at Mike. "There was a robbery here?"

"You didn't know all about it?" he asked as his eyes
burned into hers.

"How would I? I just woke up, and . . ."

"Read the rest of it."

She looked down and tried to focus on the article under
the headlines, and as she read the print, her world began to
shatter.

Sometime between ten o'clock last night and two
o'clock this morning, the luxury suite of Karl Jarkowski, a dealer for Tranoff International, a New
York-based fine-gem brokerage, was broken into. The

thief made off with a box containing Mr. Jarkowski's most recent acquisition for Tranoff, uncut diamonds worth over a million dollars.

As of press time, the Las Vegas Police Department said they have no clues as to the identity of the thief but are confident that fingerprints found in the suite will aid in the investigation. The gems, kept in a simple wooden box with a star burned into the corner, were...

Robbery. A simple wooden box. A secured suite at the Elysian. The words swam in front of her, and for a minute she felt certain she would faint. She couldn't tell where dreams and reality parted ways, where truth become lies, and lies become truth. As a trembling began deep in her being, her stomach knotted painfully.

Lincoln. The job. No, it couldn't be. It had all seemed so straightforward. Get in, test the system, bring out proof that she'd made it past the security. It had to be a mistake. She looked through the rest of the article; then, with a horrible sinking sensation, she read the last sentence.

The diamonds were taken from a well-secured safe on the thirtieth floor, a safe Jarkowski had installed himself when he began leasing the suite on a yearly basis eighteen months ago.

No mistake. No mistake at all.

"Was it another joke like Aria's?" Mike demanded, his words heavy with anger.

She had to try to explain. "Why do you think I had anything to do with this? I was with you." Her words died as she saw the pain twist Mike's face. "I was with you," she repeated in an unsteady whisper.

"Enough, Alex! Enough," he ground out. "I know you were involved in the robbery. Can't you ever stop the lies?"

She swallowed hard, her eyes painfully dry. She'd stopped the lies last night when she'd entered this room with Mike. She'd never known such truth before. She didn't care how he'd put two and two together, linking her with the theft. All that mattered was whether he would believe that she'd been set up.

She took a shuddering breath. In that instant she knew how much she stood to lose if Mike wouldn't believe her.

Mike could barely breathe. That simple act had become almost impossible after he saw the paper. Truth had leaped out and slapped him across the face, and he was still reeling from the impact.

His pain grew when Alex looked up at him. Her hair tumbled in a dark cloud round a face robbed of most of its color, and her eyes were huge. The sheet had slipped to reveal her breasts, which rose and fell rapidly with her quick, shallow breaths. The sight of her nakedness deepened his pain, and his sense of loss grew to the point where he thought he might scream in agony.

He tried to talk again, and when he finally managed it, his voice was barely recognizable as his own. "You did it, didn't you?"

He didn't know what he expected, but it wasn't her nodding in a faintly unsteady motion. "Yes, b-but it . . . it isn't what you think."

He felt as if he'd been kicked in the stomach, as if every bit of breath in his lungs had been denied to him. A thief? He'd been right! A sour taste touched the back of his tongue, and fury directed both at her and himself flooded over him.

How could he have blinded himself so completely to what she was? He clenched his hands tightly at his sides to control the need to strike out. "I knew it. I think I always knew you were a thief and a liar," he said, hating the unsteadiness in his own voice.

The fact that his words made her flinch did little to appease her own pain. "What?" she gasped.

He shrugged, the action making the tightness in his chest and stomach more uncomfortable. "When I found you, you were stealing. Then you came up with that stupid lie about the owner's wife. You said you came here for business." He ran a hand roughly over his face. "It was all a lie, wasn't it?"

She touched her tongue to her unsteady lower lip. "Yes. But I can explain. I swear I can."

"I believed you, Alex. No, I wanted to believe you. I've never wanted anything so—" He cut off his own admission. "So now you've stolen over a million in diamonds. Quite a step up from that bracelet."

As if she had just realized her own nakedness, she fumbled with the sheet and pulled it over her breasts. But that couldn't blot the memory of their beauty from his mind, or the remembered feel of her.

"I did it, but I was set up," she said.

He held out both hands, as if he could ward off her words the same way he could a physical attack. "I've heard plenty of those stories in prison. You should remember that no guilty people go to prison. Not one."

"But you weren't guilty," she whispered. "And I'm not, either."

He stared at her, unnerved by the way her image was beginning to swim in front of his eyes. It was too late to save Alex from herself, and way too late to save him from her, but he knew what he had to do. He turned from her and started for the door.

"Mike!" she called out. "Where are you going?"

"To call the police."

"No!" Alex stumbled out of the bed, awkwardly wrapping the sheet around herself as she hurried after him. She caught up to him in the hall at the top of the stairs and grabbed him by the arm, all too conscious of his body under her hand. She stopped him, all but forcing him to turn and look down at her. She tried not to flinch when she met his green eyes—cold and set. "Please, don't call the police. At least, not before you let me explain." She hated begging, but she didn't know what else to do.

He stared down at her; then, just when she was certain he was going to refuse, he nodded. "You've got five minutes to tell me why I shouldn't call the cops." His eyes flicked over her. "But first, get dressed."

A minute later Alex hurried down the stairs dressed in her jeans and shirt with the tails untucked. She hadn't bothered taking the time to put on her shoes or comb her hair.

She stopped at the bottom of the stairs and stared at Mike, who stood by the balcony door. His back was to the room, but Alex didn't miss the way his hands were clenched behind him. She had to try twice before she could say his name. "Mike?"

He turned at the sound, and when Alex met his cold gaze, her first instinct was to run. She wanted to get as far away from him and from this mess as she could, but she made herself go forward until she was five feet from where he stood. He looked unapproachable, controlled and distant. The lover of the night before might never have been.

"Five minutes," he said in a low voice and checked his watch.

She clasped her hands in front of her. "What time is it?"

"Eleven-ten."

It obviously didn't matter to him what they'd shared, what she'd given to him during the night. She was on trial now, and she knew that the judge wasn't sympathetic. He felt betrayed. And she understood his feelings, because she felt betrayed, too.

She also felt the need for Mike to believe in her. She needed to hear him tell her that he believed in her, and that he would help her. But that sounded like one of her fairy tales, one of her make-believe stories. All she could hope for was that he'd listen to her.

She went to the couch and, suddenly feeling very weak, slowly sank down onto the cushions. She pulled her feet up under her and moistened her dry lips. "I didn't intentionally steal those diamonds. I swear I didn't."

"You borrowed them?" he asked, still standing with his back to the brightness of the day outside the glass doors.

"No, I didn't steal anything on purpose. You have to believe me."

"Why should I?" he asked abruptly, his eyes and mouth tight.

"What?"

"Should I believe you because you've always told me the truth?"

She shrank at the sarcasm in his words. "You know I haven't. I mean, I have when I could." That wasn't true, either. "I never lied when it was really important."

Without a word, he went past her to the second level and the bar. Glass clinked on glass; then he came back down, but he didn't sit. He chose to stand at the end of the couch. He took a quick drink, then looked at Alex. "Do you even know what the truth is?"

She twisted her hands together. "All right, I've lied to you. But not since we walked into this room last night. I swear."

"What do you swear on, a Bible, your honor, or your mother's life?"

His words cut deeply, and she found herself admitting, "I don't have a mother."

"Oh? How about that big family of yours? Are they in on this little heist?"

He made clean hits with every word, and pain engulfed her. "No, I don't have any family. I don't have anyone. I never have." She couldn't look at Mike, so she stared down at her hands. "I was brought up in an orphanage, not a boarding school. And as for my sisters, they were the girls in my dormitory." She looked up at Mike and had to blink to control tears. "I don't have a big Italian family like you do." She bit her lip—hard. "That's the truth. And I swear I didn't steal any diamonds. That's the truth, too."

Something altered in Mike, but Alex couldn't begin to figure out what it was. His eyes seemed to change. Maybe the coolness was leaving, but there was still a barrier there that seemed insurmountable. "I believe you . . . about your family," he conceded in a low voice.

Hope leaped to life in her, but she stayed perfectly still. "And the robbery?"

"You didn't steal any diamonds?" he prodded.

She sank back against the pillows and rested her head on the back of the couch. Staring blankly at the ceiling, she exhaled unsteadily. "That's a matter of semantics, I suppose. I need to explain things to you."

An expletive from Mike drew her up straight again. She saw him toss the last of his drink to the back of his throat, then swallow. With a resounding crack, he put the empty glass on a side table, then turned to Alex. "Tell me your story, but try to keep the lies to a minimum."

"I promise, I won't lie to you again."

"Cross your heart, and—"

"No," she cut in. "I just promise, that's all."

"And what's your promise worth?"

"My life," she breathed, and knew that she was including any future with Mike in those two words.

He moved abruptly and went to the chair facing the couch. He dropped down into it, settling low in the seat, his hands gripping the arms. His gaze pinned Alex across the coffee table that sat between them. "Go ahead. Explain."

After a shaky start, she began her story, trying to make things as clear as possible. And she never took her eyes off Mike, all the time wondering whether he believed her. She couldn't tell. His expression never faltered, and he didn't say a thing until she told him who Lincoln was.

"The head of hotel security?"

"Yes."

"You're saying he set you up?"

It sounded so ridiculous when he said it out loud, but she simply nodded and kept talking. Mike didn't interrupt again until she told him about her first meeting with Lincoln.

"You just walked in and saw the man?"

She nodded. "He was in his office. He said he wanted to give me the details, and I had a feeling he wanted to meet me in person."

"Go ahead."

She did. And she didn't stop until Mike sat up and leaned forward when she mentioned Lincoln coming to her room. "Just a minute. He got into your room with a key?"

"Yes. He's security. I figured he could get into any room he wanted to."

"And it was him you were expecting when I came to your door?"

"Yes." She licked her lips, then kept going, ending with, "He took the box and gave me..." She remembered the envelope and tugged it out of her pocket, then tossed it onto the coffee table. "He gave me this as a bonus."

Mike reached for the envelope, opened it and let out a low whistle before he looked up at Alex. "Five thousand dollars?"

Alex scrambled to her feet and went around the table to Mike, grabbed the envelope and turned it upside down. She watched the bills flutter to the coffee table, staring in disbelief as ten one-hundred-dollar bills and eight five-hundred-dollar bills landed on the polished surface. She thought they were probably all hundreds—two thousand dollars.

"This is wrong." She touched the closest bills, then drew back as if they had burned her. "It was supposed to be fifteen hundred for the job and a bonus. I thought he'd probably given me five hundred for the bonus." She shook her head. "I don't understand."

"It's a meager cut from over a million in diamonds, isn't it?" Mike said. "He could probably get fifty cents on the dollar, maybe sixty cents. Uncut stones wouldn't be too hard to fence. Minimum, seven hundred and fifty thousand."

"Why would he do it?" Alex asked, turning to Mike.

"Why? You ought to know. After all, he's your boss. Or is he your partner?"

"No, he's a client." She sank back. "I swear, he—"

"Whatever you call him, you were in this together."

"Yes, but it was a job for me, an assignment."

"You test security systems by breaking into places?"

"I know that sounds crazy, but it works. When Fenner Electronics, the company I worked for, first went into security systems, they taught us how to get around them. And I had a natural ability to improvise, to figure out that next step—how to get around other companies' systems. It sounds weird, but I swear that's what I do."

"Don't swear again, and don't promise. Just let me think this through." He stood and walked over to the balcony doors.

She could see the tension in his shoulders. "What can I do to make you believe me?" she asked.

"I don't know," he said without turning to her.

"Neither do I," she admitted flatly, the heart going out of her. "But I know what I have to do. I've got to find Lincoln and find out what's going on."

That made him turn. "I can't let you just walk out of here."

Why? she wanted to ask. Because you care about me? Because of what we've shared? Because no two people can be together the way we were without really caring for each other? But she kept her questions to herself, and when Mike spoke again, she was infinitely glad she hadn't exposed herself that way.

"I know a little about the law. I had to learn. And I know about this robbery, so that makes me an accessory after the fact. If I could believe you…" He took a sharp breath as he grimaced. Alex could have sworn the expression came from pain until he spoke in a flat voice. "The law's the law. I can't change it. I *have* to turn you in to the police."

Alex knew right then the meaning of the word "heart-ache." A heart could ache. It could probably break with pain. Maybe die. She pressed a hand to her middle. "Can't you just let me leave so I can go find Lincoln?"

"No."

The single word slicked through her. "Why?"

He spread his hands out toward her, palms up. "I told you, I'm an accessory."

She turned and stared down at the money. "Can't you just forget you ever knew me?" she muttered.

"No, I can't," he said softly, unsteadily. "I wish I could. I wish I had never put myself in the middle of this mess, but I did. I can't change that."

"But the police..." The idea of being locked up made her physically sick. If the police learned that she had walked out of the suite with the diamonds, she would be sunk. But what if she could prove that Lincoln had asked her to do it. What if she could get him to admit what he had done? She realized how foolish that idea was. Why would he admit to anything? He'd set her up very neatly to take the fall. And he'd given her a bonus to boot.

She turned to Mike. "At least give me a chance."

She could see him hesitate and felt a glimmer of hope when he asked, "How?"

"Let me go and find Lincoln. You can stay with me. I promise I won't try to get away from you." She saw his disbelief and added quickly, "Look, if I could, I'd call some of the people I've worked for to prove to you what I do, but it's the holidays. No one would be working. The only thing I can do is try to find Lincoln. Just help me find him and you see what you think."

"Is Lincoln heavyset, late fifties?"

"Yes. But how...?"

"I saw him."

"When?"

"When I came to your room yesterday to ask you to dinner, I saw him leave."

"Then you know I'm telling you the truth. You saw him there, in my room."

"It just proves your partner was in your room," he muttered.

She didn't even argue. All that mattered to her now was clearing herself. "Just come with me, please?"

Unexpectedly, Mike agreed. "I don't know what good it will do, but I'll go with you to the security offices. Then, after you see Lincoln, you'll go with me to the police. And no tricks."

She closed her eyes for a moment, then looked right at Mike. "No tricks."

The phone rang, but Mike didn't make a move for it. Finally, on the third ring, Alex asked, "Are you going to answer that?"

He shook his head. "No, they can take a message." He looked down at Alex's bare feet. "Put on your shoes and we'll get this over with."

Mike kept a foot of space between them on the way to the elevator. A security guard had been stationed by the mirrored doors, and Alex slowed as they neared the uniformed man.

"I need to see some I.D., sir," the man said.

Mike nodded, took out his wallet and showed the guard his driver's license. "Is this enough?"

The guard looked at a piece of paper in his hand, then back at Mike and nodded. "Yes, sir. You're on the list for this floor. Sorry for the inconvenience, but I'm sure you've heard about the robbery."

"Yes, I have. What happened, exactly?"

"Don't really know the details, but whoever took the diamonds got away clean. The police are all over the place up there, tearing the suite apart. Milt Lincoln, the head of hotel security, he was up there with them for hours."

"Where's Mr. Lincoln now?" Mike could almost feel Alex tensing when he asked the question.

"In his office, I guess. Heard they were having a press conference, or something. The newspaper people have been here since just after dawn. That's part of the reason they've got guards on each floor now, to keep the reporters from hounding the guests."

Alex touched his arm, a fleeting connection that made his stomach clench. "We need to get going."

Without looking at her, Mike drew away and nodded. "Yes, we should."

The uniformed man pushed the down button for them, and the doors opened almost immediately. The elevator was already crowded, with seven people, all looking somber and not saying a word.

He got in after Alex and deliberately stood as far from her as he could get. He didn't look at her, and he didn't want to touch her again; he didn't dare. He'd almost believed her in the suite, a result of the weakness that had come from their night together. He'd never given himself to anyone the way he had to Alex. And he'd never told anyone about those nights in prison, the loneliness, the fears, the needs. Alex had been there for him all through the night, but for her it had been built on a stack of lies.

When they changed elevators, they entered a car with only three other people, and he chanced a glance at Alex standing on the other side of the door. He wished he hadn't. He could see a pulse beating erratically in the delicate hollow of her throat, and he remembered the sweet taste of her skin there. He saw a trembling in her shoulders, and he killed an urge to hold on to her.

She was scared to death. And she had every reason to be. She was a thief and a liar. And he was going on a wild-goose chase with her. Then to the police. He'd said it so firmly in the suite, yet he didn't really know if he could turn her over to the authorities or not.

If she had given him one glimmer of hope in the suite, one reason to doubt the evidence, he would have believed her. He wanted to. But there hadn't been a thing to prove her crazy story. The elevator stopped, and two more people got on, two more people separating him from Alex. It made it easier to control the urge to reach out and hold on to her for dear life.

Alex stepped off the elevator ahead of Mike, but he quickly reached her side, and she led the way through the lobby toward the security offices. She tried to ignore the uniformed police at the entry doors, and the man holding a video camera on his shoulder while a smartly dressed woman interviewed another man at the reception desk.

She went down the stairs with Mike two steps behind her, but they were stopped by a Las Vegas policeman right by the cigarette machines.

"Sorry, folks. No going down there."

Surprisingly, Mike spoke up before Alex could. "I need to talk to Mr. Lincoln."

"Sorry, he's got other things to do."

"It's about this robbery," Alex blurted out.

The policeman hesitated as he studied her. "You know something about it?"

She didn't know what to say. "I know Mr. Lincoln, and I just heard about this robbery, and I—"

Mike stepped in. "She just wants to talk to him for a minute."

A commotion at the end of the hall, by the open door to the security offices, drew everyone's attention. Then the policeman pointed to a group of people coming toward them. Reporters with microphones and bright lights. And everything centered on one person, a slender black man in a gray suit. He shook his head vigorously. "I've said everything I'm going to say." He tried to keep walking. "There isn't anything else."

"Just one more question." A thin woman pushed a microphone in the man's face. "Isn't one of the promises the Elysian makes to its guests complete security?"

The dark-skinned man stopped and looked at the reporter. "Yes. We have had a clean record here for years."

"Then how do you explain the robbery?" the reporter demanded. "Look right into the camera, Mr. Lincoln, and explain away."

Mr. Lincoln? Alex felt her throat constrict as the man in gray looked into the camera.

"I am Milton Lincoln, the head of hotel security, and I can speak for the whole staff in saying that we at the Elysian regret this incident and . . ."

Chapter 13

Alex tried to swallow the sickness that crowded the back of her throat as the man spoke. She'd been set up. And set up good. She turned to Mike and met his questioning look, but she didn't have any answers. All she knew was that she had to get out of there.

She turned and hurried back up the stairs. She didn't stop until she was in the middle of the lobby without the vaguest idea of what to do next.

"Alex?" She knew Mike was right beside her, but she couldn't stop staring at the police at the door, then through the glass at the squad cars parked right out front. "What happened back there?" Mike asked.

"That's not Lincoln," she managed.

He studied her from under lowered lashes for a long moment. "I know he's not the man I saw coming out of your room, but I'm afraid he *is* Milt Lincoln."

"He's not the man I've been dealing with. Mike, I don't understand." She could hear the panic in her voice as it rose. "I took all those diamonds...."

"Shhhhh." He touched her lips with his finger, the contact cool but compelling. "Quiet." His finger fell. "Not here."

"I need to find Lincoln—the man I knew as Lincoln. He's the only one..."

Without saying anything else, Mike took her by the arm and pulled her along with him toward the bar. In a few minutes they were in a fairly private booth near the back of the room, and Alex was staring down at a glass of soda. "I wish I could think straight." She ran her fingers carelessly through her loose hair, combing it back from her face, and drew in a shuddering breath. "I have to figure this out."

"Do you want to tell me the full truth now?" Mike asked.

His voice cut through her confusion, and when she looked up, she felt herself dying just a bit more. He was looking at her as if she were a mass murderer or something. "I told you the truth. That's not the man I knew as Lincoln. I never saw that man before."

Mike ignored the Scotch the waitress had set in front of him minutes ago. "Let's get this straight. The fat man got you to go into the suite, find the safe and take the box?"

"I told you that."

"But you didn't steal anything?"

She would have run this time, but Mike was too fast for her. His hand was on hers before she could stand, pinning her hand against the cold tabletop. "Sit down," he said tightly.

She'd always hated helpless females, and she fought the tears that were threatening to spill over. She was not going to cry. She was going to do whatever she had to do to make things right. She tugged her hand free of Mike's and sank back in the booth. "Why? You're just going to call the police, aren't you?"

He was silent for so long that she wondered if he would ever talk to her again. And when he did speak, he said something totally out of context. "I never told you exactly what I do for a living."

"No, you didn't, but..."

"I find missing people. I find them for clients. And I'm good at it. When I was in prison, I had a cellmate who never had a visitor. I finally got it out of him that he didn't know where his family was."

"Mike..."

"It's your turn to listen for a minute. It's important."

She had no idea how it could be important, but she closed her mouth and waited.

"Jerry, my cellmate, told me the last address he had for his family. He gave me background, anything he could think of. And when I got out, I traced them and found them. I told you that just before I was arrested I was trying to think of what to do with my life. Well, I found it. I'm thorough and logical, and very stubborn. The qualities an investigator needs. It interests me, challenges me, and I can make a living at it."

She stared at him, her mind so muddled she didn't have the vaguest idea what he was getting at.

"The man you claim is Lincoln is missing, isn't he?"

"I wouldn't put it quite like that."

He took a quick drink, then set his glass down and rocked her with his next words. "This is my bottom line. I'm willing to give you the benefit of the doubt for twenty-four hours. I'll do whatever it takes to try and find this phantom fat man of yours. Then, one way or the other, we'll go to the police and tell them your story."

Alex stared at Mike, and the tears finally came. They spilled silently down her cheeks, and she buried her face in her hands. Mike was willing to "give her the benefit of the doubt," if only for twenty-four hours, and he'd said "*we'll* go to the police." She felt an incredible sense of relief that she was no longer facing this alone.

"Alex?"

She swiped at her face with both hands, then looked back at Mike. "You believe me?" she asked.

He looked away from her and swirled the liquid in his glass, watching the motion of the Scotch. "I believe you *may* have been had in some way," he finally conceded. "But

I'm not sure how." Then he looked up at her. "If I'm going to put my neck on the line to help you, I insist on one thing—absolute truth from now on. If we don't have that between us, this won't work, not even for twenty-four hours."

She ran a hand over her face, then touched her tongue to her lips, tasting the saltiness of tears. "Absolute truth. I promise."

He sat forward, resting his elbows on the table. "Tell me everything you remember about 'Lincoln,' no matter how insignificant or trivial it seems to you."

Alex began to tell Mike everything she could remember.

He seemed to stop her every two minutes, but by the time she was finished, she could tell he was as thorough as he'd claimed. He sat back, fingering his now-empty glass, and stared across the booth at her. "Let me get this straight. Lincoln called you in Santa Monica to approach you about the job? But he didn't leave a message on your machine?"

"No, he just kept calling until he made contact."

"The note at the airport?"

"I tore it up and tossed it."

"The rose?"

"In the trash."

"The company he said referred him to you, did you really do business for them?"

"Yes." The slight suggestion that Mike was softening was a balm to Alex's frayed nerves. She thought he might be beginning to believe her. "You're good at what you do, Mike."

"I don't give up easily," he said cryptically. He pushed his glass away from him. "The logical place to start is at the security offices here."

"Why?"

"Do you have any other idea of where to start?" he asked.

"No." She didn't have a clue where to begin.

"Then trust me," he said and stood.

Surprisingly, when they got back to the security offices, they were empty. Not a soul was there. No police, no hotel employees, no reporters. The real Milt Lincoln was nowhere in sight.

Alex led the way into the offices. They looked the same as they had when she had come to meet the fat man. Not a soul was around. "I don't know why they'd leave everything open like this."

"Who knows. Maybe they're distracted because of the robbery, or maybe it's just because it's lunchtime," Mike muttered from behind her.

Alex turned to him. "Lunchtime? Maybe Lincoln, or whatever his name is, counted on that when he had me meet him here."

"Maybe." He looked around. "Where's the office you met him in?"

She turned and led the way down the short hall. She knocked on the door, in case even one person was left in the offices. When no one spoke up, she slowly pushed back the door to Milt Lincoln's office. The room was heavy with cigarette smoke, and the desk was even more cluttered. Its two ashtrays were filled to overflowing with butts. "This is it."

Mike stepped inside past her and stood very still. His eyes darted back and forth, taking in everything. "Has anything changed?"

"No, it's the same. Dark and smoky. The man who called himself Lincoln smoked, too."

"If he smoked in here, it wouldn't be noticed." Mike went to the desk and, without touching anything, studied it. "Where was he, and where were you?"

Alex pointed. "He sat there. I sat here." She tugged the visitor's chair close until it was in the same position. "He said to close the door. He apologized for not meeting me, and he asked about the flight."

"Anything else?"

"He just mentioned something about Las Vegas creating illusions, that people saw what they wanted to see. That they buy the illusion." She bit her lip. "I guess he knew what he was talking about."

"Anything else?" Mike asked intently.

"He asked how I got into this business. I told him about Fenner Electronics."

"Anything else?"

"No, I just got the details about the job, where, when and how. That's it."

"He sat all the time?"

"And smoked."

"What brand?"

"I don't know. He kept the cigarettes in a special case. He said something about not having a lighter." Then she remembered. "And he took a matchbook out of his pocket, and it only had one match left in it." She looked over at the wastebasket, but it had been emptied.

She kept talking as she crossed to it. "He played with the matchbook, then folded it all up and..." She pulled the plastic container away from the wall and saw what she wanted. She stood with the mutilated matchbook in her hand. "He tried to toss this into the basket and missed."

Mike took the book and read the logo on the front. "THE TREASURE PALACE—THE HOME OF DUNN AND DUNN."

He looked up at Alex. "Dunn? Isn't that the name he told you to use when you called him, and the one he used when he called you?"

"Yes."

"It must have some significance for him. Something must have made him come up with it." He turned over the matchbook, then flipped back to the logo. "Anyway, we know it's a start, and we know one of his interests is Dunn and Dunn... besides diamonds."

"Yes, we do," Alex agreed as she passed Mike and went out of the office. She inhaled, thankful that she couldn't detect Mike's scent out here. Then he was beside her, and she felt overwhelmed by him once again.

"I've still got the rental car, so we can go over to this place." He looked at the matchbook again. "The Treasure Palace."

The Treasure Palace was off the Strip, a casino, made for gambling and entertaining. An act that Alex had never heard of was billed on the marquee outside the sprawling stucco-and-wood building. It wasn't Dunn and Dunn. Mike parked on the street across from the casino instead of trying to find a spot in the crowded lot, and Alex stepped out into the heat that beat down from a clear sky.

Together they went across the street to the entryway in the shape of a magic lamp. Mike pulled the golden doors open, and Alex stepped past him into a dimness that rendered her almost blind for a moment.

Once her eyes adjusted, Alex could make out a huge room to her right, closed off with a velvet rope across the arched entry. It was ringed with booths, and the center was filled with small, round tables in front of a raised stage. It was empty now, but to the left she could see the casino, and it was full. Slot machines were lined up row after row, and other games of chance filled the rest of the noisy, smoke-filled area. People were packed in with little room to spare.

Mike motioned Alex to the bar just inside the casino, then settled beside her on one of the high stools. After several minutes the bartender finally worked his way down to them and asked, "What'll it be?"

"Two Scotches on the rocks."

When the bartender came back with the drinks, Mike asked, "I'm supposed to be meeting a business associate here. A heavyset man, small mustache, about sixty or so. Usually wears silk shirts."

Alex added, "And he sweats a lot."

The man looked at Alex and smiled. "Sounds like a strange one, doesn't he, lady?"

"He's different, and he loves an act you've had here before, Dunn and Dunn," Alex said.

The man looked blank. "He could be a regular here, for all I know. I just hired on with the rest."

"The rest?" Mike asked.

"The place just changed hands, and the new owners brought in their own people. All I can tell you is that Dunn and Dunn play here for three weeks, then take off two weeks. They won't be showing again until next week."

Mike laid a ten-dollar bill by their untouched drinks. "Thanks anyway."

Alex followed Mike out into the brilliant daylight and oppressive heat, wishing she had her sunglasses with her. She hurried to keep up as he headed back to the car. "That wasn't any help, was it?" she asked.

Mike opened the car door for her. "None."

"Dunn and Dunn. He used that name, and..." Why hadn't she thought of this before. "The number he gave me to call. Maybe it would help if we could find out whose it is."

"Do you remember it?" Mike asked.

She took a small slip of paper out of her purse and handed it to Mike, then asked, "What now?"

"The police," he said as he fingered the paper.

She grabbed him by the arm, the first time they'd touched in a what seemed like ages. "You promised!"

"I know. I'm just going to get information, that's all."

"But how? The policeman at the Elysian was suspicious when all I did was ask to see Lincoln."

Mike looked around, then said, "Come on. I'll show you how to do it."

He led the way to a stand of pay phones outside a convenience store just down the street. He pushed a lot of numbers, then finally spoke into the receiver. "Detective Barrows, please. Mike Conti calling."

He looked at Alex and whispered, "A friend on the police force in Los Angeles."

Before Alex could ask him why he had a friend there, he started talking into the receiver again. "Hey, Gil. It's Mike...Las Vegas. Sure, Gil. Listen. I need some more information, but it's out of your area. It's here, in Vegas. There was a robbery last night at the Elysian, on the Strip."

Mike looked at Alex, but spoke into the receiver. "So you heard it was pretty professional, eh?" His green eyes held Alex's. "All right. Could you find out what you can on it? And I need you to check a phone number for me, too. A Las Vegas prefix." There was a pause; then Mike read "Lincoln's" number to him. "I'll call you back." He looked at his watch. "Is two hours enough time? Good. Thanks. That's number two I owe you." He hung up and turned to Alex. "It's been on the news in L.A."

He didn't give her a chance to ask anything before heading back to the car. Once they were settled in, with the air conditioner going full blast, Mike tucked the paper in his pocket and turned to Alex. "All right, ask it."

"Ask what?"

"How would a man like me, know someone in the LAPD?"

"Okay, how?"

"I grew up with Gil in Santa Barbara. He was there when I got arrested, and he stuck with me—even when he went to the academy and made the force. He's been down in L.A. for a while now, and I keep promising him I'll come down and visit. This is the closest I've come."

She leaned back against the door, letting the cool air brush across her heat-flushed skin. "You never did say why you were in Los Angeles, much less in Aria's."

"No, I never did, did I."

"Well?"

He turned and gripped the steering wheel. "Is it important?"

"You said we have to be completely honest. I just want to know why you were where you were."

He looked back at her. "I came down from Santa Barbara on a case. A man named Stanley asked me to find someone for a friend of his who's dying. He thinks if the man knows he has a family, he'll fight to live."

Alex swallowed hard; the words made her feel strange. "A family's important. I hope you can help him."

"I found the missing person. It wasn't terribly hard. Stanley just wasn't too sure if knowing would help the man's condition."

"Will he live?"

"I don't know," Mike said softly. "I just don't know."

Alex turned from Mike and looked off down the street. That was when she spotted a billboard and something clicked in her mind. *REAL ESTATE, AN INVESTMENT IN THE FUTURE OF LAS VEGAS*. "Real estate," she breathed.

"What?"

She pointed to the sign. "The fat man said something about real estate. We were talking about gambling, and he said that real estate was the best gamble in Las Vegas, that he got a real rush when he came out on top."

He shrugged. "That's something to consider."

"It's more than that." Before he could say anything else, Alex jumped out of the car and hurried back to the phones. Quickly she flipped open the nearest phone book and turned to the listings under Real Estate. Gambling might be the mainstay of Las Vegas, but the number of real-estate offices wasn't far behind the number of casinos.

Then Alex did something she had never done before. She looked around, then tore the pages of real-estate listings out of the phone book. In a minute she was back in the car, excitement making her slightly breathless. "Real-estate listings," she said as she smoothed the pages on her lap.

"And?"

"I'm going to check all of them, starting at ..." She looked at the first listing. "Aaron and Aaron Associates."

"How many are there?"

"A few," she said with admirable understatement.

"What's the first address?"

She looked at Mike. "Why?"

He looked at his watch. "You still have twenty-two hours. I have this car, and I'm not letting you out of my sight." He shrugged. "Give me the first address."

Alex read it off, not about to fight with him. It was what she wanted, having him there to help. She was suddenly much more optimistic as Mike shifted the car into gear and headed off.

But by four-thirty she was getting discouraged. Not one person in any of the real-estate offices recognized the description of "Lincoln," and they were halfway through the alphabet.

Alex sank back in the car seat with a sigh after getting nowhere at the offices of Phillip James Land Consultants. She closed her eyes to shut out the glare and the sight of the elegant gray stone offices, and let the cool air from the air conditioner wash over her. "What a waste."

"Nothing?"

"They looked at me like I was crazy."

"Where to now?"

She didn't know what to do, and she felt close to being beaten. "I don't know. Maybe I should just go to the police and let whatever happens happen."

"Do you mean it?"

She turned to look at Mike, unnerved to see him staring at her intently. "Yes. I'm not getting anywhere this way."

Unexpectedly, he reached out and grasped her hand in his. It was the first time he'd touched her in hours, and it made her heart skip in her chest. "I'll stick by you," he said.

She turned her hand until her fingers were laced through his, and she held on to him tightly. She managed to whisper his name around the tightness in her throat. "Mike?"

His hand tightened on hers. "What?"

"Do you still believe I intended to rob that man?"

"No." But he'd hesitated one heartbeat too long. "I think you got involved on impulse, maybe for the excitement or something, then it got out of your control."

"It did...in a way. But I never thought it was robbery. Never."

"I don't want to argue."

"If it wasn't a holiday weekend, you could call a few of the people I've worked for. You could ask them what I did for them."

He considered her for a long moment. "Would they tell the truth, or would they lie for you?"

"Never mind." She jerked free of his touch and bit her lip hard as she looked out the side window. It was too much to ask that Mike would understand, that he would believe her. "Just take me to the police station," she said in a voice flat with resignation. "I'll take it from there."

Without another word Mike drove off down the street. But he didn't go to the police station. Instead he pulled into the first fast-food restaurant he came to, ordered two sodas and two hamburgers from the drive-through, then paid for their food.

Back on the street, he drove until he came to a series of pay phones near the road, where he stopped the car. Leaving the motor running so the air conditioner would keep working, he said, "Wait here. I'll call Gil back and see what he's found out."

She didn't argue. As she watched Mike put through his call, she was aware of his every action, every movement. She licked her lips. In no time at all, he'd come very close to becoming the center of her world, and that made her feel all that much more lonely.

She took a deep breath as he came back and got in the car. "What did he say?"

"I'll tell you as soon as I find us someplace to eat." Silently, he drove down the Strip; after they'd past the last of the hotels, he pulled into the shade of a huge tree. He left the motor idling, then opened the bags from the restaurant. He gave Alex a drink and a burger.

"I don't feel like eating," she said, the idea of food making her vaguely sick. "I want to know what your friend found out."

"First take this. You haven't eaten all day, have you?"

She shook her head and took the cup and wrapped hamburger. She took a tentative sip of the cold liquid, then nibbled at the burger. After another drink, she sat back and looked at Mike. "Tell me what he told you."

Mike washed down a bite of his burger with his drink, then said, "Gil found out that the robbery happened just about like the police said it did. The robber was in and out quickly. There were fingerprints, but they hadn't been matched to anyone's when Gil checked. But there's a bit of a shadow over Jarkowski. It seems that he's got a reputation for being a gambler."

"A gambler?"

"He's known at the tables, and he's got a thing for young girls, but he's always been honest about his job. Lots of stones passed through his hands without sticking to his fingers. They're kicking around the idea that he might have masterminded the job, but they aren't very confident that he did." He looked at her narrowly. "Do you know him?"

"No, and I didn't set it up with him." She swallowed more of her drink, then realized she didn't have any idea what the man looked like. She didn't know if she knew him or not. "What does Jarkowski look like?"

"Gil said he's about sixty, thin and balding, and given to wearing white. Not a bit like your Lincoln, is he?"

The man in the elevator with the woman in the red jumpsuit. She would bet that had been Jarkowski. "No, not a bit like him." She sighed with disappointment.

"They've got a lot of fingerprints."

She stared at her hands. "I didn't wear gloves," she muttered. "I didn't think I'd have to."

"The number the man gave you is for a hotel down the Strip. There's a room there rented to a man named Dunn, Lewis Dunn. No one remembers him, and he paid cash for five days' stay. He's called in for messages twice. That's a dead end, at least so far." He looked at his watch. "It's five-thirty. You've got about eighteen hours left, so what do you want to do now?"

"I don't know," she admitted, then glanced out the window. "Finding missing people is *your* business."

"Logically the real-estate list is still your best bet. It's a long shot, but it's better than nothing."

She put down her burger and drink on the console, then fumbled in her purse for the pages from the phone book. She stared down at them. "You're right. It's all I've got." There were a lot of offices left.

"What's next?"

"Farley and Davis Realty," she said and read off an address that was just a few streets away from where they were parked.

Mike put his uneaten food in the bag and set his drink in the console holder. "Let's go."

At eight o'clock, when the moon was rising in the eastern sky and the city was washed in twilight, Mike drove into the parking lot for Stalwart and Sons Realty. A lady was just turning over a CLOSED sign on the glass door of the single-story, glass-and-steel building sandwiched between a pizza parlor and a carpet dealer.

Alex got out of the car quickly, barely aware of the heat now, and ducked to look back inside. "I'll try and get her to talk to me."

Mike shrugged. "Give it a try. I'll wait here." She turned to go, but he spoke again before she closed the door. "Good luck, Alex."

She looked back at him. Meeting him had been the best luck she'd had in a long time, no matter what happened between them when this was over. "Thanks," she said softly and swung the door shut.

Mike watched her approach the building and wondered if he'd ever be able to walk away from her. He doubted it. No, he didn't doubt it. He *knew* he wouldn't. When the twenty-four hours were up, he'd go to the police with her, he'd help her find an attorney, and he'd call Stanley and see if *he* could help her in some way.

What scared him was that he didn't know just how he could protect her once she was arrested. And Lincoln... He believed there was a man, the fat man he'd seen coming out of her room, but where he fitted into all this was a mystery. He wanted to believe her story, but . . .

He saw Alex knocking on the glass door; then the woman crossed and opened it. After a minute she moved back and let Alex step inside. Through the glass, Mike watched Alex talking rapidly to the heavyset blond woman, and for a minute he thought Alex was drawing a blank again. Then she began to nod. She held her hand about six inches above her own head, then patted her stomach. *A fat man,* he could almost hear her saying.

The woman hesitated, let the door swing shut, then went to sit behind a desk by the front windows. She listened intently to Alex, who was leaning forward, her hands braced on the desktop. Then the blonde reached for a book, flipped through it, stopped and turned it toward Alex. She pointed to something. Alex leaned forward, intently studying the page, then straightened.

She was talking quickly again; then the blonde stood and took the book into a back room. Alex stayed where she was, standing very still and staring after the woman. When the blonde came back, Alex all but lunged forward to take a piece of paper from her. They exchanged a quick handshake; then Alex walked out of the building. When she reached the parking lot, she broke into a dead run.

In a second she was climbing into the car, and Mike had only an instant to think how beautiful she looked before she all but dove at him. "I found him! I found him!" she gasped and hugged Mike so tightly that he was stunned. He felt the console cut into his leg; then Alex was sitting back. "She knew him! His name's Peter Jessop. He lives around Las Vegas, she didn't know where, but he dabbles in real estate. He's involved in something big right now, some development thing." She held out the paper, a grainy copy of a black-and-white picture. "He's a land developer, and he has his real-estate license. This is a picture from the book of agents she had. Peter Jessop, aka Lincoln."

He took the picture and stared at the face of the man he'd seen at Alex's room, but this time the man was wearing a tuxedo, with a jacket that barely met across his ample middle. "Where is he?"

That made the smile falter a bit. "I don't know. She says she hasn't seen him anywhere for about a week." She seemed to deflate a bit with her admission that Jessop wasn't immediately within reach. "He's not listed, but she showed me this picture, and even though it's a bit blurry, it's him."

Mike wanted to tell Alex that she'd gotten more information than he would have expected, but instead he turned away from the sight of her and started the car. "I can find out where he lives. That's the easy part."

He drove down the street to a small shopping center and pulled into the parking lot. Then he got out and walked to the pizza parlor and went directly to a pay phone near the doors. He took so long making what looked like two calls that Alex was on edge by the time he got back to the car.

"Peter Jessop lives north of here, five miles beyond a bend in the road called Golden Springs. He's on the Anything Goes ranch, and the word is he's been in Arizona for a week." He let the last part sink in before he added, "He's supposed to be staying at a friend's place somewhere outside Phoenix."

Alex clasped her hands tightly on her lap. "Anything else?"

"Not much. Nothing you'll want to hear."

"Tell me."

"He's important in his own way, a gambler, but not a big loser."

"That could be a link to the gem dealer," she said quickly, grabbing at any glimmer of hope.

"Maybe, but his luck's always pretty good. He's not in hock to anyone as far as my contact knows. And he recently bought a huge chunk of land to the south, land that's being rezoned for commercial use. He's not loved by one and all, but he's not hated, either." He studied her from under lowered lids. "Now, the big question is—why would he set you up? What would he have against you?"

"I don't know." But she knew he had a fortune in uncut diamonds. And she had nothing except the money he'd given her, money she'd stuffed back in her pocket and never looked at again. And the probability of being sent to prison. "No one's going to believe my story," she said. "So I'll have to have proof before I go to the police."

"What proof? This picture?"

"No, I'm going to find his ranch. *I* know he's not in Arizona—at least that he's been around here in the last week. I need some real proof of what he did. If I can walk into the police station with something solid, maybe they'll believe my story."

Mike grabbed Alex by the arm, and the picture of Jessop fell onto the console. "You're crazy, and this has gone far enough. You know who the fat man is. If he's your partner and double-crossed you, I'm sorry, but I can't let you go after him like that. And if he's an innocent party whom you've decided to drag into this . . ."

"An innocent party like you?" she asked through clenched teeth.

"I'm far from innocent," he muttered, his hold tightening to hover just this side of real pain.

"And far from being dragged into this against your will, too," she added, her eyes burning. "You can get off the merry-go-round right here, Mike. Just forget you ever knew me. I'll take care of Jessop and get myself out of this. I've gotten out of every other scrape in my life by myself. I'm a survivor."

He looked into her eyes, and he felt a solid hatred for the man who was probably her father. Whatever the reasons, Alex had been totally alone in her life. But not anymore. Not as long as he was around. And in that instant, without a shred of real proof, he knew that Alex wasn't lying about the robbery. She wasn't lying about being alone, or being a survivor. "He really set you up, didn't he?"

She nodded, the trembling motion more eloquent than any words could have been.

"All right, then. Count me in. Let's go to the police and tell them about Jessop."

"Don't you understand that I can't? Not without proof, something to back my story." She spread her small hands. "My word doesn't mean anything. It never has. I'm no-body."

Mike saw her unsteadiness and reached out to hold her. He needed the contact, too. "No you aren't, Alex," he assured her as he held her tightly to him. He inhaled the sweetness of the perfume that clung to her hair and felt as if he'd been joined to her forever. "I'm here for you."

He felt her start to shake, and he thought she was crying. But as he held her back, he was shocked to see she was laughing. Her eyes were overly bright, but it was definitely laughter coming from her softly parted lips.

"What's so funny?" he asked, confused, as he framed her face with his hands.

"You," she managed in a choked voice.

"Me?"

Her laughter faltered. "You. I give you all these logical explanations and you don't believe me. Then all I do is tell you I'm going after Jessop and you're suddenly on my side."

A tear slipped down her cheek, and Mike gently smoothed it off her silky skin with the ball of his thumb. "I might not always have believed you, but I've always been on your side," he said softly, a bit in awe at the intensity of his feelings for her.

"Thank you," she whispered and covered his hands with hers as she leaned toward him. When her lips touched his, Mike felt as if he'd suddenly found his center, the core of his existence. His soul settled, knowing that Alex was what he wanted.

When she drew back, he let her go, and he didn't reach out for her, even though the urge to do so all but choked him. He knew himself better than to chance it. If he touched her again, he wouldn't let go of her. "You're welcome," he said, her taste still on his lips.

She moved farther from him, and the gathering shadows of the coming night softly blurred her features. "Mike, I promise, the first thing I'll do when I get my life straightened out is call you."

"No, you won't." He held the steering wheel because he didn't know what to do with his hands. But he did know he wasn't letting her walk away, even for a little while. "I'm staying with you. We'll call Gil to find out the best way to handle this."

She shook her head. "No, I'll do this my way. I don't want you getting mixed up in this any further. I've got a lead. I know where Jessop lives, so that's where I'm going."

"What?"

"I'll go out to his ranch and try to figure out what's going on. With any luck, I'll find something that will prove what he did."

He studied her narrowly. "How do you plan to do that? Just walk up and ask him for proof that he set you up, that he's the one who took the jewels?"

"I don't know yet. But I'll figure it out. With any luck, he'll be sloppy, he'll leave evidence.... Maybe even the diamonds are there with him." She licked her lips and smiled weakly. "If there's one thing I can do, and do well, Mike, it's get into a place without any one knowing until it's too late."

The idea of what she was suggesting made his breath catch. "That's breaking and entering."

"So? I'm already wanted for that plus grand theft."

"And if there's nothing there, no Jessop, no jewels, no clues?"

"Then I'll go after him in Arizona. I don't have a choice."

He ran a hand roughly over his face, then exhaled as he looked back at Alex in the shadows. "You're determined, aren't you?"

"Yes."

It didn't take more than a heartbeat before he laid every-thing he'd worked for since getting out of prison on the line. "I'm coming with you."

Chapter 14

The partial moon and scattered stars cast an eerie glow over Peter Jessop's ranch. The Anything Goes sprawled over hundreds of sage-covered acres on either side of a deserted two-lane road. Through the six-foot-high chain-link fence topped with barbed wire, Alex could see open fields far off to the right; ahead of where she and Mike stood, there was a stand of orange trees, their sweetness heavy in the night heat. At the end of a sweeping drive that led from main gates fashioned like a huge golden horseshoe, was the main house, high on a hill in the distance. Low outside lights bathed the house in a subdued glow, showing a single-story home with a heavy tile roof and manicured grounds.

Alex stared at the house. She couldn't see any movement at all. Nothing stirred at the house. The night was still, and not a car came down the road.

"The old man at the gas station wasn't kidding, was he?" she said in a whisper, her eyes beginning to burn from trying to make out anything through the darkness. "This place really is isolated, and look at that fence."

"It doesn't look like typical ranch fencing," Mike said, matching her hushed tones. "And it also doesn't look like anyone's home."

The ranch was well past Hank's Oasis, and she and Mike had found it only after stopping at a small gas station about five miles back. The owner had told them, "Go straight for three miles, then swing a left by the big signs for Golden Creek. Go five miles down the road. Jessop's is the only place you'll come to. In fact, it's the only place on that road until you get over the rise and into sheep country. You can't miss it. They've got a big, gold horseshoe gate at the main entrance."

They'd found the horseshoe gate, driven past it, then found this place, a gate marked Deliveries. Mike had parked out of sight behind a stand of cactus on the far side of the road; then they'd crossed to the fence to get a better look at Jessop's home.

Alex had felt her heart sink when she'd realized the place looked deserted. But she had no where else to go, no other lead to follow. Now she moved back from the fence to study the delivery gate. It was chain link swung inward and was the same height as the fence. It was also cross-framed with metal trussing and had a hasp fastened with a heavy chain and padlock. A box by the side post was closed. Probably an intercom. She scanned the surrounding area as far as she could see into the darkness. No cameras. No real security. She looked back at the distant house.

"Alex?"

"What?" she asked, keeping her voice as low as Mike's.

"Do you know what you're going to do?"

"Get inside."

"That's it?"

"Get inside and look for anything to prove my story."

He motioned to the house. "It's huge. Where do we start?"

"I'll find the study, or the library, or his office, if he has one."

"Have you thought about why he did this to you?"

She *had* wondered about that, then realized that he hadn't done anything to *her,* per se. She had just been a means to an end. She had a unique ability that he'd exploited. Yet she knew there had to be some reason why he wanted the diamonds, although, with what she knew about him, it didn't seem as if he would need the money. She looked at Mike, his features stark in the moonlight. "Why do *you* think he set me up?"

Mike shrugged, a sharp movement that tugged at the cotton of his shirt. "The question of the year. The man owns enough of Las Vegas to be considered rich. Maybe it was all a game, or the product of a crazy bet, or maybe he gets off doing things like this. Maybe it's a rush for him."

A rush? *Real estate. That's gambling. Laying everything on the table and coming out on top—one way or another. It's a real rush.* Lincoln's words echoed through her mind. "No, it's something to do with the land, with real estate," she breathed. "I don't know what, but I'll find out if I can get in there."

"How do we get inside?"

"There is no *we*, Mike, just *me*." She spoke in an intense whisper. "You said it yourself. This is breaking and entering. You can't afford to get messed up with that. You could be arrested, and even though you were innocent the first time, you wouldn't be this time. I can't let you do that."

"Sorry. It isn't up to you to let me do anything. I'm coming with you. You can't stop me."

"You'd risk prison for me?" she asked, barely able to form the question.

"I'd risk a lot more if anything happened to you," he said simply. "I can't take that chance."

Her heart lurched in her chest. He would do that for her? He would put everything on the line? Their time had been so short and so intense, there had been so many lies, yet so much love. Love? She looked up at him, stunned by the simple realization that she loved Michael Conti.

"I'm coming," Mike whispered when she didn't say anything. He came closer, close enough for her to feel the
warmth of his breath brush her face. "No arguments."

The realization that love was exactly what she felt for
Mike burned through her. A need to share it, to shout it into
the night, up to the moon in the sky, all but overwhelmed
her. *I love you!* she wanted to say, to hear it echo around the
two of them. But she didn't. She couldn't. Not now, when
she had disaster hanging over her head. When she knew she
could go to prison. "Mike, I . . ."

He reached out, and his hand rested on her shoulder. "We
don't have time to argue this, Alex."

"No, we don't," she breathed, praying there would be
time when this was settled.

"How do we get in?" he asked.

"Over the fence." Focus, focus, she told herself. She had
to think about what needed to be done, but with Mike
touching her, she could barely concentrate on breathing.

He looked up at the top of the fence and let go of her to
point to the barbed-wire strands. "Over that?"

"Can you think of anything we could throw over it for
protection?" she asked, never taking her eyes off him.

"Not a thing," he whispered. "Unless I give you the shirt
off my back."

That idea made her mouth almost dry. "No, not thick
enough," she murmured.

"Just a minute." He ran across the road to where the car
was hidden behind the cactus, and in less than a minute he
returned with a loose floor mat. "Thick enough?"

"Perfect," she said.

"You're the boss, so just tell me what to do."

"Let's go a bit farther from the gate."

With one hand he held the mat, and with the other he
reached for Alex. His fingers laced through hers, the action
as familiar as if they'd been doing it forever. Alex walked
through the heat of the night with him, her heart pounding
not only from the fear and excitement of getting this close
to Jessop, but from her newfound knowledge. Yes, love. It

felt right. She'd never believed in love at first sight, but she knew that was exactly what had happened.

"How often have you done something like this?" he asked.

"Never."

"A first?"

Just like falling in love, she thought, but simply echoed, "A first." There would be so much to say when this was done. The whole truth, without the need for stories and hedging. A new experience, as new as this love she felt for him. As new as this fear of prison, too. Prison.

She stopped and let go of Mike. The trees came almost to the fence here. "Here," she whispered. She pointed to the top of the fence. "Toss that mat up and over the barbed wire."

Mike lifted the thick mat, then flopped it over the triple strands of sharp wire. He looked at Alex. "One other thing, before we plunge headlong into this."

She looked at him and waited.

But he didn't say a thing. Instead, he pulled her to him. For a precious minute she simply let herself lean on him, let his essence seep into her being. If this was what was meant by two becoming one, she fully understood it. She felt complete and whole—finally.

Then he kissed her, a hard, fierce kiss that seemed to forge a bond made of steel. Almost as quickly, he was setting her away. "We're going to talk, really talk, as soon as this is done," he said in a husky voice. "All right?"

"Promise," she whispered.

He brushed her cheek with the tips of his fingers, then moved back. "Let me go first, and I can help you over."

She shook her head and reached for the cold metal wire. "I've gone over higher walls than this," she said as she pulled herself up and shoved the toe of her tennis shoes into the mesh. With little effort, she was at the top, slipping over and landing softly on the dusty ground on the other side.

Mike hurried after her, then dropped down beside her. "The mat?" he whispered by her ear.

"Leave it. We might need it in a hurry." She squinted into the distance, trying to see a way through the trees.

"This way," she said softly, pointing toward an irrigation path that led away from the fence.

They hurried through the trees and found a gravel drive that looked like a route for truck deliveries. Staying just inside the cover of the trees, they followed it, stepping over the snaking dark shapes of irrigation pipes along the way.

When the trees thinned, Alex stopped and swiped at the perspiration that trickled down her face. The heat was tremendously oppressive now, and the sweetness of the orange blossoms made the night seem heavy. Ahead was a scattering of trees and beyond them, the house. She motioned to Mike that she was going to go first; then she led the way across spongy ground still crisscrossed with irrigation pipes.

As they came to the last of the trees, Alex looked out at a small, tree-strewn expanse of thick lawn. The ground lights bathed the rough brick walls of the house in softness, and she could make out one light in a room shaded by the trees.

Alex turned to Mike and whispered, "Wait here. I want to look inside, where the light is. I'll see if anyone's there, and if there's a security system. If there isn't a digital alarm, and there isn't anyone in the room, I won't have any trouble getting in. If I'm not out in ten minutes—"

"No." The single word was spoken against her cheek; then his lips caressed her ear. "Together," he said softly.

"You're crazy, you know," she said, her voice unsteady.

"I know," he agreed in a whisper and kissed her ear. "Get the hell back here if there's an alarm. If not, signal to me."

Alex touched Mike lightly on the check, needing that fleeting contact to ground herself. Then she turned and headed for the house. When she reached the wall, she pressed close to the rough surface in the shadows of the trees and inched toward the nearest window, then reached to touch the heavy wooden frame with the tips of her fingers. No wires, no raised areas to indicate sensors.

She cautiously looked around the side of the window, and when she didn't see any movement inside, she stepped even closer. She cupped her hands on the cool glass and looked inside, into a den of sorts. Bookshelves lined two walls; maps covered the others. A huge desk stood right under the window against the wall, with a gooseneckeded lamp giving off a low glow, and blueprints were rolled and stacked to one side.

French doors farther down looked like the best way to get inside, so Alex hurried over to them, felt around the knob, then slowly turned it. It clicked, and she pulled the door open. She stared into the room; then, satisfied that there weren't any movement sensors, she turned to where she knew Mike was hiding and motioned, but she couldn't see a thing. For a split second she felt completely alone, and hated the feeling. Then Mike was with her, his body close enough for her to feel his heat and his hand on her arm. "I'm impressed," he whispered, looking at the open door.

She bit her lip hard, almost afraid to have one person be so terribly important to her. Yet pleased. God, it felt good to know someone was there, that someone cared enough to stick with her.

He motioned for her to go in first, and she quickly stepped into the silent room. Hard tiles met her feet, and the air was cool and welcome. Mike moved behind her silently, closed the door, then stood by her side in the silence. He touched her shoulder, a comforting gesture, and bent close to her ear.

"I'll keep an eye for anyone coming," he said. "You do the looking." Then he moved silently across the small room to the closed door. He leaned against it with one shoulder, and Alex realized that he was actually pressing his ear to the heavy wood. He listened intently, then gave her the thumbs-up sign.

Quickly, she began to search the room, starting at the desk. She sorted through the papers and blueprints, but she didn't understand any of them. She rolled them back up, pushed them to one side, then picked up an address book. Flipping through it, she found it filled with names. One had an address in Arizona. With a shrug, she pushed the small book into her back pocket. Then she tried the drawers one by one. Paper, envelopes, matches, mail addressed to Peter Jessop. Clutter. Nothing more.

She looked around, then went to the shelves. She looked for wires of any sort in the walls, books that looked out of place—too new or too old—or pictures that sat too far from the wall. Nothing struck her right away. One by one she tugged at the books, then caught her breath when she tried to pull out an impressive leather-bound copy of *Real Estate Laws of Nevada*. She heard a click, and the book swung out, attached to a part of the shelf. Alex stared at Peter Jessop's safe.

She turned to tell Mike, but didn't have a chance, because he looked at her and pointed to the door. "Someone's in the house and coming this way," he hissed.

Before Alex could think of what to do, Mike was right by her. He motioned to the knee space under the desk. "Get under there, as close as you can to the wall. You're small enough."

"What about you?" she whispered.

He looked around. "I'll be okay. Just get in there."

Quickly, Alex shut the safe and scrambled under the heavy desk, getting as far back as possible. She pressed against the cold wall and held her breath. All she could see were Mike's feet as he crossed and stood to one side of the door. Then she understood what he was doing. And he'd be fine—as long as the door swung open and stayed that way.

Right then it did open, slowly, swinging back to hide Mike. Alex stared at white loafers under black, shiny slacks coming into the room; then the owner stopped. She heard a hissing, then caught the pungency of cigarette smoke in the air. Jessop. No one else wore white loafers and smoked those terrible cigarettes. Without swinging the door shut, he went to the left, to the bookshelves. She heard a soft thump and vague clicking. The safe being opened.

She closed her eyes tightly, willing herself not to gasp for air to compensate for the thundering rhythm of her heart. She concentrated, listening to each action. A three-number combination, a simple safe. There was a soft thud and then a click, and she knew the book had been snapped back into place.

She looked toward Jessop as he walked to the desk and dropped heavily into the chair. She heard the sound of the phone being dialed; then the chair tipped back on two legs, and one hand hung low over the arm. The cigarette, caught between pudgy fingers decorated with gold rings, smoldered not more than two feet from Alex.

"It's me. I can't come until tomorrow. I went all the way in and made the call, then he tells me we can't do the exchange until tomorrow."

The cigarette lifted out of sight, and a low hissing echoed in the stillness, then, "Nine tomorrow morning." The chair hit the floor with a thud, and the loafers were planted firmly on the floor in front of Alex. "I put the stuff away, but I hate the waiting. This wasn't the plan, and—"

His voice stopped abruptly; then he snapped, "Bull! I had this set up so pretty. Then it gets all screwed up. That girl got into the suite without a hitch, and she gave me diamonds. Now all I have to do is make the exchange, get the money, and it's done."

There was a long pause; then a conciliatory tone came into Jessop's voice. "Sure, sure. It'll be there under the wire. Barely. Don't worry." The receiver hit the cradle with a crack. "Damn," Jessop muttered and stood.

Alex found herself willing the fat man to leave, but he stayed. He stood very still in front of the desk; then she heard the rustle of paper, things being lifted, then set down again. He began to hum tunelessly, then finally stopped with a sigh.

Get out of here, she wanted to say as he moved again to the safe. She heard him open it, then close it. Finally he walked to the door and out into the hall. Alex waited a few seconds after the door clicked shut before she scooted out from under the desk. She took one step toward Mike, who was still in the same place, then stopped dead when the door flew open without warning.

"Well, well, what do we have here?" Peter Jessop said. He was holding a small handgun, and it was pointed right at Alex's middle.

Chapter 15

The sight of Jessop robbed Alex of the ability to do little more than stare.

"So, set a trap and catch a rat," the fat man said as smoke from his cigarette drifted out of his nose and mouth.

It took all her will not to look right at Mike, hidden from Jessop by the partially open door. Instead she forced herself to stand her ground, look Jessop in the eye and talk.

"Did you think I'd let you set me up, then just go off like a lamb to the slaughter?"

"Actually, I considered the fact that you could pull some trick out of your bag and get out from under the whole thing. I just didn't know one of those tricks would be finding me and breaking into my house." He smiled. "I could shoot you right now and tell the police I found you vandalizing my office."

"Sh-shoot me?" she stammered, aware of Mike moving slowly behind Jessop. But she couldn't tell what he was doing without looking right at him. "How did you know I was in here?" she asked.

His smile turned sly. "That perfume of yours. I could smell it when I got off the phone." He flicked the gun toward the desk. "And everything has its place here. Especially on my desk. You shouldn't have taken what wasn't yours." Then he laughed, a rough sound that grated on Alex's nerves. "I figured I'd get this gun out of the safe, then leave and give you enough time to come out of hiding."

Mike was moving, coming up behind Jessop silently. Look at Jessop, not at Mike, she told herself. And keep talking. "So, you caught me. What are you going to do?" she asked, hugging her arms tightly around her middle.

He sighed, then shook his head. "I could shoot a thief, as I said before, but to tell you the truth, it's against my nature to hurt a woman. Then I have to consider the bigger question of self-preservation. That's something that can't be underestimated." He took a long drag on the cigarette. "Sorry. But if it comes to you surviving or me, it's got to be me. That's the way it is. But first I want my address book back."

Mike was two feet from Jessop.

"You understand, don't you, little lady?" Jessop said, the gun leveled at Alex.

A foot from Jessop.

"Now give me that address book."

Then Mike moved so swiftly that Alex wasn't quite certain what he was doing until he had one arm around Jessop's neck and the fat man's hand twisted up between his shoulder blades. The cigarette fell to the floor, and the gun skittered across the hard tile. It hit the toe of Alex's running shoe.

"Wh-what?" Jessop sputtered, his face a brilliant shade of crimson.

"Alex, get the gun," Mike said.

She stooped and picked up the small gun. Then she raised it, annoyed that her hands were shaking so badly. "All...all right. Now it's a matter of my survival," she said to Jessop. "You understand, don't you?"

"You bi—" Jessop gasped when Mike twisted his arm higher.

"Watch your language," Mike said, then let go of Jessop so quickly that the fat man staggered sideways before he could get his balance. Mike ground out the smoldering cigarette on the tile, then came around to stand by Alex and take the gun from her hand.

Jessop's eyes darted from Mike to Alex, then back to Mike. He rubbed at his shoulder, and his breathing sounded labored. "I don't know who you are, but..."

"I'll call the police," Alex breathed, afraid, yet knowing she had to make the call.

Jessop took a half step toward Alex, but Mike stopped him immediately. "Don't move, Jessop. I didn't check to see if this gun's loaded, but I'll bet your life it is."

Stopping dead in his tracks, the fat man dropped his hands to his sides and curled them into fists. "It's loaded. Go easy with it," he muttered.

"You stay where you are."

"Hold off on calling the police." Jessop held out both hands palms up, and they were shaking almost as much as Alex's were. "Listen to me, both of you. We can work a deal. This whole thing's gotten out of hand. There's no reason to call the cops. No one needs to get hurt."

"Oh?" Alex asked. "Just a minute ago you were going to kill me."

"No I wasn't. I was just going to scare you, little lady. I'm no killer. God, I'm not even a thief. That's why I needed you."

Alex frowned at him. "Why *did* you pick me?"

"I needed the diamonds, and I certainly couldn't have pulled off the robbery myself, and God knows I didn't want some thug helping me."

"But..."

He exhaled heavily, his shirt stained with sweat at his underarms and neck. "No one was going to get hurt...ever. The man you took the diamonds from, Jarkowski, I know him. God, I've played poker with him for more than two years whenever he came into town. He'd get his girlfriend, and we'd have parties, and we'd gamble. Not much money involved, but a good time. Then my life's going down the tubes, and he tells me about this big deal he's doing for his company. A million-five in diamonds. Uncut. Easy to fence for at least fifty cents on the dollar. A godsend, a real godsend. The timing was perfect."

He was talking so fast that Alex was having trouble catching every word. "I made sure he was insured, that he wouldn't lose his job. It's the first time he's ever had problems in ten years with the company. He's not out anything. It wasn't life and death to him like it was with me. Damn it, I need the money!"

"From what I've heard," Mike said, "you own enough of Las Vegas never to worry about money again."

Jessop frowned, the expression a mixture of pain and disgust. "I've mortgaged everything to buy a chunk of land south of the Strip. I got an inside tip that it's going to be rezoned and a mall put in. I got it dirt cheap, just three million, but I had to mortgage everything to get it. Now the zoning's taking longer than I thought it would." He tugged at the collar of his shirt. "Hell, give me another two months, and when the zoning comes through, I'll make it big. I'll win on the gamble, but right now I've got interest payments due. I'm not going to lose everything, not when I'm this close.

"All I've got to do is meet the interest payments to buy time, enough time for the zoning to be finalized and for the land to sell for ten times what I paid for it."

The rush of gambling on land? That was what he'd said. "You've done all this for some piece of land?"

He looked at Alex as if she were crazy. "Some piece of land? For thirty million dollars. That's why I did it. I'm meeting a guy tomorrow who'll give me fifty cents on the dollar, seven hundred and fifty thousand, for those stones. Uncut diamonds are virtually untraceable. They're as good as gold. And it was all working out. I can make the payments tomorrow and survive while . . ."

"...Alex goes to jail?" Mike finished in a low, rough voice.

Jessop shook his head nervously. "Naw. She wouldn't have done time. She'd be off scot-free as soon as the cops figured out that she was telling the truth. Her work sounds strange, checking security systems from the inside out, but she could have proven it. She could have gotten satisfied customers to vouch for her. No one would have been hurt. Insurance will take care of Jarkowski's company, and the little lady got paid really good for her trouble. I even gave her a bonus."

"It would just be a minor inconvenience for her, is that it?" Mike asked.

"Exactly. Still can be. And we can all get on with our lives. Nothing big. No problems. If you'll just listen to reason." He took a hissing breath and tugged at his collar, popping the two top buttons open. "Listen to me, mister. I don't know who you are, but we can come to some agreement. How about if I offer each of you a percentage of the profits on the land when it's sold? One percent each of at least thirty million could fix you both up for quite a while."

Alex looked at Mike, then back to Jessop. The stillness in the room was nerve-racking.

"All right," Jessop finally said. "Five percent each."

"And we're supposed to trust you?" Mike asked. "Is your word good?"

The sarcasm was heavy, and Jessop colored. "I...I could make a show of good faith. How about that?"

"Good faith?" Mike asked.

"What would you be happy with?"

Alex had a sudden idea and spoke up before Mike could say anything. "How about a written confession?"

"God, woman, you're crazy," Jessop sputtered. "I'm not about to—"

"The show of good faith was your idea," she pointed out, aware of the way Mike was staring at her. "I'll just hold on to the confession."

The fat man stared at her. "Why don't I just take out an ad?" he asked sarcastically.

"Alex?" Mike said, reaching out with his free hand to touch her arm. "You can't..."

She looked right at him, his green eyes meeting her gaze. "Trust me, Mike. I know what I'm doing," she said.

She could almost see him thinking, remembering his doubts about her, the lies she'd told. She knew he didn't have any real reason to trust her, but she hoped he would. "Go ahead," he finally said.

"Thank you," she breathed.

Mike motioned Jessop to the desk with the gun. "Sit over there and do what the lady says, or the news will be reporting that they just found your body."

The fat man glared at Alex. "You can't—"

"No, but Mike can. He has the gun," Alex said, and she moved back to let the man pass her. With a crude oath, Jessop walked to the desk and sank down heavily into the chair, then reached for a drawer. "Hold it, Jessop," Mike said. "Just tell Alex what you need and she'll find it."

The fat man looked at the gun still on him, then at Mike, but he spoke to Alex. "Paper's in the top right drawer. Pen's in there, too."

Alex moved past Mike, making sure not to block the direct line between Jessop and the gun, and she pulled open the drawer. She took out a sheet of paper with the heading *Anything Goes* at the top, then a pen from the side of the drawer. She laid both on the desk near Jessop's hand.

Jessop took out a handkerchief from his pocket and dabbed at his forehead. "What do you want me to write?" he asked Alex.

"Just put down the truth."

"And keep Alex's name out of it," Mike added.

Jessop hesitated. "How do I do that?" he asked.

Alex wanted to know, too. That and why Mike was making such a request. But she didn't ask. If Mike could trust her, she could trust him.

"Figure that out yourself," Mike murmured and motioned sharply with the gun. "Just do it."

Jessop picked up the pen and began to scribble furiously on the white sheet of paper. When he sat back, the page was almost full. "There. Good enough?"

"Alex, read it and see if it's what you want."

She grabbed the paper, read it quickly, then looked at Mike. "Everything's here except why he did it."

"Finish it off, Mr. Jessop, then date it and sign it—legibly," Mike said.

Jessop let out a hissing sigh, then began to write again when Alex laid the paper in front of him. "Is that enough?" he asked as he finally sat back.

Alex looked down at the sheet and read the addition. "Fine," she murmured.

"All right," Jessop said to her. "Take it, and within the next two months—"

Alex looked at Mike. "Now I'll call the police."

Jessop struggled to get up, but Mike was there before the other man could make it to his feet. Mike thrust him backward into the chair. "You said this is loaded," he said, standing over the man. "Should I test it to see if you're lying?"

Jessop glowered up at Mike and grabbed the hankie that had landed on the desk. He wiped his face nervously, but didn't say a thing.

Mike spoke without looking at Alex. "Look around for some rope or some sort of cord."

The fat man sputtered. "We had a deal."

"I lied," Alex said, then looked at Mike with a smile. "That's excusable, isn't it?"

"Very excusable," he said, his gaze meeting hers in an intimate acknowledgement of what was growing between them.

Alex had to force herself to break the contact. "I'll find some rope." She remembered seeing something in the bottom drawer. Quickly she took out a roll of nylon twine. "How about this?"

He took it without looking away from Jessop. Then he handed Alex the gun. "Keep this on him, and if he even looks like he's going to try anything, shoot."

"I've never..."

"Just squeeze the trigger. I don't care where you hit him." He looked down at Jessop. "Push your chair back from the desk."

"What?"

"Do it, and don't get up."

Jessop skidded back until he was about five feet from the desk. Mike tested the twine, then went around behind Jessop and tugged the fat man's arms back behind the chair. Then he tied each leg to the chair.

"You can't do this, you damned lunatic! You're ruining everything. Who the hell do you think you are?"

Mike straightened up and stared down at Jessop. Then he took the man's handkerchief and jammed the linen in his mouth. "The name is Robie. Mr. John Robie," he said and cast Alex a slanting glance. "Isn't that right?"

"Sure."

"Keep that gun on him," Mike said as he crossed to the desk and reached for the phone. Alex moved closer to the desk, uncomfortable with the way Jessop was glaring at her. But he was securely tied up, and a written confession was on the desk. It seemed as if everything was going to be all right after all. She just had to face the police.

Mike punched in the long-distance number for Stanley. After only one ring the line was picked up. "Yes?"

"I need to talk to him."

"He'll call you back in one minute. What's your number?"

Mike read it off the phone, then dropped the receiver back in place.

He turned to Alex. So much to say, so much to explain. When this was finally over, then... He reached for the phone when it rang, but he didn't say a thing until he heard Stanley.

"Conti, is that you?"

"Yes."

"Where have you been? I've been calling your number for hours!"

"Things have been—"

"Later. Everything about the girl checks out. I need her here. I've got everything waiting, but—"

"Listen to me," Mike interrupted, then quickly told Stanley everything that had happened. "What do you want me to do now?" he finished.

There was a pause, then Stanley spoke quickly. "Get out of there. Leave everything the way it is. Make sure this Jessop is secured, and that the confession is on the desk out of his reach. Then get out."

"No problem, but—"

"Exactly where are the diamonds?"

"Behind a stack of books on the shelf behind the desk. In a wall safe."

"Open or closed?"

"Closed."

"Any way to get it open?"

Mike looked at Alex, her eyes wide with confusion. "Can you open that safe?"

"I could try."

"Yes, we can get it open," he said into the phone.

"All right. Open it, then get out. But don't go back to the hotel. Have you got a place you can get to where no one will find you?"

Mike had the perfect spot in mind. "Sure."

"Go there. Then call me as soon as you arrive. Whatever you do, get out without being seen, then—"

"What about Alex?"

"Let me worry about her, Mike. You just get her to safety, make sure you don't leave any prints and let me take care of everything else."

"The hotel?"

"They'll forget you two ever existed. Call as soon as you can," he said, then hung up.

Mike put the phone back in place, then looked at Alex.
"Open the safe."

"Who was that?"

"I trusted you. Now you trust me," he said. "We don't
have much time. The safe needs to be open before we get out
of here."

Mutely she nodded, then moved slowly, as if she were
having trouble putting one foot in front of the other. Shock
was setting in.

She looked pale, delicate, and he loved her. The idea came
of its own accord and settled deep in his soul. And he wasn't
a bit shocked. Yes, love. Four days and he'd fallen so hard
for this woman that she could literally take his breath away.
When she came close, he reached out. He touched her, badly
needing the contact. "As quickly as you can. All right?"

Alex nodded without saying a word, then went to the
shelves. Mike glanced at Jessop and for a minute feared that
the man as going to have a stroke; then he saw the burning
rage in the man's eyes. "It's all survival, Jessop," he muttered and pushed the linen further into the fat man's mouth.
He couldn't resist saying, "And that bit of advice comes
from John Robie."

Mike looked around for something to secure the gag, then
tugged the desk drawer open. Beside the notepaper was a
stack of neatly folded handkerchiefs. "Bingo," Mike whispered, then took out two of the linen squares and tied one
around Jessop's mouth.

Then he unfurled the other one and spoke to Alex, who
hadn't moved. "You do the safe, and I'll wipe our prints off
everything in here."

When he looked back at Alex after he'd wiped the door
and the shelves, the door knob and the desk, she was staring at Jessop, the safe open, the wooden box in her hands.
"Alex?"

She looked up at him. "What are we going to do?" she
asked in a tight, small voice.

"Get out of here," Mike said and went to her. He took
the box, wiped it off with the handkerchief, then put it back

in the safe. Taking Alex by the arm, he looked back at Jessop. "We're going to ride off into the sunset, Jessop, and if you know what's good for you, you'll forget you ever knew Alex."

Jessop struggled against his bonds, his eyes alive with pure hate.

Mike tugged at Alex and led the way to the door. He urged her out into the warm night, then followed. Carefully he reached back inside, wiped the door edges, then tossed the soiled linen back into the room. He grabbed Alex by the hand and ran off into the night with her.

Stanhope walked into the hospital room, knowing his three long-distance calls had set things in motion that would take care of this Jessop and protect Alexandria. Now all he had to do was tell Ian he had a daughter. The decision about the orphanage had been right twenty-seven years ago. He could admit that now. Ian could never have dealt with a child, Meg's child. And the child hadn't been turned over to strangers. She'd had a good life with Elizabeth, and Elizabeth, his own sister, had loved the girl and cared for her. It had been the right decision. Elizabeth had been as much of a mother to her as Meg could have been.

He looked at the pale man in the bed, met his dark-eyed gaze and took a deep breath. Would Ian understand? That didn't matter now, he conceded. The truth had to be told.

"Ian," he began, annoyed that his voice was unsteady. "I have something to tell you, something that might make you hate me. I'm past worrying about that now. All that matters is that you survive. It's time you knew the full truth. Twenty-seven years ago..."

There was no time for talk until Alex and Mike were back in the car and heading away from the Anything Goes. She felt stiff and uneasy, filled with questions that needed answers. Finally, when he reached over and touched her hand clenched on her lap, she looked at him.

How she loved him. How confused she was. "Mike, what did you do back there?"

"Got us out without you taking any heat." His hold on her tightened comfortingly. "You're going to get out of this scot-free . . . if things work out."

"Who did you call? It wasn't the police, was it?"

"A friend."

"And . . . ?"

"He's going to take care of everything. I don't know how, but he will. He can make believe you and I never existed."

They had just reached the main highway when they heard a high-pitched siren. Alex looked ahead at flashing lights coming toward them, then three police cars sped past and took the turn onto the road to Jessop's place.

"It seems that Jessop is going to do some time. Deservedly."

"Amen," Alex whispered and held on to Mike. "Where are we going?"

"We need to drop out of sight." He glanced ahead of them. "Then I need to make a call."

"Who to?"

"My friend. He'll tell me what to do next." Mike shifted, taking his hand from Alex's only long enough to put his arm around her shoulders. He pulled her to his side, and even though the console between them bit into her hip, she didn't resist. She rested her head in the hollow of his shoulder and looked out at the night, at the moon slowly being shrouded in mist.

"That's a liar's moon," she said softly, thinking how ironic it was, since the truth was finally coming out. "A real liar's moon."

Hank's Oasis looked the same to Mike, even though his life had undergone changes of dramatic proportions since the previous time they'd been there. Under a sky dominated by streaky clouds that drifted across the face of the moon, Mike drove into the parking lot, then got out and came around for Alex. Taking her hand seemed the most natural thing to do as they walked into the tiny café.

The man behind the counter glanced up, looked blank for a minute, then smiled at them. "You two. How's it going?"

Mike urged Alex forward into the coolness of the dingy room. "We need a bungalow."

"Sure thing," he said with a knowing nod. He reached under the counter and held out a key to Mike. "That's forty bucks."

Mike didn't care what the man thought. He just wanted to be alone with Alex, alone to look at her, to relish having this thing behind them, a solitary place to finally tell the truth...the whole truth. He dug into his pocket, then counted out almost all of his available cash for the man.

"The last one, number 10," the man said.

Mike took the key and nodded. "Thanks."

He took Alex by the arm and went out the back door, the way he'd gone the first time, with the man leading. They walked through the heat, past the cottage they'd been in the first time, and went all the way to the end. Mike unlocked the door, let Alex step past him into the cottage, then followed her. He flipped on the light, then tossed the key onto a low white dresser and closed the door.

This room was about the same as the other one, but the color scheme was blue mixed with pink—and mirrors over the bed reflected back the multihued spread.

Mike put the safety chain on the door, took a deep breath and turned to face Alex.

"I need to make a call. Then we have to talk."

When she simply nodded and stood by the door, he crossed and picked up the phone by the huge bed. He put in his call, then spoke quickly, "What now?"

The other man said simply, "Your number?"

He read it off the phone, then the man on the other end said, "He'll call within the hour. He's taking care of things. Stay there and wait."

Mike hung up and turned as Alex crossed and sank down on the bed, her hands clutched tightly in her lap. "We'll wait for a call. Then I'll know what we'll be doing."

"I don't understand what you did back there, but I really owe you," Alex said softly. "I thought that if I got him to write a confession, the police would believe me more easily. But I wasn't sure. Jessop's smart."

"You're smarter," he said. "The confession was a terrific idea." He exhaled as he ran both hands over his face. "Hopefully by the time tonight's over, that will all be done and past. It's now and the future that I want to talk about, Alex. We talked about truth, absolute truth."

She nodded. "Yes, absolute truth."

He hesitated, then began to pace, needing the movement to keep his thoughts straight. "I haven't told you everything about me. There are things—"

"—about both of us, Mike," she interrupted. "I can't begin to remember what truth I've told you, or what lies. I was told once by my..." She bit her lip, then kept going. "...by Sister Elizabeth at the orphanage something Mark Twain supposedly said. 'If you tell the truth you don't have to remember anything.'" Her small hands clenched and unclenched in her lap. "Well, I can't remember anything anymore. And I'm tired of trying to. Any lies I've told, they haven't been meant to hurt anyone. They were a way of compensating for what I didn't have. But I don't want that to be the case anymore."

"Most people tell lies for very good reasons, Alex." He wished Stanley would call; then the truth could be told. "I know some lies aren't meant to hurt, but maybe to protect, or because a promise has been made not to tell the truth."

"Yes, that too." She blinked rapidly. "Jessop told me no one could know about our deal. That's why I made up lies to tell you. I was working for him. At the time I thought he was legitimate, and a business confidence has to be honored."

"Yes, it has to," he agreed with real feeling.

She looked right at him, her eyes wide but dry. He could see the way her jaw lifted and her hands clasped each other tightly. "I need to tell you things, to make things clear. Then you can forget anything else I've ever told you."

When he would have objected, she stopped him with one word. "Please."

Mike nodded, pushing his hands into his pockets, and leaned back against the wall by the door. "Go ahead."

He watched her carefully and listened to her low, halting words and he knew that she was stripping herself to her soul for him. She trusted him enough to tell him about her loneliness, her nights of crying herself to sleep, her wishing for a family. She told him about Elizabeth, Stanley's sister, who had obviously loved her a lot. At least Alex had had that much. She told him about girls who came and went, adopted or claimed by distant family members.

What she didn't tell him, but he knew anyway, was about a time when she had decided to survive on her own, to do whatever it took to get by. And his love for her deepened incredibly. This awareness of her hadn't taken years to take shape. It had burst into his existence, full and completely formed—incredibly perfect.

He felt tears burn his eyes as he watched Alex, and he grieved for lost years, for things not realized. An anger burned in him directed at the quirk of fate that had kept her father from her, that had kept that father from loving her and caring for her and being there for her.

Would she understand why that secret had been kept from her? Would she understand why he hadn't been able to tell her once he had known? But he knew that wasn't the real question. The real question was, would she still want him in her world when she found out she wasn't alone? That she had the family she'd longed for? He wasn't certain, but he knew she had to be told the truth. He glanced at the telephone, willing it to ring, but it remained silent as Alex kept talking.

"When Sister Elizabeth died, I didn't want to stay at St. Thomas's any longer. My 'family' was gone—all gone. So I headed down to Los Angeles. You know the rest."

She stared up at him expectantly, and he let himself go to her and reach out, taking her cool hands in his to gently tug her to her feet. "Alex." He went to brush her forehead with his lips and thought how much he loved the flavor of her silky skin. "You aren't alone."

He felt a shuddering sigh shake her, and he tilted her face up with one finger until he was looking into her liquid brown eyes. "Not anymore," he breathed.

Her smile came with the suddenness of a flash of summer lightning, brilliant and potent. And it fused her with his soul.

"Do I have you?" she asked, her voice soft but steady.

"Forever," he breathed and bent to taste her lips. "Forever."

That single word meant more to Alex than any other word she'd ever heard. *Forever.* From now on. Never alone. Together. Joy burst inside her, shimmering through her until she thought she would burst from it. She gladly met Mike's kiss as he bent low over her, opening her mouth, inviting him to possess her, to be one with her.

Together they tumbled back onto the bed. His hands on her shot fire through her, and she moaned deep in her throat. Forever. Yes, that was what she wanted, what she'd wanted since first seeing Michael Conti.

"Alex," he breathed against the heat of her throat. "There's something else, something I need to tell you, but I can't. Not yet."

"Then I'll wait," she whispered back through the stillness. "And while I'm waiting all I want . . . all I need . . . is you."

His feelings for Alex edged toward real pain. Their intensity shook him and wouldn't let him go. When she arched toward him, fitting into the lines of his body, he gratefully took her. Forever. He knew that was how long it would take him to get enough of this woman.

And now he needed her, too. He needed her with him, against him, her taste in his mouth, her heat under his hands. Gently, with hands that shook, he began to undo her blouse. He trembled with anticipation, and her hand covered his, helping him undo the last button; then the fabric was pushed aside. One by one the barriers fell, and in the strange light of the room, he looked down at Alex, at the perfection of her face flushed with desire. Then to the line of her throat, the swelling of her small breasts.

She was everything he wanted in life, everything. He felt centered and alive. For the first time he could remember, he knew the meaning of the word commitment. He was hers, and nothing would change that. Ever.

Alex looked at Mike above her and felt herself tense as his eyes roamed over her nakedness. His eyes caressed her as surely as if he'd touched her. With an unsteady hand she touched his cheek, and as the bristling of a new beard brushed the tips of her fingers, she knew that home was encompassed in this man. Life went in patterns; she'd realized that years ago, but then it had been patterns of loneliness and aloneness. And although she and Mike had been through hell, she knew that new patterns were beginning, good patterns.

She helped him free himself of his shirt; then the rest of his clothes landed with hers in a heap on the floor by the huge bed. Side by side, legs entwined, they lay on their sides facing each other, holding each other, neither one daring to move in case reality evaporated in a mist.

This was like a dream, but with heat and strength and aching desire filling her.

"The last time we were here," she whispered, "I thought it was all a dream. I couldn't begin to know what happened or what I dreamed happened."

He stared at her, the green depths of his eyes alive with fire. "Do you remember this?" he asked softly and touched her.

"Y-yes," she gasped, an ache of need heavy in her, but she didn't move.

"This? Do you remember me doing this?" he whispered unsteadily as his hands moved again.

"Yes," she said, biting her lip hard.

"And this?"

"Yes."

"How about this?"

She nodded, her breathing coming in short gasps.

"And...this," he asked, his voice as unsteady as she felt.

"Uh...huh," she managed and closed her eyes, the feelings so intense she felt unable to breath.

"This?"

His voice echoed around her, and she moaned, her head thrown back as she arched toward his hand on her. "Yes," she gasped. "Yes."

"This isn't a dream, love, this is the truth," he vowed.

Yes, the truth, she echoed in her heart, and with stunning ability, Mike showed Alex where dreams ended and reality began.

The telephone rang, shrill and demanding in the gentle softness of the room. Alex stirred beside Mike, her fulfillment as complete as his. Mike knew the call was from Stanley, and that now Alex could finally know the truth. For just a minute he felt uneasy about what would happen when she knew everything; then he admitted the truth wasn't his to play with. She deserved to finally hear it, no matter what the cost to him.

Chapter 16

After a lingering kiss on Alex's flushed cheek, Mike reached for the ringing phone. "Yes?"

"Mike?"

At the sound of Stanley's voice, Mike slowly sat up and held Alex more tightly to his side. He looked into her heavy-lidded eyes and mouthed the words, It's him, then asked into the receiver, "What do we do now?"

"Get the girl to the airport as soon as you can. There's a charter flight waiting for her there. Get her on the plane. Then your job is finished. We'll take over from there."

Mike felt the heat of Alex against him; then her hand spread on his diaphragm. "Where's she going?" he asked.

"To Paris to meet her father. And Mike? One more thing."

Wasn't it enough to feel his whole being sink when he thought of what was about to happen? "What?"

"I'll be using the name Jon Stanhope with the girl. Now put her on the phone. I have a lot I need to say to her. When I'm done, get her to the plane any way you can."

"The mess with Jessop?"

"Taken care of. You and the girl were never in Las Vegas. Now, put her on."

Mike exhaled, closing his eyes for a moment; then he turned to Alex. "The man on the phone is named Jon Stanhope. He has a lot of explaining to do to you."

On impulse, he kissed her, tasting her softly parted lips and letting her fill him. Then he got out of bed and handed her the phone. He waited until she had pushed herself up against the headboard, her dark hair tumbled around her face, and when he heard her say, "Hello," he walked into the bathroom and closed the door.

Alex listened to the man begin to talk, to tell her about a man called Ian Hall, a man who met a woman in Egypt. Her mind took it in, but through a strangely detached haze of shock and disbelief. When he told her that she was the child he'd arranged to have placed in the St. Thomas Home, that his sister had been a nun there, Sister Elizabeth, who had loved that child and taken care of her as if she were her own, the haze began to scatter.

Phrases echoed in her mind. "Your father...in Paris...sick...doesn't know about you. Come to him...be with him...your father."

Alex held the receiver so tightly that her fingers ached, yet she couldn't seem to ease her grip. "My father?" was all she could manage.

"Yes. He needs you. He never knew about you."

"How?" she asked, needing to know how he could not know about her, and Stanhope explained his lies, lies born out of concern, out of caring, even out of love of sorts. But lies that had cost everyone dearly.

"I want you to understand one thing, Alexandria. I had no choice about what I did. There was no way you could have been with Ian, could have been a family, not then. And I made sure that you were taken care of. Elizabeth loved you very much." The man stopped talking, and the line stood open.

Alex stared at Mike as he came back into the room, his hair spiky from a shower, his Levi's his only clothes. Elizabeth had loved her. She knew that was the truth. But Mike... He knew about her; he must always have known.

"Mike?" she asked softly. The question was for the man in the room with her, but the man on the phone answered.

"He found you for me, and stayed with you until we knew you were what Ian needs now. For a while we thought you were..." He cleared his throat. "...a thief... a liar."

Mike stayed on the far side of the room, his gaze never leaving hers, his arms crossed on his bare chest. "And if I had been all of that, a thief and a liar?" she breathed unsteadily into the phone. "What then? Would my... my father ever have known about me?"

"No." The single word came without hesitation. "Mike would have walked away. I regret the deceptions involved, but I've always tried to do what was best for Ian. I'm doing that now. I want him to live." A long pause, then, "Alexandria?"

"What?" she asked, her insides beginning to shake in the strangest way as Mike's image began to blur.

"Mike will get you to the airport, and a private jet will be waiting there for you, along with a passport and a visa. As far as the thing with Jessop—it never happened. You will be in Paris as soon as humanly possible." A hesitation, then three words were said quickly, the most important three words of the conversation, "Will you come?"

She felt like a commodity, something to be used, to be bargained for. If she'd been less than perfect, she would have been shunted aside, discarded completely. She would never have known that she had a father. She hated Stanhope for that; she hated this clipped voice over the phone line telling her about a father who apparently hadn't even known she existed. And Mike? She had no idea what she felt about Mike. There were none of the crystal-clear feelings of just moments ago. None of the certainty she'd felt. Love? Confusion blurred everything, confusion and a growing pain.

"Alexandria?" Stanhope asked again. "Will you come?"

A father? A part of her? A past? A family? "Yes," she said, because she couldn't say anything else. "I'll come." And she held out the phone to Mike. "Your employer wants to talk to you."

Mike moved to take the call, his hand brushing hers, and she drew back so abruptly that the receiver tumbled to the bed. He reached for it, and as he straightened, his green eyes met hers, harsh lines etched deeply at the corners of his mouth. "Alex?"

"It's like something in a bad movie, isn't it?" she asked in an unsteady voice. "P.I. finds the lost child of a dying parent, and on her birthday, too."

"Your birthday?" he asked flatly.

"Maybe it is, maybe it isn't." She stood up before Mike could do or say anything else, and hurried into the bathroom. "I'll be ready to go in just a few minutes," she tossed over her shoulder.

"Alex?" he called, and she stopped dead, but didn't turn.

"What?"

"I love you."

Without trusting herself to say anything, she went into the bathroom, the space still steamy from Mike's shower and, in some strange way, still holding his scent. She closed and locked the door, then pushed back the shower curtain and turned on the hot water. Quickly she stepped under the needle-sharp stream, and, while the sound of rushing water echoed in the small cubicle, she cried.

The south of France
August 15

"Dad?"

Ian Hall looked up as Alex stepped out onto the balcony of Stanhope's villa. She had no idea what either Jon Stanhope or Ian Hall did for a living, but as she looked down at the formal gardens that grew to the edge of the bluffs, then turned her gaze to the ocean, blending into the horizon, she realized neither man was poor.

"Alexandria," Ian said. He smiled as he reached for her, his hand linking through hers as she sat by him in a matching recliner. "Did you make your call?" he asked.

"I can't get through," she said, settling back. She looked at her father, thankful Stanhope had finally gone off to do some "business" and left her alone with Ian.

"Overseas lines can be impossible sometimes," Ian said. He knew what she was trying to do, and his hold on her tightened. "Don't give up, child. Never give up."

She looked at him and smiled. She knew what he was thinking behind those words. He'd given up, but she wouldn't. Now he was doing so well that she could consider leaving him for a while. "A remarkable recovery," his doctor had said more than once. "Incredible."

Incredible, Alex whispered in her heart, and she held tightly to her father across the distance that separated the two chairs. The past month had been incredible. From the moment she and Mike had left the motel and driven to the airport, it had been as if another person inhabited her body, a little child filled with pain and longing and eagerness to see her father. When Mike had stopped her at the foot of the stairs leading to the door of the private plane that would fly her to New York, then to France, she'd looked up at him.

She hadn't known what she felt. She couldn't begin to think about her feelings for him. Her focus had been on France, on getting there as soon as possible. Mike had looked down at her, then cupped her face in his hands. "Whatever happens," he'd said, almost shouting over the noise of the private jet, "I'm here for you. That's the truth."

I'm here for you. His words had drifted around her, but they hadn't meant anything. Not any more than his "I love you" had at the motel. There hadn't been a place for them then, but now they beat in her brain and made her eyes smart. A sudden emptiness filled her, and she swallowed hard. She had her father, and he had her, as well as Stanhope. There had been no need for forgiveness on Ian's part for what Jon had done twenty-seven years earlier. There had been an explanation, anger, pain, then acceptance and, finally, happiness.

And now Alex had such a complete connection with her father that it was almost as if there had been no gap in their relationship. She loved him. If he had died on the operating table, her grief would have been as deep as any child's when a parent died.

He smiled at her. "I'm going to rest. You try that call again," he said. "Indulge me and take my fatherly advice."

"I will," she said, feeling the prick of tears behind her eyes. She had what she'd been looking for. Her father. A friend. Someone she could talk to. Someone she felt connected to. And over this past month she'd needed nothing else. Until now.

She stood and bent to kiss Ian quickly. "I'll try again," she said, then turned and went back into the silent bedroom. She crossed to the bed and dropped down on the edge as she reached for the telephone. There was time to think of other things now, time to see just what her life was all about.

Santa Barbara, California
August 17

Mike turned off the lights in the office and headed out the door. The night was almost balmy, with a refreshing hint of ocean air in the gentle breeze. The streets were quiet and all but empty. Santa Barbara didn't have a wild nightlife, he conceded, and knew that was part of the reason he'd never moved away. He liked the city's settled peace.

He went down the steps into the parking lot and got into his car. A white convertible, his only extravagance. But he liked the freedom, the feeling of the air rushing all around him.

He drove out of the parking lot and within minutes was headed south on the 101 freeway. One month, thirteen days and several hours tumbled all together. His last glimpse of

Alex had been as she went up the steps into the private jet. He'd told her that he would be there for her, but he knew his words hadn't meant a thing to her. And in minutes she'd been gone.

He'd kept track of her, had found out that her father had lived, that she'd never left the hospital for the first five days, staying in a room down the hall from him. Then she'd moved with him to a villa in the south of France. And she hadn't called. Hadn't written.

He gripped the steering wheel tightly, the pain as fresh as if Alex had just walked away. What had he expected? She had what she'd always wanted—a family.

He smiled tightly. Family? He'd worked late the past three nights because he didn't want to go home, and he hadn't wanted to go to his parents' house, either. He didn't want any more questions. "Why are you so sad? Why don't you find some nice girl and get married again? Cousin Estelle works with this very nice girl, and she . . ."

Mike cringed. He'd found a nice girl, a very nice girl. And she was half a world away, while he stayed at home and waited. He didn't even know what he was waiting for. He sped up as he neared the turnoff for his condo near the beach. He didn't have to stay here and wait. He didn't have to, and he wasn't going to.

He could catch a flight out tomorrow. He could go to France. He knew exactly where Alex was staying. He'd given her enough time. All the time he could endure, at least. If he could see her, if he could just talk to her, just touch her . . . If he could hold her . . .

He turned off the freeway, headed west and swung into an underground parking area, then turned off the engine. He sat in the dimly lit parking garage for a long time before he finally got out of the car. His shoes clicked on the hard concrete floor as he walked to his door, then stopped. He looked up at a crescent moon high in the sky, shadowed and elusive, with fragments of clouds skittering across it.

He heard the voice at the same time that he caught a hint of flowery perfume on the night air.

"Now, *that* is a liar's moon, Mr. Robie."

He stood very still, thinking that his obsession with Alex had brought a ghost to haunt him, a ghost with a voice as soft as warm honey and a scent as special as anything he'd ever experienced in his life.

"Mike?"

The sound of his name brought him back to reality, and he turned slowly until he could see her not more than five feet from him. She came slowly toward him in the darkness, through the gentle night, and in that instant he recalled everything about her—her taste, the feel of her, the oneness they'd shared. And his insides drew up into a painful knot.

"Alex." Just saying her name made the moment real.

"Hello." She stopped less than a foot from him. "You must be very dedicated to your job."

He didn't understand that statement any more than he understood her being here. "Pardon?"

"I've been waiting here for three hours, since six o'clock." She laughed, a small, nervous laugh. "I was beginning to think you might not be coming."

He felt foolish just standing there staring at her, at the dark halo of her loose hair around her face, at eyes that were lost to the night. Minutes ago he'd been going to fly to France to see her, certain he would know what to say and do once he got there. But now he had no idea where to start. Everything faded into insignificance in the shadow of this love that stirred him.

"I thought of sending you a report on Jessop. He's going to trial for grand theft. He's got lawyers who'll probably get him off easy, but he'll do some time." The words were meant to fill space between them. Maybe they were meant to keep him going until he figured out what to do.

"I heard. Stanhope told me." Her voice ran across his nerves, sending awareness to every part of his body.

"Your father?"

"He'll be fine. I'm getting to know him."

Getting to know her father? Was that what she'd wanted? Was that *all* she wanted?

Alex could hardly breathe. All those miles, all those hours of flying, and when she was finally facing Mike, all she could do was stare. Her whole being seemed incredibly alive, as if part of her had been hibernating while she got to know her father. Now that part burst into life, filling her world. But she didn't know what to do about it.

She stared at the man in front of her, every feature as precious to her as life itself. He was just standing there staring, waiting. All she wanted to do was jump into his arms, to feel his heart against hers, yet a part of her was afraid to take the initiative.

So she found herself talking about the moon. "A true liar's moon," she said, pointing to it in the inky sky. "It gives light, yet you can't see what it really is, because of the clouds."

"And?" he asked softly.

"The truth is I'm Alexandria Elizabeth Hall. My real birthday is April Second. My mother's name was Margaret, but my father called her Meg. I look like her, he says, but she had blue eyes. She and my father met in Alexandria, Egypt, on July Fourth, and they loved each other very much. They weren't together when she had me, or when she was killed in an accident when I was a baby. My father, Ian Hall, is alive, and he's going to live for a long time to come. And I love him." She bit her unsteady lip. "That's the truth about me. That and the fact that I love you, Michael Conti."

There, she'd said it. She'd put everything on the line. And she waited.

He finally asked, "We agreed on complete truth, didn't we?"

She nodded, unable to speak.

"The complete truth is that I'm late because I didn't want to come back here all alone and spend another night thinking about you. I didn't want to go to my parents' house and hear another lecture on poor Michael being all alone. And

I didn't want to go to my brothers' or sisters' houses and see them with their families." He took a deep breath. "Basically, I hated being here while you were six thousand miles away. I hated being here and aching with loneliness while I gave you time to sort out your feelings."

Alex felt air rush into her lungs and her whole life solidify. "Mike," she whispered and went to him, holding him. He loved her. She felt as if her life had come full circle, that it had just been made whole.

His arms were around her, tight and compelling. She was in the place she'd wanted to be forever. And she had everything she'd ever wanted. If she'd tried to make up a story she couldn't have thought of one this perfect. She tipped her head back. The moon was casting sharp shadows on Mike's face, yet she could see the gentleness there, and the wonder that she felt echoed in him.

She felt sure enough of herself to ask, "You do love me, don't you?"

He stroked her gently. "The truth?"

"The absolute truth," she said unsteadily.

The clouds drifted away from the moon, and its full light shone down on the two of them as Mike whispered, "I love you, and that's the truth."

* * * * *

Silhouette Sensation

COMING NEXT MONTH

NO PLACE TO RUN
Marilyn Tracy

Dave Reynolds was the sheriff of a sleepy little
town in New Mexico and when the pregnant widow
of a State hero moved in over the road he just
naturally was interested. He was even more so
when strange accidents started happening to that
little lady. Janey knew that the good guys could get
hurt or killed so she welcomed neither the sheriff's
professional nor his personal interest. But it was
hard to rebuff the man who'd delivered your
child...

CHILD OF MINE
Mary Anne Wilson

Stuntman Cade Daniels had to convince Megan
Lewis that his job didn't make him a bad father. He
was fighting for the custody of his baby son and
Megan would be making a recommendation to the
court, but Megan didn't like risk takers... Cade
needed to find a way to make her change her mind
because Megan made him aware that he'd been
alone too long...

$\mathcal{S}$ilhouette Sensation

COMING NEXT MONTH

SUSPICION'S GATE
Justine Davis

Travis Halloran thought Nicki Lockwood should have believed in him fifteen years ago. She'd only been a child, but she'd known him as well as anyone. Finally, he could prove his innocence. But how could he use his proof when the truth would destroy Nicki, the woman for whom he'd waited for so long?

SEA GATE
Maura Seger

The work Andrew Paxton did was secret, classified and, therefore, valuable to interested parties. So when a raven-haired beauty washed up on the shore behind his home, he was suspicious. Prolonged exposure to Marina did nothing to alleviate that suspicion—she was definitely hiding something. Where did this unusual woman come from?